Soldier for Christ

Soldier for Christ

A Novel

JOHN ZEUGNER

RESOURCE *Publications* · Eugene, Oregon

SOLDIER FOR CHRIST
A Novel

Resource Publications
An Imprint of Wipf and Stock Publishers
199 W. 8th Ave., Suite 3
Eugene, OR 97401
www.wipfandstock.com

ISBN 13: 978-1-62032-932-0

Manufactured in the U.S.A.

for Alice

"The God who is with us is the God who forsakes us (Mark, 15:34). The God who lets us live in the world without the working hypothesis of God is the God before whom we stand continually. Before God and with God we live without God. God lets himself be pushed out of the world and on to the cross. He is weak and powerless in the world and that is precisely the way, the only way, in which he is with us and helps us …"

—Dietrich Bonhoeffer, July, 1944

"For God hath concluded them all in unbelief,
that he might have mercy upon all."

—Romans, 11:32

Part One

1

Foreigners sometimes came through on Sundays to the church toward which Owen walked, but they came in black chauffeured vehicles and behind darkened windows so that their alien faces never upset the scene, or intruded on the dazzling views down toward Kobe harbor. But this *gaijin* was carless . Worse yet, as he walked he was visibly sweating. Had no one told him to purchase those thick towel-like handkerchiefs by which the Japanese fought off the summer heat and rainy season humidity? The greatest mischief in summery Japan was to be seen glistening, copiously gushing that meat-saturated sweat redolent even at a distance. The required white short sleeved shirt soaked onto his back, so that even the over-the-shoulder draped poplin jacket had darkened on its right lapel from his exertion.

Owen separated the ascent to the Kobe Union Church from Rokko Station off the Hankyu line into two parts: the initial trudge up the mountain beyond the drab/dirty concrete university buildings, via the macadam ribbon between rows of attached housing, stuccoed and with metal roofs; and then as perspiration began to gather along his sides, the more glorious struggle on the suddenly cobblestoned roadway flanked on either side by larger and larger Japanese single family houses with garages, tiled water drainways edging the cobblestone, and terracota tile roofs with cocked satellite dishes—tiny, immaculate gardens viewable over narrow granite flecked walls—the constant delicate rush of artificially falling water within those gardens, and occasionally very frail, elderly Japanese in lightweight summer *yukatas* standing at the end of the glistening driveways to their garages watching him, measuring him somehow, their puzzlement reminding him how out of place a foreigner was in this richest area of suburban Kobe. What was this youngish, overweight *gaijin* doing among such opulence , at the restricted top of the mountain?

The climb to the Kobe Union Church, not quite at the summit of the mountain (Owen imagined that position was reserved for a Buddhist temple, either actual or contemplated) was not equivalent to the Via Dolorosa of Owen's imaginings. Nonetheless he liked equating his own perspiration with Jesus' travail. The arrogance of the equation amused Owen and filled his blossoming sense of irony concerning the Word in Japan. Besides, the son of the living God didn't have to deal with the constant humidity of Japan, did he? Jerusalem was dry, parched, stark, hostile. Japan was warm, muggy, welcoming, puzzled, green, cooperative and abhorrent of judgment, castigation, suffering itself. That was perhaps the difference and why conversion never occurred, or if it occurred had no recognition of, no conception of, redemption. What was sin in silk-soft Japan?

A month ago when Owen had tried to explain Jesus' redemption of the world through agony and suffering, to an elderly Japanese who listened so respectfully in the vestibule of the Kobe Union church, who finally said, with apparent instant grasp. "Like Hiroshima." In answer Owen mumbled in Japanese, "So desho" ("I guess"). And the conversation terminated. The old gentleman bowed and back-stepped out of the narthex.

As a sometime assistant, would-be curate, to the rector, Owen had volunteered to lead the adult Sunday school class, and today he was determined to try something new—something to forge at least a common ground among his well heeled students: gaijin vice-presidents of Proctor and Gamble and their flowery wives fresh up from enormous western style apartments (homats) on Rokko Island, the latest filled-in real estate in Kobe harbor; a lean and committed missionary couple, Jena and Archie Hesseltine, who peppered their conversation with Japanese phrases and puns; and three Japanese women who were regulars at the service—Yasuko the church secretary, who may have come only because she felt it was expected of her position, Myumi whose children attended Christian elementary school and should therefore have a mother who, she explained, understood "what the very kindly teachers of that school believed"; and Mariko who was a simultaneous translator and needed to keep her edge speaking English, as well provide Owen with exquisite distractions of aggressive sinning. They were the core students around the gleaming varnished table on the church's third floor. Sometimes the core group was joined by visiting gaijin, a lonely American college student or two, or military types who had strayed far from the bases in Iwakuni or Yokosuka, and heard that the brunch after the Sunday service at the Kobe Union Church was free and plentiful.

The church Rector, Father Bob Bonneau, often mentioned in his homilies his own long attachment as a Navy Chaplain in the pacific fleet, and perhaps that nautical connection accounted for the sailors who also turned up at very specific and predictable times. "God is most evident in burning bilges and mortar-fired foxholes," Reverend Bob frequently said, either during the homily or afterwards at the brunch. And those who listened always nodded smiling. Owen had never been in a fox hole or a bilge, and therefore resented, if he thought about it, the implied camaraderie of combat. Still he envied the apparent linkage between deprivation, fear, and conversion. What could account for the near total absence of conversion experience among Japanese Christians? Certainly they knew throttling and sudden panic at disasters, yet at no time did they link such experiences with ultimate power beyond nature itself, or so it seemed to Owen. Indeed if conversion required acknowledgment, then the Japanese preference of silence was literally unthinkable, or at the lower frequencies unattainable. Did that make the "practice" of Christian worship any less valid for them or for Owen himself? Was redemption merely the form of religion, its most evident ritual recitation, with no more meaning, as the poet noted, than "tomorrow's bread?" Saved or slain one trudged up the mountain to the Kobe Union Church. One waved to the chauffeurs out of their Mercedes dusting them with large feather dusters, white sweatfree shirts in the soft sunlight of the mountain top, slicked down black hair, thick waists and sparkling black shoes. Nodding back to Owen in that silently assented camaraderie of subservience to nobler masters—or at least better heeled ones.

Owen admired the selfless arrogance of the Proctor and Gamble VPs—"This church ought to be more Christ-centered and helping toward the Philippines," they might have said during their tenure of two years in Kobe. "Money is a given. The church needs to involve younger people more directly in service," they intoned. "We need more potluck suppers." And most emphatically, "This church should never invade principal. The endowment guarantees the long term survival of this effort. Good stewardship begins with husbanding resources for the future." Store up not riches Owen often thought, hearing these sentiments, but never said out loud. The P & G VPs were, in fact, his preferred target audience. They were articulate, open to challenge, full of grace and guile—worthy sparring mates.

This particular Sunday Owen had resolved on a novel tack-—an exposition of not Christ but Judas.

"I thought we might embark on a kind of quest for the historical Judas," Owen said and checked to see if anyone got his little joke. No one nodded, although Owen imagined there was some subterranean appreciation among the Hesseltines. "Notice what Christ says to Judas in various gospels—let's try some reading. Could you?" "Owen pointed to a thick-waisted American at the far end of the oval table.

"Luke 22:47 says . . . He drew near to Jesus to kiss him; but Jesus said to him, 'Judas, would you betray the Son of Man with a kiss?' and Matthew 26: 47 says, "Judas said Hail Master' and Jesus replied, 'Friend, why are you here?' Mark says Jesus said nothing to Judas, although he mentions to others that his betrayer is at hand when he sees Judas and the priests arriving; "

"Let's stop there and compare, 'Would you betray the son of man with a kiss,' and 'Friend, why are you here?'"

"Compare what?" the thick waisted reader said, easily, without a speck of hostility.

"Good question," Owen countered—"maybe Christ's state of knowledge about Judas at the time."

"State of knowledge?"

"What was Christ thinking?"

Jena said, "In Luke he knows what's going to happen, but in Matthew he doesn't seem to know."

"Yes," Owen said, too loudly. "And what does that suggest?"

"That a part knew and a part didn't."

"Yes," Owen answered, "a part knows and a part doesn't—the part of Christ that knows we might call, what?"

"Maybe it means Matthew and Luke disagree about what happened." Archie said.

"Yeah, maybe." Owen answered," But what can we do with that thought?"

"Do we have to do something with the thought?" the thick reader said, again without hostility.

Owen thought, he's like a hillbilly philosopher. "I'd like to," Owen answered, "but maybe we should consider why Judas acted as he did?"

"It was the money," the husky American reader said. "The thirty pieces of silver."

"Profit then?" Owen answered.

"He wanted to ingratiate himself with the Sanhedrin," Archie said.

"He knew he was on the wrong side and he was going to avoid losing by betraying Christ," Jena added.

2

LATER THE RECTOR SAID, "You know Owen, Yasuko said you shouldn't spend so much time on Judas, when most people don't even know Christ."

Owen watched the rector carefully—was there a trace of smile in his tone, a put-on, was that it? Or was there a message beyond the irony and the knowing comradeship of being evaluated by Yasuko.

"I wanted them to think about God's will and Judas, God's plan and Judas. Wasn't Judas necessary?"

"Betrayal was necessary. Judas wasn't necessary. And fully culpable." The rector said, running a fat hand through his thinning hair, slicking it straight back off the red ellipse of his birth marked forehead. "Fully culpable."

"I think it's like being a Christian in Japan, isn't it?"

"How so?"

"You have to reconceptualize it—in different terms, beyond the categories in the Gospel."

"I don't follow," the rector answered, peering beyond Owen toward the French doors that blocked entrance to the wide circular room, for dining or meeting downstairs.

"Maybe we're too hard on the Japanese Christian community—" Owen said.

"There is one?" the rector replied.

"Oh, I think so, but it's not the same as we might like. It's not had an easy time."

"What's the point?" the rector smiled "Maybe only that—I don't know." Owen answered.

"Pray on it, my boy," the rector continued "Ask and it shall be given to you."

"If you say so."

"I don't say anything." the rector corrected him. "Now why don't we get some coffee and rolls." He motioned toward the doors.

"I only meant that I didn't understand how hard it was to be Christian for Japanese, until I came here. How unusual it makes you, how vulnerable, how separated from the flows of life here." Owen continued while the rector nipped slowly at a tiny cinnamon roll. They stood against the vast curving windows of the meeting room, looking down the hill past the train lines, past the accumulated concrete apartment complexes and small shops to the erector set, shipyard cranes in Kobe's harbor.

"It's no stand to be a Christian in the states," Owen continued.

"Try it in the Navy" the rector said.

"It's still within the norm, still permitted, admired even."

"Admired?" the rector's eyes sparkled.

"Still within the parameters."

"Ah, parameters—there's a recent concept."

"I'm only saying that within the category of thinking, you could imagine all the Christian message and still feel as if you were normal, acceptable, worthy. There might be embarrassment, but surely no shame. No shame."

"So what's the point?" the rector said, still staring down the hill. The windows were thick and imposing, lined with bronze straps and ratcheted into chrome holders.

"The point, the point is that it's not that way to be a Christian here— nothing provides for that decision. Nothing makes it all right. Everything makes it wrong."

"Everything?"

"Yes, everything, and you have to admire any Japanese who does it."

"Most do it to learn English," the rector said, smiling at Owen now.

"I don't think so."

"The Lord moves incomprehensibly, my boy. And I wouldn't have it any other way."

"I concede all that, "Owen answered, dumping off the rector's sardonic stance. "It's very hard to be so, so unplugged in this society as to be Christian."

"There's a rather tight knit Christian community, in fact," the rector answered—perhaps a trace of exasperation with Owen.

There was a pause. Yasuko joined them. She carried a green mug and vapors off the top of the mug seemed momentarily as grey as the grey of her hair, close cropped, just to the tops of her ears.

"Ah, Yasuko, just in time," the rector said. "You can explain how easy it is being a Christian nowadays in Japan."

"Compared to when?" Yasuko said.

"Let's say World War II—maybe that's what Owen needs to do, fill in Church history during World War II. Maybe some oral interviews and a little update on the church history text, a few more pages on the easiest time to be a Christian in this country.."

"It must have been the hardest," Owen said, rejecting the tone of the rector's remarks and puzzling over them at the same time.

"You have read the church history?" Yasuko said to Owen.

"The little yellow book?" Owen asked.

"Yes, "Yasuko answered.

"You see that building up there beyond the water tower, way up?" The rector pointed away from the harbor to the pines above the church. "That's the main classroom of Oxford University here in Japan."

"I know that," Owen answered.

"Dons in robes, walking around the top of the mountain, looking at the harbor and wondering why no students come, but they're here for life since Fuji steel has committed to offering Oxford. I tried to get one of them interested in the church's history during World War II, but that looked like work to the 'historians' there. Would've disturbed their posturing—their slow strolls around the empty campus—their musings about the absent students. So nobody bit, but now I see I should have looked closer to home. Why don't you do it? It's an interesting story—this church was saved by Nazis from a takeover in '42."

"By Nazis?"

"Well, by the local German community and Pastor Rielmann."

"And by Mioko, "Yasuko said.

"Oh yes, she'll have to give you her side of the story. That should be your first interview—how she saved the church from her people. Single-handedly."

"She and Mogens Nielsen."

"Ah yes, the Danish saint. Mioko and Mogens saved the church from the dread Thought Police. Or so she'll tell you, and tell you and tell you. Very strong willed woman, Mioko. Now I must speak to the trustees at the coffee line." And the rector was gone.

Yasuko sipped her tea, "Have you read the yellow book?"

"Only parts of it," Owen answered. The sun off Kobe bay seemed a chrome brilliance; he squinted at it, determined to find the cranes that had suddenly blurred into sun spots on the water.

"I will get you a copy," Yasuko said, "from the office."

"I suppose I should read it—charged to do so from the pastor himself."

"I think the Mission is not so demanding. If you would like to read it I will put one on the table upstairs. You can pick it up before you get on the bus."

"How much you know about my comings and goings," Owen said smiling, but it seemed she saw no edge in the remark.

"If you want to interview Mioko, I can take you there. I've been meaning to visit her for a long time anyway. She's in a home outside of Akashi; she has no family—only the church, and I should be paying her a visit."

"Did she save the church?"

"She found out the government was going to takeover the church and she and Mogens went to see Pastor Rielmann and then Pastor Rielmann and Mogens went to Tokyo to the German Ambassador, pleading for the church to remain under its own control."

"And it was?"

"Yes, Pastor Rielmann jointly held the rectorship for the German church and for this one—he gave sermons in English all through the war. Then in the last month of the war the church was bombed, almost totally destroyed. If she had not heard the threat of takeover; if she hadn't told Mogens and involved Pastor Rielmann, then perhaps the church would have been absorbed by a Japanese church or the government directly. The German Ambassador really saved the church, however, not Mioko. It's all in the yellow book."

Yasuko put out more than just the Little Yellow book for him. The brown envelope on the table upstairs contained several documents, including three prior histories of the church—pamphlets only about 12 pages long, but the ones in 1952 celebrating the re-enclosure of the church, and in 1969 at the opening of the second class room building, and 1978 commemorating the move out of Kobe to property near Ikuta shrine and in 1990 at the opening of the new church on the mountain top, all contained the same story of Mioko Tanaka, meeting a Dr. Sugiera on the train back to Kobe from Osaka on the night of March 23rd 1942 and hearing from him that the government planned to takeover the church, the only English speaking foreign church in the area and close it down—since it was mostly Brits and Danes and Dutch who came to services, all enemies of the Rome/Tokyo/Berlin axis. And that Mioko had gone home and immediately phoned Mogens Nielsen, who immediately called a meeting with Pastor Rielmann. Together they went to Tokyo for a direct appeal to the German Ambassador; allegedly the Ambassador intervened at the foreign ministry and the takeover stopped; instead, Pastor Rielmann assumed pastoral duties—the church's regular rector had been arrested the day after Pearl Harbor, and Rielmann kept up English services, monthly communion, and even Sunday school classes right through until the church was bombed.

In each post war history, then, Mioko Tanaka was the first fighter for the church, the Paul Revere of Christian salvation during the long night of fascist pagan attempts.

3

Was Yasuko related to Mioko?

Yasuko laughed at the question as they waited for the limited express at Sanomiya station in Kobe. "No, indeed. There are 18 million Tanaka's in Japan. No relation at all. Besides, as old as Mioko is, I'm still too old to be her daughter."

"I should have remembered you said she had no family."

"Only the church"

"The church she saved."

"Yes," Yasuko answered. "She always stood up to anyone—it was only natural she should stand up to the imperial government. But she didn't have too many friends in the church, at that time."

"Or since, if the rector is correct."

"He is partially correct."

"I can conceive it..."

"She was, is, hard to get along with—that's true enough. She's very different from most Japanese; she was a long time in California studying music. Maybe at Claremont—you should ask her."

"And that made her lose friends?"

Yasuko smiled, "it made her strange to many Japanese, I suppose."

"And being Christian couldn't help much."

"Perhaps not. Still, it gave her a place to retire to eventually."

"The real function of the Christian community." Owen said. "Old age retreats. In the U.S. a lot of retirement homes are denominational."

"Denominational?" Yasuko asked.

"You know specific branches of the Christian church—Lutheran homes, Episcopal homes, Presbyterian homes, Baptist homes."

"So many names."

When they were on the train passing out from Suma along the Inland Sea, Owen watched the steel gray water so opaque, motionless, and thought it was the back of some infinitely placid and deep creature. The sky was grey too, hazy and stroked with darker tones toward the horizon.

"Tell me about the home." Owen said.

"I've only been once before," Yasuko answered. "It's very modern and very clean."

"And very depressing." Owen volunteered.

"Yes, that too, I think. She seems to like it there. She has a group of friends, her team, I suppose. And they look after her."

"Does she leave much?"

"I don't think so. She plays the piano."

"What kind of a room does she have?"

"Six mat with a very nice mahogany wardrobe—the rooms surround a courtyard. She has a view of that, and the dining room is close by. She likes visitors."

"I would think." Owen answered, still watching the Inland Sea.

He wondered if it ever got blue or blue/green. Just this endless solder color. "The authorities never punished her for intervening in the church's future?"

"Did they know about it?" Yasuko answered, "I think they only dealt with Pastor Rielmann and Mr. Nielsen. Most likely they never connected her with it. She had no real power."

"Still, you'd think they'd want a scapegoat."

"Later they did arrest Mr. Nielsen."

"And what happened to him?"

"I don't know. I don't think he ever contacted the church again."

"Not a good sign."

"I suppose so. But it was a difficult time—often you didn't hear from someone for years and then they turned in okay at the end—is that the expression?"

"Maybe 'turned up okay' is slightly better." Owen answered.

The home was further from the station than Yasuko remembered. Twice she paused to puzzle out signs Owen couldn't read. The signs for the home usually were on brown backgrounds and that meant occasionally Owen saw directions before she did. Only when they came to a short steep hill did Yasuko acknowledge she was certain now of the way.

The sky had turned a solder color too, and Owen regretted not carrying an umbrella.

Mioko Tanaka wore a long grey skirt and brown sweater. Her hair was yanked back in a neat bun and she struggled standing with a cane, leaning forward a bit to watch them more intently as they came across the cement walk into the flagment portico.

"I've been standing here for forty minutes waiting for you and now at last you've come." Mioko said rather too loudly, Owen thought, but the receptionist to the right and the nurse hovering nearby did not seem to understand what was being said.

Yasuko slipped out of her shoes and into slippers effortlessly but Owen struggled with the entry procedure, as always. Yasuko covered by handing Mioko her gift of a box of eight wrapped cakes.

"Good," Mioko said, "we have a special visiting room and we can eat these there. I'll make sure we get some tea. I've not had one of these in years. And I'm so glad you didn't wrap the box up."

Owen worried about his heavily wrapped gift of handkerchiefs.

"And is this the historian, you've promised me?"

Yasuko immediately turned and said, "Yes, I'm so sorry, this is Owen Mathias."

"Owen what?" Mioko said, cutting her off. "I'm hard of hearing now and everything else."

"Owen Mathias," Owen said, extending his hand.

"Spell it."

"M, A, T, H, I, A,S." Owen said slowly.

"Oh math-eye-as," Mioko said. "But you say it differently like math-ee-us."

"Yes, that's the way my family pronounces it."

"Well, at least I can understand it now. Let's go to the room. Although it looks like you've got something for me, too."

"Yes, but it's heavily wrapped."

"I hate that—it's my hands, I can't work my hands so well anymore, and I hate asking for help."

"You don't have to ask," Owen countered, "I'll do it directly when we get to the room."

"Good." Mioko answered, "I suppose you want to lead there too."

"Not a chance," Owen laughed, "you, only, know the way."

"Well, you've got that right. I know all there is to know about this place and how to get around here, even if I can't walk very fast. I used to hate Japanese *omiyage*, little gifts for every occasion, and I never did it, except when I had to, but now and here I think it's quite wonderful. And I quite like these cakes. You don't often see something new here, isn't that odd? Collecting new things all your life and then at the end you seldom see anything new."

"I see new things everyday," Owen said.

"Oh but that's because everything is new to you here in Japan."

"I've been here before," Owen answered.

"Not here you haven't , I'll bet."

"Right again."

"Right as rain," Mioko said. "That's an expression I remember from my days in California. I was a musician once, in your country but a very long time ago. But I date my differentness from then. I never imagined I'd end up in such a room as this," Mioko motioned to the green walls and the noisy fan unit mounted near the ceiling. "It's like a little coffin isn't it? The whole place is a slow rehearsal for a little coffin and then the flames."

"Mioko," Yasuko interrupted, "I've not heard you so sad."

"It's not sad or morbid. It's what's going on. I agree I didn't know it until fairly recently, but that can't change things. It's what's going on. The rector in good health?"

"Yes," Yasuko answered.

"He doesn't come out much anymore."

"He's very busy."

"That's not it. He doesn't like me, and I can't say much for him either."

"Not like Pastor Rielmann?" Owen asked.

"Rather too much like him," Mioko answered. "I'm not a typical Japanese, you know."

Owen did not answer. There was a sudden silence.

"Let's have a cake,"Mioko said. "And, Yasuko, make us a little tea from that machine." She pointed to the tea unit on top of a file cabinet at the end of the room.

While Yasuko filled the tea cups, Mioko said, "Are you sure there isn't a second T in your name?"

"Not the way my family spelled it. Maybe at some time. "

"At some time, I'm sure," Mioko answered. "Now you've come about what?"

If there was a hostility, Owen chose not to hear it. "About the church during World War II."

"What about the church?"

"How it survived."

"Quite nicely thank you—no trouble at all."

From the file cabinet Yasuko said, "He wants to hear how you saved the church."

"Saved it? From what?" Mioko asked.

"You know, from the government, from the police, from a takeover."

"There was never a takeover."

"Yes, because you intervened and got Pastor Rielmann and Mr. Nielsen to speak with the German Ambassador."

"I don't think so," Mioko said.

"Oh, you know you met Dr. Sugiera on the train ,and he warned you about a takeover."

"No," Mioko said.

Yasuko brought the cups over on a circular plastic tray. "You know what I'm talking about, Mioko. You know the police were going to join the church to a Japanese congregation down in Kobe, and you got wind of it, and you frustrated the security police. It's all in the church history."

"Whenever I saw the security police all they said to me was 'thank you.' For what I never knew."

"But the church," Owen interrupted, "was in grave danger—the pastor had been arrested. The *Kempeitai* were talking as if the place was a hot-house of sedition."

"Whenever I saw the security policy, they'd say 'thank you'—for what I don't know. The church was never in any danger."

Owen warmed up to the questioning—"There was no takeover attempt?"

"Of course not. Was the church ever taken over? Of course it wasn't."

"Pastor Rielmann didn't have to serve double duty —one for the German congregation, and one for the English-speaking congregation?"

"He may have, but what does that show?"

"The church was in danger, doesn't it?"

"No, of course not. The church is here now, was here then ,and no takeover occurred or was talked about."

"And the church was never in danger?"

"Of course not"

"You didn't get Pastor Rielmann and Mr. Nielsen to go to Tokyo to plead for the church before the German ambassador?"

"Of course not, it wasn't necessary. The church was quite safe."

"Was the church not bombed at the end of the war."

"Of course not."

"But the pictures of the previous church, surely you've seen those."

"I've seen all the pictures, never one about a bombed out church."

"That's astonishing," Owen said.

"Mioko, you surely remember the *Kempeitai* talking about the church as an enemy."

"Japan never moved against the church—everything functioned right through the war. And the security police whenever they saw me would say, 'thank you'—for what I don't know."

"Mioko, surely you remember Dr. Sugiera."

"I do not."

"Or Mr. Nielsen?"

"I remember Mogens,—he pronounced his name 'moans', isn't that odd? As odd as 'Ma-THEE us'. don't you think?. He was always worried about his children. He missed his children. He loved his children so."

"You were worried the police would pick him up."

"I don't think so. The police weren't so awful. Whenever they saw me, whenever I ran into them, they'd say 'thank you,' for what I don't know."

"And Pastor Rielmann didn't listen to you and Mr. Nielsen and decide to go to Tokyo that night?"

"Why should he go to Tokyo? The church was here. And it was safe, entirely safe."

Owen came in, "Then the little yellow book's account is entirely inaccurate."

"Oh I don't know about that, but I do know I never authorized it ."

"Mioko, you wrote most of it."

"Well, I never wrote a single word about any threat to the church. The church was in no danger and whenever the security police saw me they said, 'Thank you'. For What I don't know. I never knew."

"And even the bombing of the church."

"The church was fine, is fine, will be fine." Mioko said, then peeled the cellophane away from her small circular cake.

Owen looked at Yasuko who only smiled weakly and pushed his tea over toward him on the narrow table top.

"When you were in California, did you study music full time?" Owen asked.

"Of course. That's why I went there."

"How was that—studying full time?"

"It was wonderful, surrounded by music. I'm a very different sort of Japanese, you know. "

Owen wondered if different meant she wanted to be asked about the church in a certain way. Have the answer ready from a specific code given only to her.

"What do you remember of Pastor Rielmann?" Owen asked.

"I remember he gave very boring sermons and that his English, which was very clear, tended to go on for a very long time. But I could tell he was very convinced."

"Convinced?" Owen pressed.

"Absolutely, he was ...." Mioko seemed, uncharacteristically to struggle for the right word in English. "Faithful, full of faith."

"What happened to him?"

"I have no idea."

"I mean was he arrested too?"

"No,of course not. No one was arrested. I attended every Sunday right through the war, and Pastor Rielmann gave the sermon in English every 3rd Sunday right through the war, in fact right through till some time in 1946, when a missionary came part-time."

"And you can remember that very well?" Yasuko said.

"Yes, of course, I can."

"But not warning Mogens Nielsen and Pastor Rielmann?"

"Warning them of what? The security police only said thank you to me, for what I don't know."

"How many children did Mr. Nielsen have?" Owen asked.

"Four,—one he had never seen, but three he could describe to you in great detail. He spent too much time doing that, describing his children to anyone who would listen. I had met them, and they weren't so angelic as he described them."

"He thought they were angels?" Yasuko asked.

"He thought they were the most special creatures on the planet. I remember that very well. Especially the oldest Johanna. and little Peder and the baby until the new baby came, Soren. He was always showing pictures of them."

"Did he ever see them again?"

"How should I know?"

"I thought you might have stayed in touch somehow, or after the war."

"We didn't. I assume he got back to his family and had everything he had longed for.—Why write then?"

"But you don't know for sure?"

"No, I don't know what happened to him. I could imagine I suppose, but I don't know."

"What would you imagine?" Owen pressed.

There was a long silence. Mioko unwrapped another cake. She smiled first at Owen, then at Yasuko. "You are so kind to visit me, but I had better get back to my group; we are in some kind of competition today and maybe I am the fittest." She quickly ate the cake, then got up putting the shards back in the plastic bag. "I will walk you to the entry and then I must get back to my group."

On the train home Yasuko said, "I can't imagine Mioko being told to join her group. I can't imagine her wanting to live that way. She never lived that way, couldn't live that way."

"She was younger then. Maybe as you get older..."

"Only if you lose your faculties."

"So what have we then? Was it because I was there, she wouldn't talk. She didn't want *gaijin* listening to her story, is that it?"

"No. She likes talking to *gaijin*. Probably no one speaks English to her there. No one. Her mind is going. She truly can't remember anything as it actually was, only as she might want it to have been. That happens—my mother doesn't remember fighting with my father; she remembers only golden times, wonderful moments. She delights in telling and retelling those. But it is not what I remember."

"You'd think she'd recall her own heroics."

"Yes, it is very sad."

"Well, she's not sad about it. "

"We can be sad for her."

"I don't think so." Owen said, watching as the sea near Suma drifted out to absolute blackness. The train swayed almost soundlessly.

4

"So old Mioko's gone round the bend," the rector said just after Owen's second Sunday school class on Judas.

"Apparently—I wonder. If I hadn't been there, maybe she would have talked to Yasuko."

"Ahenh, no. Not a chance. I've seen it so many times before. Past a certain age, everything starts to dissolve. The Church wasn't bombed. The church wasn't bombed. The simplest, most direct impressions give way, till there's nothing left. It's called getting ready for the end. Course, being in that home hasn't helped much—nothing to keep her alert or focused. I've seen it all before. Lots of times. Poor old Mioko."

"Well, I'm not ready to write her off yet."

"Who's writing her off? I'm just saying as a historical source she's a dead loss. I'm sorry I put you on to her."

"She seemed pretty lucid most of the time." Owen said.

"It's like short term and long term memory. Some older folks can remember exactly what happened on July 12, 1951 but can't remember whether they talked to you this morning or not."

"That's not her problem."

"Well it's like her problem only reversed, I guess. Anyway I've seen it plenty of times before. I'll put you on to some other sources—the church has had plenty of amateur historians. You've got to roll better with the punches, my boy. But you will, I know. I know it exactly. Now I can't be late. You can, but I can't."

Owen thought, I can be more than late, I can miss the whole service. And he did. He went downstairs, turned away from the open chapel doors and went outside. The sunlight was harsh, brittle, crisp and the trek down the mountain to the train station was severely steep, upsettingly tilting so that he pushed toes against the pavement to prevent pitching off balance. It seemed he was always lurching ahead of himself, struggling to keep upright. The roadway was narrow, slick black macadam and there was a treacherous seven inch wide concrete trench on the side where he walked. Mercifully no car came up or down the slope. He walked gingerly along the edge of the drainage trench. Japan was no country for the infirm of step, he decided. After a certain age there'd be no way to walk to church. The taxis were expensive.

He imagined the rector had reached that part of the ecumenical service called The Pardon. The rector's phrase was always predictable; "And so my friends believe the good news of Jesus Christ crucified, died, and resurrected for our sins. Believe the good news."

Judas's fate had been the subject of some debate at the lesson. Did the Jewish elders purchase the burying site for paupers or did Judas himself? Did he throw himself off a cliff or did he simply swell up and explode in blood on the ground? Akeldama meant exactly what, another stocky American executive wanted to know. Owen was unsure, but that is not what the fellow wanted to hear. He wanted an answer, opaque, solid, and significant. Something to hurl at skepticism, indeed to banish unbelief. Owen could not answer or mollify him.

"There ought to be some way to look it up, don't you think?" The executive said.

"I'm sure there is—a lot of ways," Owen lamely offered.

"Is the term Greek or Aramaic?" Jena asked, tossing Owen a dubious lifeline.

Owen couldn't say, promised to look it up, but wondered now what sort of dictionary would have the term. And more importantly where he'd find basic biblical guides in English. The bookstores in Osaka and Kobe had a myriad texts on mastering English, and then spinning racks of Penguin paperbacks, but he was not sure about Biblical lexicons. Owen remembered hearing a strange lecture in divinity school on the term—a tortured linguistic tracing, all related to the classical notions of blood—but he could not recall the central point of the lecturer, or even who the lecturer was.

Owen's western style house (for foreigners) was just beyond the college's main gate a mile from Nishinomiya station. Near the gate was a short wall of 20 mailboxes arranged in three horizontal rows . Each box had a narrow, side-hinged door with a gap large enough above and below the door so that you could reach directly in and take your mail out. There was a coupling on each door for a small lock, but most boxes didn't have one. Like most Americans Owen was bemused and awestruck by Japan's safety.

"Who, after all," his neighbors asked him, "would want to steal another's mail?"

"Not even cash envelopes?" Owen once countered.

Yes, those would require some care—please be careful with them came the inevitable answer.

There was a large envelope in Owen's mailbox, almost a packet. The return address was written in Japanese, with "Mioko Tanaka" in English at the top. He tossed the envelope on a table near his two-burner kitchen unit while he made tea. He suddenly felt skeptical about the packet. He decided to make *hojicha*, a stronger tea for staying awake—a student tea, a little bracing for the message from Mioko. He thought, while the tea steeped, that perhaps he had left a handkerchief, or maybe a flat notebook. But he sensed that would not be the case.

She wanted him to know something—she wanted to share something with him. He was sure of it. Then he thought about throwing the envelope out unopened. Curiosity was too strong, however.

Mioko's note was terse, direct, entirely characteristic. "I've tried for several years to find someone to give this to, and then there you were—surely God's will. Just as sure, I 'm certain, that there was an extra T in your name some time back. Come and see me after you've read the enclosed. You'll want to come alone."

The enclosed were pages, each one with Mioko's name at the top, on notebook lined paper, folded neatly in half twice. The paper was fragile, yellowing, flaking at the edges:

"*Mioko*—

I'm writing you on the extra page—or what Kawabata calls the extra page. I have to write two pages each day for the interrogators, but Kawbata brings me three. I can write you on that page and Kawabata says he'll arrange for it to get to you via his own family in Kobe. Do I believe him? Or is it a ruse to get access to my honne thoughts beyond the official two pages? Is Kawbata a traitor to my friendship or is he a good man who understands the disease of this place and wishes to redeem himself somehow? You will have to ask him, should you ever meet him someday, after this war is over. Will it be over? I know now I won't see the end of it. The world will surely end for me, my world at least, soon enough. And good riddance. But I have things to say to my children, and that's where you come in. On the 'extra page,' I will document some of the horror here, and you can use that. But between those horrible things I want my children to know something better, something more hopeful. Will you help me in that need? Please.

This morning two boys, my son Peder's age, ten, were taken outside and put into rain barrels, strapped in and left to freeze to death in Harbin's minus thirty degrees. Left, but monitored every ten minutes by nurses in heavy fur coats, taking blood pressure, heart rate, consciousness and entering the data in green notebooks. I could watch and listen to their deaths from my window in the infirmary. After an hour another fur coat came and using a small curved saw severed the right arm of the boy nearest the building. He had mercifully already passed out from the extreme cold—maybe the arm itself was frozen, I couldn't tell. And then they monitored the blood flow and whether the sawed-arm boy died more quickly than the other boy. It seemed they may have been twins. Pray for me. Mogens."

Owen stopped reading, put both hands around the very hot handle-less cup of *hojicha*, felt the heat flood into his fingers. He squeezed harder on the cup. He recognized it was the accepted Japanese way of banishing winter chill. From a department store you could buy a *kotatsu* table with a heating element underneath, so that you could sit with your kneeling legs covered by a thick blanket at the table and that would heat your lower extremities. And then you could grasp the tea cup to warm your arms. You could lean over the tea vapors and the steam would bathe your face. Three specific actions for three guaranteed results.

But with no one to monitor your warm descent into death. Owen wondered, why show me these things?

"Mioko, today buboes under my arms are oozing again, and even though the infirmary is warm I feel like I'm in an ice barrel myself, or floating on an ice floe. Kawabata says I've been given plague, but a mild kind. I'll live. Pray for me. Mogens."

"Mioko, fellow soldier for Christ!

Too sick to write. Mioko, too sick to write. Can't write. But still writing. See what that means."

And another page:

"Mioko, Children die here. You hear them crying. You hear them scream-ing. This morning I got to watch two of them die from exposure. Outside, in tanks—a green tank and a blue one. They were twins. Both about eleven years old. Chinese boys in identical black bathing suits. Immersed in water and left to freeze to death. But after two hours doctors came and fitted them with

sensors. The boys were shivering so hard they had to use adhesive straps to keep the sensors on their upper chests. Their eyes were rolling, pleading. Then in another hour, the doctors came back. Lifted the blue tank boy's arm and hacked it off at the elbow, then strapped the remainder to the boy's side , then pushed him back in the thick, icy water. Kawabata says they were studying (yes studying!) how long it would take him to die of exposure while bleeding. His brother was intact. By standing on my cot I could see through the translucent window their rolling eyes and hear their softening screams. Children die here. In another hour their heads dropped. The shivering stopped. And I could hear the soldiers sent out to fetch the bodies, complaining that they had been forced to wait too long because the bodies were in semi-ice now and very difficult to extract. They were forced to use long iron spike poles to chip the boys' hips loose. I wondered if they would want to reuse the tanks.

Children die here. A month ago Kawabata took me to another wing, a much warmer, much nicer area, something like a hospital to a really fine room with two beds and two chairs, and a toilet curtained off. "This is 'medical research'" Kawabata said with evident pride at having mastered yet more English vocabulary. "We can have a nice chat, is that it? A chat?" "Yes," I answered, "A nice chat. Good English." But we didn't chat. He left. Twenty minutes later he brought in a small Chinese girl, and said she was eight years old. He patted the bed for her and she obligingly lay down. He pulled the thick gray blanket folded at the end of the bed over her. She rather quickly fell asleep. "You'll stay here with her. They want to study what happens." "They?" "Well, Dr. Matsuno at least." "What kind of doctor tortures children?"

"A researcher," answers Kawabata, as if impressed by the term. "Researcher," he repeats as if to sound it out. "To look again," he says smiling at his memory of the dictionary.

This morning I began throwing up and when I tell Kawabata this, he nods and says we should go to see Dr. Matsuno, who turns out to be very young. Maybe still in his twenties and looking like a schoolboy. He wants to know when I began vomiting. The exact time, but I have no way of knowing. "You took my watch," I tell him. But he insists we can estimate very exactly if I describe the light in the room when I first threw up. We spar about this issue for another few minutes. And finally I ask, "What did the girl die of?" "A kind of neurological trauma," he answers automatically, earnestly. Then adds," But not from fleas. Do your feet feel numb?" he asks in the same level tones. "No." "Interesting," he says. "Please take off your shirt. When your feet begin to feel numb, please tell Kawabata-san and he'll bring you back." 'You have some medicine to cure that?" I ask. "No. There is none. At least there is none now. But I have an idea to keep the numbness from spreading. Neurology is so experimental, so trial and error. That's why I like it. You can stumble on things no one could have thought of. You may urinate some blood. I studied in Seattle." You may piss blood and I studied in Seattle. Some connection there. I answer in nauseated level-tone, "I understand everyone urinates blood in Seattle." "Do you really think that?" "I've never been to Seattle." "So you are joking, but joking is not appropriate to your situation." I answer, "So desu neh."

My feet do go numb, numbing and tingling. It seems golf balls of pain are shifting around on the soles of my feet. And the numbness moves up my ankles toward my knees. Kawabata, good solider, takes me back to Dr. Matsuno. "Did you eat any of the girl's food?" "No." "Hmnn, well we need to put you in the infirmary and watch what happens." "What is going to happen?" "I can't be sure, but I assume the numbness will move north." "And then what?" "We'll have to watch, you will be advancing research greatly." "It hurts to walk. In fact I'm not sure I can walk." "That's an important sign. We'll get you to the infirmary, even if we have to have soldiers carry you." Kawabata says he cannot bring me extra paper in the infirmary.

Owen held up the page to the light on his desk as if to imagine mysterious writing able to appear on the remainder of the whitish yellow sheet. But there was nothing. He turned to the second packet and pulled off the thick rubber band, but then decided not to open the pages. He tossed the collection on his desk and went into the *tatami* room and sprawled out on the rush mats. The cool give of the *tatami* was, as always, relieving, inviting. The pages needed explanation Mioko's covering note said almost nothing. He wondered if she were playing coy with him, or had, in fact, simply lost the thread of coherence as she gathered them up for mailing. And why send them to him? The pages were fragile all right, almost brown on the edges, almost brittle and the ink had faded in some places to illegibility. So Mioko wanted to draw him back, was that it? Or was she just scattered and confused? He wanted information and without Yasuko around to deflect his inquiry. He assumed Mioko wanted that too. Why wouldn't she?

Part Two

1

THAT AFTERNOON MARIKO PHONED. "I figured out the link between base-ball and *sumo*," she said without even a mocking "*moshi, moshi*" opener. "It's a short timing thing. Compression. Squeezing everything into the shortest possible time, in baseball only a tenth of second—in *sumo* maybe longer, but maybe it could be argued (that's a good collection phrase—one giving you time to do some internal translations, isn't it?), yes, it could be argued that the key balance thrust is only a tenth of a second in *sumo* too. That's why we Japanese thrill to both *sumo* and baseball. Do you agree?"

"At such conferences," Owen said, "the key question is always—'would you comment on that?' You never ask for agreement in Japan."

"You've been reading your guide books again, "Mariko said, after a pause.

"There's a similarity in body shapes," Owen said.

"In the guide books?"

"No. Between *sumo* wrestlers and baseball long ball hitters. Why are you thinking about it?"

"It came up at the American center during the conference. A professor asked why the Japanese liked baseball and *sumo*, since they were so differ-ent. And I've been thinking about it ever."

"I think the expression is 'ever since.'"

"Ever since? How does that make sense?"

"Since. Not sense. Since," Owen corrected.

Again a pause. He wondered if she'd hang up, but finally she said, "No jokes. I've told you that. Jokes don't translate."

"That's a shame. I wonder why we get along."

"Do we?"

"I like your company," Owen answered. "And we share the church."

"Yes," she replied hanging back a bit.

"Although I know you're not a Christian."

"*So desu ne.*"

"But you have an interest," Owen paused, "maybe even beyond learning English, is that it?"

"No interest," she answered. "I'm not for the three in one, you know. And the guilt bores me."

"I know that."

"I wish it bored you."

"You can teach me how."

"Now—there's a good idea. Why don't we meet for dinner at Gaylords. You like Indian."

"Done," Owen answered. "In one hour."

"I expect you to be free of guilt by the time you get to Sannomiya."

"Not possible. Too much sin in the world."

"Ever since," she answered and hung up.

Over onion bajis and cheese pakoras and before the palak paneer she always ordered, moving the chunks of paneer to the edge of her metal serving dish, and the lamb vindaloo, his standard, she said to him. "Here's how to think about natural functions."

"Natural functions?"

"About what we'll be doing. Here's what a student told me just a few days ago—he's very earnest about learning his English, so he could talk to his Canadian lover—a fellow who works in the consulate. 'I like him so I give him my front, but I don't love him so I don't give him my back.'"

"And what did you answer?" Owen asked.

"I couldn't think of anything to say."

"And you want my advice?"

"No, I wanted you to know how he thought about such things. I wanted you to see how he looked at sex, the naturalness of it."

"Front not back. Of course, the naturalness of that. It's positively 'off hand'".

"Off hand?"

"A joke, sorry. Casual. Without emotional investment. Unthinkingness."

"Yes, all of those things and none of those things too. Just something natural."

"Yes, natural. In front, natural."

The raita and nan came late. She used pieces of nan to mop up the remaining spinach.

Owen alternated bites of vindaloo with spoons of the cooling raita. The closing chai tea came with complimentary cognac delivered somewhat unctuously by the owner himself, Ray Bannerejee; Mariko addressed him in Japanese and they seemed to be discussing whether he should move the restaurant out of this mammoth office building—it seemed being the first floor under 34 other floors made the operation vulnerable, or compressible. Besides there was no view, the owner said, smiling. As always, Mariko charged the bill to her business account. "So long as we talk in English, I can get funds for these meals. Or I can be recruiting you to teach in my language lab."

"Ah yes, the native speaker. The idiot who makes perfect American sounds."

"Bannerjee-san used to make tapes for me, before he opened this restaurant. And I hear he goes to South Korea to make more tapes, every time he has to leave to get his visa renewed."

"So the English market has moved to South Korea?"

"Everything's more prosperous over there."

"Will the Koreans here be moving back?"

"I don't know and I don't care," she said, smiling. "Time to go south."

He smiled acknowledgment, "For my lesson in naturalness?"

"Yes, of course," she answered.

Going south meant leaving and walking away from the water toward the dismal *Etta* district full of ramshackle apartment complexes and floppy single houses holding the poorest residents of the city, descendants of meat cutters and tanners, as well as never-assimilated Koreans impressed decades ago into forced labor and left in limbo after the war. On the edge of the district were the Love Hotels they always used, although lately Mariko had favored a mock American deep south mansion called, appropriately enough, "Tara". Their first venture had been in a placed called "Cinderella's Pumpkin" painted a lurid orange and with constant strobe lights playing on the front porch littered with giant green carriage wheels.

"Tara" seemed understated beside it. Huge columns ala Louisiana mansion and clapboard lines drawn in the white stucco walls, as if wood had somehow cohered into something more durable. The clerk always wore a Rhett Butler-length suitcoat and sported a charcoal drawn mustache—altogether a slenderer, smaller, would-be Clark Gable. As always Mariko booked the Scarlet O'Hara suite for two hours.

As always the first hour was given over to water libations. There was a mammoth marble round deep tub with the interesting touch of outside wall spigots and plastic stools so that bathers could lather up properly in Japanese fashion before entering the piping hot waters. She undressed Owen, slowly, thoughtfully, carefully folding his clothes in the wire baskets provided above the spigots. As always she encouraged him to create heavy suds over her narrow breasts, even as she lathered his genitals and slowly worked soap into foam around his stiffening penis; just as he seemed unstoppably cresting toward ejaculation, she poured a bucket of severely scorching water over his back.

"Slows down everything," he said. They squirmed off their stools, slithered on the marble floor toward the deep mammoth , sunken deep tub. For a moment he thought they should mount there on the slick marble, but she was too quick for him and slithered into the piping hot water. She pulled at his shoulder, yanking him into the tub. The enveloping heat indeed wilted desire immediately.

"You must have thrown the switch," he said, fighting the urge to flee from the searing water.

"You must always turn the lever before you start washing," she answered, fitting a folded towel on her forehead.

"I think it's burning my skin," he sighed.

"It's not," she answered smiling. "We need to rest a while, to gather our strength and increase our pleasure."

"Is that natural?"

"Ever since," she answered.

"Ever so, is better," he said.

"Ever so, ever since," she said slowly turning the phrases over.

"Ever again," he said.

"Ever green"

"Ever a tease," he said, putting his own folded towel on his forehead.

"Oh, you have no idea," she said.

They treaded water facing each other in the deep tub; it seemed to water got hotter still and after ten minutes she admitted as much and reached to throw the lever that turned off the heating element. He felt near sleep, his muscles melting into near jelly. Then she glided over to him and pushed gently on his shoulders, shoving him back toward the edge of the tub. When he got there she shoved harder, directing him to hoist himself up out of the water. "Leave your legs in, and lie back," she said quietly. He obeyed, but the marble had cooled and was momentarily shudder-inducing.

The effect was dizzying and stiffening. And soon enough she was licking him and slowly enveloping him in her mouth. He rose and swoll toward her patient plying. He half sat and could not resist pushing his hands on the top of her head, guiding her. He pushed down hard as the tide of heat rose further, sending him ascending the escalator of paroxzm; she began gagging, but he could not stop himself from pushing harder on her head. She flailed her arms out from the water, attacking his arms now clamped like iron bars on the top of her head. But he was irresistible until sudden explosive deliverance that turned her gagging into vomiting. In panting relief he eyed the streaming black, white-flecked bile pouring out of her mouth and momentarily thought of Mogen's reaction to plague gushes out of the little girl's festering body, but realized with some relief that Mariko's deposit was only deeply darkened palak paneer spinach. Mariko continued heaving.

"I'm so sorry," he said, "I couldn't stop myself." But she extended her hot palm across his mouth.

"Say nothing," she said softly. "Say nothing. We've only started."

2

ON THE NEXT TRIP to see Mioko he brought Mogens' account of that little girl's death, but rather than review its atrocities he slumped into the rocking rhythm of the train to Suma and re-experienced Mariko's supremely soft, slippery stomach—the incredibly inviting slopes of its deliciously lickable terrain. In an extravagant oral reciprocation he had lolled his head down those soft slopes, kissing the freshly shorn mount and plunged his tongue, his heart, his resurrected longing, into her, her calves flung out over his shoulders. Pausing only long enough to swig from the plastic cup of tepid green tea on the train window ledge, then breathing through her swaying, sweet secretions, breathing harder and harder, finally tearing himself loose long enough to continue the exploration with his longer, firmer member so that he imagined momentarily that he had found the bottom of her throat from below and inside her. She squirreled herself tighter and tighter against him, legs pushing down harder and harder on his shoulders as he rolled higher and higher into that perfect ball of delerium and delivery. It seemed at release they could have rolled across the firmament a perfect bouncing beach ball in an endless envelope of gorgeous, softly-spreading, moist darkness.

He said to Mioko, before the inevitable red bean paste sweets and the tepid tea, "Tell me how you knew Mogens Nielsen, and what you thought of him?"

But she didn't tell him. Rather it was all girlish giggling and reticence and apparent confusion at his questioning. So he broke off and tried another tack: "Why did you send me the letters from Nielsen?"

"Did I send them?" Mioko asked smiling insanely at him in the lobby of her silver housing.

"I gave you my *meishi* with my postal address, and, remarkable to say, the letters came in the mail."

"And no one else has your address? You never receive mail? Only from me?"

"Well, did you send them?"

"You say I did."

"So, Savior, you are the Queen of the Jews?"

"It's swell bantering with the scriptures, isn't it? Of course I sent them to you. Now you tell me what do you think of them. Let's have tea and you tell me what you are thinking. Better yet, let's go to the reception room and I'll play Chopin. Yes, Chopin softly, and you can whisper to me what you think the letters—are they really letters—or are they something else? Maybe not even Mogens'. I'll play Opus 72. No.1 in E-minor; it, like the letters, came out after his death. And it's softly done, a kind of contemplation of death. Yes, perfect for our discussion. For our chat. I like that word chat."

She slipped out of her slippers never breaking her slow walking rhythm when they came into the large tatami room that served group functions. The mahogany upright piano had dug its double wheels into the matting. He kept his slippers on, even though she scowled at that insensitivity. The black bench was mounted on a wooden tray to keep the legs from driving into the tatami.

"You have to tell me quickly. It's a short piece." The slow repetitive rhythm in the left hand began softly as a mournful melody in the upper register limped out—an infinite legato line that seemed to calm itself into the rhythm, only to nudge upwards as if to escape the lower relentlessness.

"You have to think of them in terms of their audience. In terms of his situation."

"Of course," she said, watching her right hand climb further away from left. "Of course."

"I'd like to know how you got them."

"Oh, I bet you would like to know that. Maybe I went to Harbin after the war. I always wanted to go to China. But it's not really China is it?"

"I don't think anyone went to Harbin after the war. Russians everywhere."

"Maybe I had a Russian lover," she said, closing her eyes, nodding to the rhythm.

"Maybe you are a Russian lover," he answered.

"And what does that mean?"

"It means you didn't go to Harbin."

"Well, you are right there. And now I'll have to play it again. You're a slow thinker."

"I think the clearest thing is to accept the extra page explanation. If you accept that, then they are for real, aren't they? He had a chance to tell you what he really thought, what he imagined was actually happening, if he could understand it at all. But he had to know someone at the place was looking over what he wrote, don't you think?"

"I think Chopin was wise to keep this music in his closet. It's pretty dull stuff don't you think?"

"I didn't find it dull stuff. Did you?"

"I could not read it at first. It was horrible. Horrible."

"I didn't find it that horrible. It was pretty threadbare, if you want to know."

"Threadbare?" The left hand stopped playing.

"Pretty open between stitches, so that you had to fill it in with your own threads—if you see what I mean. For example I say 'eye' and you think 'pull it out with pliers.'"

"But you only said 'eye' didn't you?"

"That's all Mogens said."

"I think they killed him in Harbin."

"Presumably."

"Our lord was killed deliberately—as part of God's plan, isn't that so?" she stopped playing.

"And Judas made it happen, blamelessly....is that it?"

"Yes, of course. And the church was never absorbed into the Japanese Christian Church, and after it was bombed, it was properly rebuilt and then properly moved to Rokko."

"Properly?"

"Yes, properly, according to God's plan."

"And it was God's plan to send Mogens to Harbin?"

"I don't think so, but it was God's plan to bring those letters to me and to you."

"Yes but how?"

"Oh, but we cannot ask that question, can we? It shows lack of faith."

"Faith has nothing to do with it, at least as I understand it. It's simply a matter of logistics. How did you get the letters? They were written, presumably, to use your term, in Harbin. How did they get to you in Kansai?"

"We need to stop for some tea," she said, getting up from the piano. And they went out of the reception room—effortlessly she slipped back into her slippers at the edge of the *tatami*. And they skittered slowly down the linoleum hallway to her room, pausing along the way only to gather up a tray with tea pot and cups. Owen wondered if magically little cakes would be waiting from them on the low table, but it was bare and he struggled to settle onto the *zabuton* placed there for him. He tried, unsuccessfully to cross his legs before his torso, then thrust them out under the table. With an easy envious grace she settled onto her calves on the other side of the glistening mock Formica of the table's surface. She poured two tea cups, ever the geisha of his imaginings. And between sips of the tepid tea she explained that she was from snow country in Japan, along the base of the Noto peninsula where the snowfalls were so constant that drifts along the edges of the road were sometimes 12 feet high. Cars had to put red pennants on their aerials so that collisions could be avoided at intersections. Still it was never terribly cold—her village fought the snow in the center of town with running water—special hoses down the center of the street melted the snow as it fell with no risk of freezing so long as the water was running. She missed that kind of snow in California—gigantic unthreatening snow banks—most of the newer houses in her village put the living rooms on the second floor, the bedrooms underneath, so that at night you could look out at your neighbors before sleeping in the snow cased rooms below. She found piano playing in America very competitive. The Japanese emphasized imitativeness—the very soul of uncompetitiveness.

Everything should be aimed at triumphing in auditions, pushing through to individual unique but defensible interpretations. It was better to adopt a model and precisely duplicate the intonations, didn't he think? Mogens understood, she said , that bending your will to another's was the greatest freedom, the best discipline of liberty, and in that sense he was most profoundly Japanese—indeed, most Danes were. They easily fit in, didn't he notice that? They deliberately bridled their inclinations to see what would happen if they duplicated the sentiments and actions around them. Only the rarest American could do that, didn't he agree? The Danes were patient because they welcomed the information that someone had actually planned well before hand what should occur. Planned even down to reversed expectations. And gradually it became clearer to him that the simple logistics he wanted to know would not be revealed on this visit. At the foyer she mentioned it was God's plan that he would see her again, she was sure of that.

He wondered on the swift train back from Suma if God knew whether his answers were correct or off the mark, and consequently, whether there would be further revelations or only smiling silence and feigned ignorance.

3

"Well, of course the coy tease is her favorite pose," Reverend Bonneau said. "You can't blame her, can you? How could she keep you coming around if she spilled the beans entirely.

Or more likely she's just floating in and out of coherence. It happens all the time."

"All the time?"

"All the time, my boy. It's the most time consuming of all your pastoral duties. It is, you know. No getting around it. Listening to the endlessly waffling bleatings of people nobody else cares to hear. You should hear the stories I'm partial witness to. On shipboard the toughest bos'nmates would come slobbering to me, about the woman who left them, or the parents who never cared one whit about them, or the incredible anger they felt toward some sibling. Or the money they owed."

"But they came to you. She's not coming to me."

"True enough. Maybe you're not sympathetic enough, although you seem pretty sympathetic to me, and to lots of others around here. Maybe you need to give her time. Or more likely she's drifting around in some fog that only death will lift. That happens a lot too, you know."

"She seems to be playing with me."

"Of course, my boy. That's in their nature you know. Learned at mama's knee. Little fillips here and there to keep the groceries coming. Keep your interest up. Actually, the more I think about, I'd bet she's got some dark secret eating at her and it's only worming its way out over several attempts at dislodgement. She probably doesn't know herself what is going on, but sooner or later, the truth will come sweltering out. You can count on it. Unless, of course, she's already way around the bend. And that's possible, you know. Highly possible. And if that's the case, waiting around for some revelation is pointless. Often is. Very often is. So if you're looking for solace, don't look here. I'm no solace dispenser. Never have been, although I could easily have been I guess."

"She just won't tell me how she got Mogens' letters, if in fact they are Mogens' letters. Although she admitted Rielmann and Mogens did go to Tokyo, did somehow preserve the church from takeover. She admitted that."

"And soon enough her part she'll also admit . . . . or not, I suspect. Maybe she truly can't remember what actually happened. Does she weep about it?"

"About what?"

"About what happened to Mogens, about reliving the whole episode."

"No she doesn't cry."

"And how true that is. Mioko's no crybaby. A lot of steel in the little lady. Yes indeed. A lot of damn steel. She showed me the blade once or twice and I got the message to give her plenty of room at the church. A wide berth in a very narrow berthing area. In the war we used to sleep four stacked high. Sometimes you'd be lucky to get a fist between your nose and the hammock overhead. Just a fist. But I'll tell you something." Bonneau stood up from the Sunday school table. "If she's posing it's because she's got something she wants to tell you, something eating at her that she needs to get off her chest. "

"She has a very tiny chest."

"All Japanese women do," Bonneau answered. "My boy, you can't shock me. I spent 27 years in the U.S. Navy. Mioko could shock me, maybe, but not you, my boy. Maybe you need to shock her. Did you think about that?"

"How shock her?"

"I have absolute confidence in you, my boy. Trust in the Lord to find a way."

And on his next visit to Suma Owen believed the Lord wanted him to make Mioko listen to the most disturbing of all of Mogens' pages—a choked passage detailing the contraction of plague. But although Mioko listened carefully enough she did not seem to absorb it as Owen assumed anyone must. To overcome her evident comfort in the silence of her reaction, he asked, "Do you want me to read it again?"

"Of course not, why would I want to hear it in the first place. It's so terrible, so unthinkable."

"Maybe if I read it again, slower this time, you'll remember how you came by it."

"Buy it. A favorite American expression, I understand. Buy it, now!"

He started in again on the flow from the buboes in the little girl's armpits—the almost metered recitation of her labored breathing and the rats gnawing at her rotting calf.

"Oh stop. It's inhuman."

"Oh, I agree. Inhuman but by humans concocted. The cement buildings weren't there naturally—they were constructed. Mogens wasn't a tourist longing to see ice sculptures in Harbin, was he?"

"What do you want to know?"

"I keep coming back to the basic question—how did you get the letters?"

"That's not what you want to know," she said firmly, suddenly looking directly into his eyes.

"A calculated distraction, but I'm not buying it. Not buying it. Did they arrive in the morning post?"

"I suppose they could have, but someone delivered them."

"Who?"

"Someone I didn't know. Someone I'd never met."

"Who?"

"Someone you've encountered."

"What?"

"Yes, someone you'll recognize. Perhaps I should play more Chopin for you."

"That won't be necessary. No more Chopin. No more tea. Just the information—who gave them to you?"

"Surely you know that information is all that old people have, their only currency. They have to be chary trading it away casually. You'd stop coming. It's not my appearance they brings you here, is it?"

He thought about how she might have looked in her twenties. For a moment he could meld her into Mariko's body and the thought was exciting, embarrassing. Did she catch that, he wondered. "You're attractive enough," he said. "A rose in this dismal setting."

"Dismal it is," she answered. "But leaving takes such energy, and essentially I have no one." She motioned to the outside beyond the courtyard.

"There's the church."

"A community for transient *gaijin*," she observed. "Transient *gaijin* in need of some reminders I guess of something they left behind. And father Bonneau reliving his youth in the Navy."

"Or maybe his earlier youth in Kobe," Owen said.

"Yes, he's home in Kobe, isn't he? Unlike his parishioners. He's more Japanese than I am. People don't understand that. Can't understand that. But Jesus wasn't Japanese, was he?"

"Definitely not," Owen answered.

"Too judgmental, don't you think?" she asked.

"He never picked up the stone."

"So he didn't. But he expressed perfect displeasure, often enough."

"They cut off Mogens' ring finger with his wedding ring on it and sent it to Copenhagen, on the very same flight he was supposed to continue on from Harbin. I bet you didn't know that." Owen said.

"I did know that. I know about Unit 731 and their 'medical research.'"

"How?"

"Kawabata told me."

"Kawabata?"

"Yes." Her sudden self-satisfaction seemed tinged with regret at his name.

"So he survived the war?"

"Of course he did."

"Then he brought you the sheets himself."

"It's possible."

"It's possible? Such coyness, lady, doesn't become you."

"Yes, he brought them. There may have been others involved."

"What others?"

"Why don't you ask him?"

"He's alive?"

"Of course. Sometimes Japanese live long lives. Longest in the world , you know. Are you surprised I'm alive? I don't really think so. Kawabata is probably younger than me."

"He's alive ? Where is he alive?" Owen was furiously calculating. Kawabata would have to have been young in Manchuria, but that made perfect sense. The youth would see the atrocity clearly, and find a way to overcome it. Or at least live in conscience with it, but he'd read conscience was not a Japanese property. Those who argued God existed because something had to explain the presence in human beings of a sense of right and wrongness needed to live in Japan, Owen had decided.

There were no interior voices. Conscience quite kayoed. Instead, the antennae were supremely fixed on messages from the group outside. It was not that Kawabata was diligently listening to outside voices; a good

Japanese he had never heard anything else. He knew he existed because neighbors existed. If they vanished so did he, was that it? But still he brought extra pages—the young supremely obedient, supremely fixed person opted to bring an extra sheet. Perhaps he was part Danish? He managed to store extra sheets safely somewhere and after the war bring them safely home. In the midst of the inferno a hand took hold of him and simply guided him through a simple kindness. The Samaritan paused on the roadway out of what? Messages directly from the supreme being? The example of Christ? It made no sense to think of Christ as a modest risk-taker, did it?

Owen repeated as if to savor the syllables, "Kawabata is alive?"

"Oh yes and very fit. A tennis player. I used to play tennis and I was very good. But not now," her voice trailed off.

"A tennis player?"

"I said that."

"Not a saint. A tennis player."

"Yes, not a saint, but I suppose he might be—mightn't he? No I think not. Too worldly. Like you."

"And he comes to see you?"

"He came once. Just once. He's not a regular. He's not a 'returner'. I didn't have information for him." She smiled.

"And tea sweets."

"Boxes and boxes of them. This place is littered with them. And of course I offered him some, but he wasn't much interested. Do you play tennis?"

"Avidly," Owen answered.

"Then you must play with him some time."

"Why?"

"Because I think he'd teach you something. He's very precise in his demeanor and very serious. He always turned down the sweets. Unlike you."

"I understand Japanese relentlessly push away proffered food," Owen said quickly, smiling at her.

"And they squat on their haunches to smoke at train stations," she replied.

"Before they serve and run to net."

"They seldom go to net, as well you know. They're back court players, and so is Kawabata, I bet."

"So he came here more than once."

"Never. I just surmise certain things. It's a generalization I can offer after a long and thoughtful life."

"I wonder if Mogens died thoughtfully."

"I do wonder that myself, sometimes. And I wonder if he might be waiting for me in the afterlife."

"Waiting with vengeance?"

"Oh yes. He might not believe, as we Japanese do, that the dead are all good. So there I'd be quite dead and quite good, but he might not believe it."

"And would he have reason?"

"Perhaps Kawabata-san might know that."

"You confided in him?"

"No. But perhaps Mogens did. He'd after all, be the one to know if vengeance was required, wouldn't he?"

"Was it?"

"Perhaps. But we're forbidden vengeance, aren't we?"

"We are indeed," Owen said. "But Kawabata might not be. Is Kawabata a Christian?"

"Heavens no!" she answered.

Her instant response surprised him, and he suddenly realized that in the non-Christian world, which presumably Kawabata inhabited, retribution might be more than just possible. It occurred to Owen that delivering the scribbled, emotional sheets to Mioko might have been more than simply informing her of Mogens' situation——rather a sharing in its degradation, a sharing of pain. Or more than that, a getting even, perhaps a direct assault on her for whatever role she might have had in Mogens' fate. Or might Kawabata be simply the supreme naif who did as he was asked—out of some strange very Japanese amalgam of obedience and compassion?

On the train back from Suma, the gentle rocking summoned Mariko again and her slick softness blended off into the darkness of the Inland Sea to his right, undulating in the reflected light of the train car in the window, gathering him up in the steady clicking of the steel wheels, spinning him back into that wavy beachball hard breathing so that he felt like a child slowly congealing in freezing slushy water whose arms were being hacked, then sawed off. He heard Mogens' coughing question, "Why, Lord, do you show me these things?"

And he heard Mariko's sly answer, beckoning him onward, "So you may go more deeply into them—more and more deeply."

4

In the backroom of the second floor Chinese restaurant at Hankyu Rokko station, Archie Hesseltine, having introduced Mathias to his "kept bottle" of Suntory Special Reserve directly answered Owen's question. "You're asking me about Unit 731 in Harbin? That's rich. I translated maybe half of reports coming out from that place, right after the war. In Tokyo, for Ambassador Atcheson. On a top secret basis since a lot of the doctors involved in the Unit were going to the U.S. to help bio-warfare there, and the other half were escaping judgment in Tokyo. They were held long enough to determine their accurate status, and then eventually tossed back into Japanese life, where most of them found good work, good pay, and local status as having passed through the toughest container offered by the Occupation—jail until D.C. decided what to do with them. I went home, and, bingo, the great change of '47 suddenly made all those sadists and butchers, a pretty pathetic and very, very silent lot indeed, made all of them wonderful Japanese citizens again, and dispersed them back into Japanese life. Some of them run hospitals and med schools in every major Japanese city, especially Kanazawa. It turned out perfectly for them. We forgot to bomb Kanazawa and so, the old Japan was wonderfully preserved and who should return to the old Japan, but the cream of the old Japanese medical profession. Not jail terms, not execution for savagery or atrocity or whatever you want to call it. No. Just reclaimed status. Healers of the sick, keepers of the flame of Japaneseness. Talk about *tatemae/honne*. Jesus! Can you hold bifurcated views in your same brain? These people sure can. Some of the best were taken to the good old U.S.A. for 'extended debriefing,' but most just reabsorbed, as if they had never been gone. 'What did you do in the war, Daddy?' 'Well, let's see for a good while in Manchuria I dissected living human beings without anesthesia, so their blood and organs would not be fouled by anything to make the suffering less. And then on the weekends I got to freeze and hack children to death. I got to saw off arms and soak kids in salt water and watch them freeze outside and monitor how their breathing eventually stopped. That's what I did in the war. And now of course I took all that knowledge, after I shared it with the Americans in their heavy smelly boots, and now I put it to use to ease the suffering of my fellow citizens.' 'Oh Daddy, you were so brave in the war. How we love you.'"

Hesseltine poured another four ounces of Suntory Special Reserve and nodded at Owen who thought the sunlight off the varnished table was glitzy-dizzying for a moment.

"They put me in a room near the makeshift initial embassy and I reported directly and solely to Ambassador Atcheson, who seemed to get more and more agitated as we brought him more and more details of the Unit's wonderful work."

"We?" Owen asked.

"Sumi and me. They sent me a fellow from Waseda's law school, Taro Sumi He teaches at Keio now. There's an irony, the Waseda boy is now a Keio boy—only the Occupation could have arranged that. We had a bitch of time translating terms from medical Japanese to English. Even Sumi, who knew just about everything, couldn't crack some of the writing. Who had knowledge of the Japanese terms for 'Lycophilization' for example, 'excision of phelgmon ascites?' We used to go to Roppongi bars at night after all day reading through atrocity after atrocity. We'd sit in some creepy *nomiya*, some crappy *sake* bar and we'd recite the Japanese phrases we'd struggled with all day. We'd ask the distinguished parties on the other bar stools for their best translations, and they'd look at us as *henna gaijin henna* Japanese fruitcakes. God, that was the best part the fun of playing those word games in the bars around Tokyo. I think we'd gone nuts, if we hadn't done it. Even now when I go to Tokyo we go back to Roppongi—although it's nothing but posh bars and young people, but still we find some bar somewhere—probably playing Samba music and after enough Suntory, old Taro will start reciting the phrases and he'll ask the patrons nearby to help with the translation. He'll get warmed up to it, and he'll say to anyone nearby who'll listen: 'Here's what we did to the children of Jiln, the Children of Jiln and out will come the litany of mutilation. Induced disease, induced deprivation, denial of nourishment. How long can a ten year old boy live without water? How are his arms different on the seventh, tenth, and twelveth day? If you are six years old, a girl in a barrel of saltwater, and someone comes by and hacks off your right arm, say precisely ten centimeters below the shoulder, and the barrel is outside in Harbin in winter, will you freeze to death before you bleed to death? Those were important questions. Troops lives could be saved by them, couldn't they?"

Owen was aware that Hesseltine's energy, conviction, passion seemed to escalate as he recited statistics, questions, issues from 731 Unit's functioning. Owen wondered if Archie was reflecting Sumi's tension or his own, or indeed if there was any way to separate the two.

"He'd asked these questions and toss out terms in Japanese that no Japanese could understand, explaining that killing children requires a special, acquired vocabulary, but that the all encompassing Japanese language could provide that vocabulary and none of it need be written in *katakana*, all of it would be native to these magnificent little islands. These magnificent little people." Hesseltine stopped as if to draw himself up for another burst, but decided instead to sip his drink in silence.

Owen said to cover the sudden stoppage, "Recitation of atrocities?"

"Here's the thing," Archie answered, "it was the beginning of thinking about God differently. . . . The litany of butcheries gave me wonderful ammunition to taunt my old man. He was the veteran Japanese speaker, the cream of the translators, who refused to help in the occupation. He stayed up in Niigata and said he'd have nothing to do with a regime that could incinerate 200,000 people in a tenth of second. But he took the money I sent back up to him, used it to keep my brother and sister, my mother in food supplies and water through the worst of the postwar stuff. Oh, he even was grateful for it, but always claimed he's seen too much of what the Americans did to Japan to throw in his lot with MacArthur. So I could tell him about the Japanese regime and its nasty little history of slaughter and dissection. And since having listened to his innumerable intoning sermons I had decided that God was a silly concept and an unhelpful one at that. And the notion of omnipotent goodness presiding over the hacking freezing death of children Well, that was a wonderful thing to toss in the great believer's face.

"We're talking innocent, totally innocent victims, here aren't we, Dad? So from a little mud and spit God fashions this child, blemishless, sweet-natured, even tempered, softly addressing the skyshine of innocent life, and what then does big Daddy do? Why he pops this child of his fashioning in a barrel of salted water and saws off an arm, a leg, puts a trowel through the stomach, injects some kind of dye and watches to see whether bleeding or freezing triumphs first and records oh so meticulously how the organs shut down, records meticulously the moaning, the crying, the beseeching—the decibels of despair. Notes it all down in green ledgers and black notebooks.

When precisely do the eyes roll up, when does blood begin to congeal in the salt water, when do the finger nails turns green blue? All of it, everything is copied down, everything is recorded, so that I can translate it bile by bile, blood by blood, pus by pus, vomit by vomit, excrement by excrement. I get to write it all out again in another language, relive in another culture, universalize it and for what? For what? To save future lives? To wallow in the delicious viciousness of it? To show that the tower of Siloam falls on the just and unjust, is that it, Dad? To illustrate what? That we cannot comprehend such evil? Where were you Dad when I fashioned the earth and all its glory? Were you here before the sun? Is that it Dad? What sort of redemption could there be for such atrocity. It's like Hiroshima magnified isn't it? Nagasaki cubed isn't it? And yet you take your stand on those? You make your gesture, your grand stance on those, while I translate and translate, and translate one butchery one sadism after another. Do numbers make any real difference? I don't think so, they all point to the same conclusion. The same writhing emptiness, the same blank curtain yanked across —across, across what, across nothingness. And the great literate father replies slowly: 'I will pray for you and Taro.' It was in his mind, only Taro's infiltrating Buddhist bullshit that corrupted my belief."

"Yet," Owen said, "we worship together—every week at the Kobe Union church. And you take the Eucharist as if it meant something."

"It's true enough. I let the pressed bread dissolve in the hope it makes the sorrow swallowable, in the actual hope that somewhere somehow there's a place where inexplicability itself dissolves. But of course it doesn't. The ritual is a way of acknowledging the absurdity of any response, a way of getting across the divide—a genuflection toward inexplicability toward the purity of inadequacy before life itself. Bring on the rituals, the best armor against absolute infinite jokedom."

"What is the joke?" Owen asked.

Hesseltine looked at him skeptically. "It's soundless laughter, can't you hear it, young Owen?"

"I've heard long- term *gaijin* in Japan go crazy."

"At the very least, "Hesseltine said, "they end up speaking very slowly—at least in English very slowly. That's the kindest thing to do, and in Japan doing the kindest thing is terribly important, but you already know that."

"Perhaps seeming to be doing the kindest thing is even more important."

"How Japanese you've become. And that tells me you'd much rather slip over into intercultural musings than talk about what's really bothering us."

"Bothering you."

"No. Bothering us. The unspeakable longing to get around the divide. You know something? Those whackos actually tried to spread anthrax using pigeons. Can you believe it? Pigeon feathers holding anthrax powder. The idea was to have the pigeons fly around a village and spread the germs as white mist falling from the overly blue skies. Jesus! It apparently didn't work, or at least the evaluators didn't get a chance to do the follow up surveys. The war ended and the evaluators went home to Tokyo, to face the music. But of course the music didn't crank up at all. Atcheson was upset by that, but the military said the information was too valuable to be lost in mere moral judgment on these sweet investigators. Sweet indeed!

"Okay, Daddy, God we know is just a symbolic structure a human contrivance to explain the end of life, but how match up the symbol with the reality of anthrax proliferation? Conscious proliferation. What kind of mind fashions the all-loving symbolic God and then in the early afternoon injects children with plague germs, so the buboes can be counted and monitored, the fluid in the lungs carefully quantified and recorded?"

Hesseltine poured himself another few ounces; the link necklace on the bottle clinked as he fumbled with the bottle. "You're doubtless familiar with the argument that God exists because we have an innate sense of right and wrong, an innate moral compass. Ergo it comes from somewhere and all rational creatures have it. So the great father must have imbibed our soul with those sweet calculations that we always make." He paused and looked a long time directly into Owen's eyes, "I think you've probably used the argument yourself. But at least my pious father didn't have the brass to toss that fulsome garbage out as a reason. He was nobly embarrassed by that contention. So am I. Comes of living here, doesn't it? Live here for a while and you know moral compass goes spinning as the neighbors dictate, doesn't it? You bet it does. But what's the difference. Today what's on the docket? At 10 a.m. we get to inject Log 23 with sulphuric acid' at 10:30 check on log 46's deprivation of water for the fourth day—is he frothing or sighing or merely inert, his dry eyes rolled upwards toward the light we hold over him? At 11:00 little Log 9 having been fed nothing but roots and cauliflower for the past eight weeks provides interesting but smelly commentary on intestinal gurgling. At 11:30 the *gaijin* Dane without a finger gets taken outside to check on frostbite relief through direct flame treatment. At noon we get to go to the commissary for a light lunch, of real *tonkatsu* with tired *miso* soup and slivered cabbage. Then it's on to afternoon rounds. And endless notations in the grey notebooks for little Archie and Taro to translate years hence for the American occupiers.

"And do we get profound Christian shudders at the information—from these most moralistic of all outsiders—these weeping Christians shining through with consciences scored to the apex of human perfection? Do we get their shocked registry? We do not. They are only interested in the data, interested in the record of what they could not, would not, might well undertake if they had the right incentive."

"The *gaijin* Dane?" Owen interrupted.

"Yes, the occasional foreigner, just to leaven the load. After x number of Logs, one finds a foreigner—there were even three American pilots I think. Taro liked translating the bits about Americans. They were screamers apparently. Most Logs were stoic sufferers, but the Americans screamed, whined, complained. Sometimes Taro would chuckle at their antics, chiding me about their utter lack of self-discipline." Hesseltine poured more whiskey into his glass, nodding toward Owen but not filling his—an easily acknowledged rejection of Japanese drinking etiquette.

"What happened to the *gaijin* Dane?"

"How should I know? Just one more Log on the fire. I only know his frostbite didn't respond favorably to direct flame thawing. The flesh burned and didn't repair. I think they must have amputated his feet. Taro said further investigation revealed boiling water didn't help either, just immersion in reasonably warm water, around 115 degrees Fahrenheit. That was very valuable for the American army in North Korea later I understand. So you see—our careful, our meticulous, our loving translations saved lives . The Americans were vindicated—they salved and saved the investigators, the atrocity makers, and learned from them, and all were better. Not a fragile reed was broken, no ill wind blew across our efforts. Atcheson told us we would have had commendations but the work was secret. Still he was so proud of us. God was watching over us, he said. And I found that fascinating. Why I wondered was God watching over us—had he grown tired of watching over Unit 731, bored in Harbin, and liked it best as slowly translated literature, cracked open by two bumpkins struggling on the cultural gap? Had God found the only way to consider the issue—through the negotiated dictionary-dictated maunderings of two lightweights who understood nothing of the information anyway? And when I went home to

Niigata I'd read the choicest passages, the most deliciously depraved ones, slowly to my father and ask him for help getting the language exactly accurate, so I could watch him swallow each morsel I brought him. And I'd wait for him to choke on his righteousness, on his sacred beliefs, so that I could point to the vomit of his conviction as it erupted in the hideousness I carried on the train to him. But you know what? It didn't really shock him into my unbelief. The shards I brought him merely convinced him that spreading the Word in Japan was more complicated than any missionary had imagined. But God would show the way, he asserted, in that maddening, utter confidence that colored everything he did or thought. I thought then, think now too, that was the kind of fellow who pulled the whiskers off cats, or set fire to small animals. Rather like the good doctors of Harbin."

"In war," Owen said—

But Hesseltine cut him off. "Oh, don't go there. Don't go anywhere near there. Just don't give me the nature of warfare crap. I won't absorb it, won't listen to it. Won't excuse anything, anything at all. In point of fact I was just the facilitator of a very basic bargain—the Americans got the information their consciences would not have allowed them to collect, and they could and did apply it, believe in their weird hearts that God had not judged them."

"God?" Owen asked.

"Supreme power," Hesseltine quickly replied. "The source of the sun, okay? Call me Pharoah. The great unconscious moral judgment implicit in human life."

"Implicit?"

"Or maybe explicit. Why not? The point is only Atcheson was upset by our data. He was more than bothered by it. He wanted to get the medical fraternity, wanted to hang them all. His brother was killed in the Philippines, I think. Or at least he talked about death there all the time. All the time. His staff had a running joke for new people—'Have you been on the Bataan death march yet? It's a real treat. You're gonna love it.' Friday afternoons, Atcheson had sherry in his office. Sherry, if you can believe it. Do you know how hard it was to get Sherry in Japan after the war? If you stayed long enough he took you step by step on the death march. It was important that 'these pernicious people,' his favorite term—'pernicious people' pay for their transgressions. But did Atcheson's supreme being deliver in the end?

"No. His brother died in the tropics. His pernicious doctors, his super sadists slipped back into high status in Japan, staffing the best hospitals, the finest clinics, the most prestigious research institutions. And everyone nodded and bowed to these powerful Sensei. And in Harbin somewhere people went on spitting up blood, bursting black buboes, pissing brown while their brains split open from fever or some pigeon delivered disease. And Atcheson drowned in a plane wreck heading back to the states. And suddenly, as God himself decreed it, the Pentagon took over the 731 translation efforts and Taro and I were sent back to other important work. I can't remember what it was. My father was delighted. No more damn recitations, son, about atrocities laid at the Lord. And then my father, like Atcheson just up and died."

"An accident?"

"No. Not an accident, except maybe in so far as everything is an accident. Isn't that so, young Mathias?" Hesseltine cocked and dropped his head so that it almost touched the black Formica of the table top, then he nodded a few times still keeping that position. "He just up and died. Time's up. In grammar school do you remember waiting for sixth period to end, because seventh period, activity period was mostly fun and besides at the end of seventh period you got to leave the school. Do you remember that? That's what I remember. That's where we all are, waiting for sixth period to end. Then maybe we can transition to something else. Or maybe Christ's pain his delicious blood floods over us and we can float in the plasma right beyond seventh period, to what?" Hesseltine brought his head up. "To What? To What? A Gigantic Garage Sale. The mall of all, the dream of dreams, bigger than Osaka's *San Ban Gai* with a billion little shops and *nomiyas*. Still, with enough spine to avoid total collapse into consumer madness. Into this Japan that the Lord so wisely levels in an instant. The plates shift and forty thousand die. And still they cry out for more living space. And the Lord moves the plates again and another forty thousand die. And another forty thousand die. If you cannot remember that first forty then I send you another and another until no one can remember any of them.

Any of them. And each of them, like my father, before they died had annoying habits of tucking their lower lips beneath their front teeth. Raking the teeth over the lip itself so that it became reddish and inflamed. Unconsciously doing it constantly—so that their sons might wonder at the habit. Might wonder at the habit. . . ."

"Do you know anything about the Dane?" Owen asked, to fill the sudden silence of Hesseltine's nearly nodding off.

"What Dane?"

"The foreigner you said probably died in Harbin."

"All the foreigners died in Harbin."

"I meant the Dane specifically. You mentioned him."

"As a Dane?"

"Yes."

"And what did I say about him?

"That he probably died."

"Well, that's a safe enough statement. You give enough people enough lethal diseases and you can safely say 'they probably died.'"

"Is that all you know about him?"

"Yes. That's all I read."

"He was in our congregation. In our parish."

"Our parish?"

"The Kobe Union Church."

"Ah, our parish—you mean that common place where scarcely two or three *gaijin* gather so that amidst them can come Proctor and Gamble, the U.S. armed services, and an unlucky Dane? Is that what you mean?"

"Exactly."

"So I should remember him, or someone should."

"Someone has."

"I did speak of him."

"I mean another spoke of him too."

"Well, marvelous! But now I'd rather go home than hear about him, although I'm sure he was a fascinating fellow. Sage, equanimous, surely long-suffering. My father should have met and blessed him, listened to his confession and lessened his pain. Lessened his pain. I think they gave him malaria and anthrax, maybe cholera and frostbite. *Maruta* Dane. *Maruta* Dane. That's 'log Dane'—the Chinese they called logs, but I rather doubt, actually, they used the term 'log' for him. You know they're rather scrupulous that way. Selecting terms carefully to establish hierarchy and worthiness. You have to be scum to be a 'log'—and by birth some must avoid the term. And God sees to that. God watches to make sure hierarchy is achieved. Otherwise how could the last be first, the weak triumphant, the best the worst? You need to know the order to understand the message. Blessed be the order. It's such an obvious compensation, isn't it? The first Christians were criminals and rich women. The same thing actually. Identical in the eyes of that world. Don't you agree?"

"I don't."

"Ah, not conflict averse! A rare thing in a believer, unless, unless of course you're an evangelical. But you're not. I perceive that you're not. Say you're not."

"I'm not."

"Say it three times." Hesseltine laughed, "before the passing vendor shouts, '*Yakii imo*.'"

Owen said, "*Yakii imo. Yakii imo. Yakii imo.*"

"And so, the Dane felt betrayed and went quietly to his death. Not so much disappointed as heart-broken that his champion had forgotten him. Picking his intestines up and pushing them back in place with frostbitten fingers, popping his plague boils so that the pus froze before it fell three inches from his leg. Oh my father, forgive them for they cannot remember what they are doing. But you Owen Mathias, the replacement one, will remember, won't you and you will make it all better some day, won't you? Some day after you get me home."

In the cab back to Danchi where Hesseltine lived, Owen noticed that Archie slept with an enviable lassitude, oblivious to the mangled way Owen, whispered "*migi, toh mas- su-goo*" (right and straight), then "*hidari*" (left) until he could say enthusiastically, "*coco de eii desu*"—"here is good."

The cab didn't wait for him to return after he dumped Hesseltine off in the *genkan* of his flat. They both heard Jena's somewhat dubious question from inside the apartment someplace:

"Is that you Archie?" and miraculously Archie answered "*Tadaima*" (I'm home). And then chuckled as he slumped onto the ledge of hallway to the western style living room. Owen remembered hearing that "*Tadaima*," from John Wayne as he entered a frontier log cabin in a Japanese dubbed American western on the T.V. in the seminary lounge in Tokyo. He remembered Wayne riding up on a horse, dust flying, getting off the sweating animal, hitching the reins to a post near the walk to the cabin's door, remembered Wayne lumbering toward the cabin with the powerful lurching of American not-to-be-trifled-with corpulence. For a moment Owen had been transported. He was home, things were recognizable and he listened for Wayne to speak, calculating his soft toned confidence, his certitude of command, assurance, the will of God itself. And then came the startling whine of "*Tadaima*," and Owen knew he wasn't home, wasn't certain, was surely not in command. Nor was Archie his Wayne.

5

PER DIRECTIONS OWEN THE very next Saturday morning just before 9:30 turned up outside the Bampaku Tennis club in north Osaka. Mioko had said, "He told me he plays every Saturday morning at 10:00, a special doubles match arranged with two members of Osaka University tennis club, and his partner, another *gaijin* who teaches at the university. He will be dressed in long white trousers, and in a Fred Perry white tennis shirt with a fluffy white towel wrapped around his neck. He'll wear, as he always does, a beige floppy hat concealing his very bald head. But you will notice his eyes through their alert quick movement. And his happy demeanor, as if truly the worst was well behind him and the future deliciously ahead. How I envy that! I suspect you will too."

It seemed the dull gray overcast morning had kept most of the 32 courts empty. The courts stretched out beyond the single storey concrete building that provided an entrance way.

Owen imagined Kawabata would either come from the parking lot opposite the building or along the roadway that sloped down a small hill, leading to a highway with a walking path eventually to Yamada station on the Hankyu line. He figured Kawabata would not drive himself and so faced watching the road. But after a while he grew tired and sat on the cement bench beside the entry door. Some tennis players did come by him, eyeing him strangely, occasionally nodding as if he had some official role before the doors. Owen moved to the far end of the bench and kept his eyes averted from players going in. But that only increased his discomfort, made him more vulnerable to the question coming from his unguarded, unlooked on, left side:

"Are you waiting for a partner?" The old man's voice was gentle and sweet, his manner deferential and reluctant. The long flannel trousers— Owen was reminded of a picture of Bill Tilden he had seen years before— the fluffy towel, and the rain hat, all perfectly matched Mioko's prediction.

"You must be Mr. Kawabata," Owen said, getting up and extending his hand, then pulling it back and bowing too rapidly. "I'm a friend of Mioko's—at the Kobe Union Church. She told me you often played here."

"Did you bring a racquet?"

"Oh, I'm not here to play. I wanted to meet you and perhaps talk with you sometime. Am I speaking too quickly?"

"Not so far. I can understand you."

"You speak English very well."

"No, but I'm learning and practicing."

"Better than most people at the church."

"*Honto?* I thought most of those people were English speakers." Kawabata seemed very interested in Owen's comparative remark.

"No. Foreigners who speak a lot of English and a few Americans I guess," Owen answered.

"I'm the assistant at the church to the rector, Father Bonneau."

"Bonneau? He's French?"

"No. From New Hampshire in the U.S. Maybe originally French-Canadian." Owen said, bowing again, beginning to feel extraneous and intrusive. "I was hoping I could have a chat with you sometime. I'd buy you lunch if you'd like."

"But why?" Kawabata said without any hostility, just puzzlement.

"I'm supposed to be writing a history of the church after World War II to the present, and Mioko thought you might have some information about that early period."

"I don't know anything about the church. I'm not a Christian, you know."

"Yes, Mioko told me that. Not about the church so much as things that happened during and right after the war."

"A very long time ago."

"Yes, certainly. And I can imagine you wouldn't want to talk about it."

"Not that. My memory probably isn't good, that's all I think. But if you wanted to have a chat in English, I'd like that."

"So we could have a chat?"

"Yes, a chat. One of my tapes says I should always accept an invitation to chat in English. Chatting is important for learning English."

Owen thought, he's near 80 and practicing his English. What would be the payoff? Owen almost asked that question but something stopped him. For a moment he thought the conversation had concluded. Kawabata picked up his tennis bag. "I'm sorry to delay your game."

"Oh no, the students are not here. Not up yet I think."

"Yes, especially on Saturday morning."

"They will come shortly. On Wednesday afternoon, I go to Senri Chuo to shop for groceries. We could meet in a coffee shop there at 4:00 p.m. if that would be convenient."

It seemed Kawabata was smiling, apparently delighted he could pluck phrases from his English tapes and put direction into this interchange.

"Yes, that would be wonderful. I don't know Senri Chuo very well."

"It's on the Midosuji line, the last stop in fact. You come up and directly across the—directly across the square, or maybe the plaza? Is that it, the plaza?"

"Yes, an open space, a kind of campo."

"Campo?"

"Probably square. Campo is an Italian term. Across the square."

"Yes, there is a shop called, 'Marvel' a coffee shop. Let's meet there at 4:00 p.m. Could I bring my tape recorder? I would want to catch your pronouncing."

"Sure. That would be fine."

"And you want to talk about the war?"

"Yes."

"Good I will review war words. But I was very young, you know."

"Yes, Mioko said you were."

"I remember there were no clouds there. Not like now," Kawabata gestured to the sky.

"I hope it doesn't rain." Owen added, getting up.

"It won't rain now for two hours, I think."

"Well, good luck in your game."

"You mean tennis?"

"Yes.Of course."

"We will need luck, indeed." Kawabata bowed and drew a small black leather notebook from his pocket. "I will write down our chat next Wednesday," he said, bowed again, then went inside.

As he went back to Yamada station Owen thought: cloudless Harbin and endlessly hammering cold for Mogens Nielsen. Children unsocketed in the slush tanks, and inside—delirium, erratic fever, festering buboes, injections or flea bites to be recorded, meticulously documented in the deep freeze of Manchurian winter—all to be recollected in coffee shop "Marvel." Recollected and recorded for the sake of English pronunciation. Owen imagined:

"Here's how you say 'ah-trah-suh-tea.'"

But on Wednesday the term did not come up. Instead they sparred over tennis—it seemed the university students were rather more fit than the aging Kawabata and his American professor partner.

"You would have to say that," Kawabata said. "There was nothing of difference in our abilities, only in our condition."

"Nineteen is fitter than seventy-nine, I suppose," Owen said.

Kawabata laughed, "But I liked best that those students came over afterwards and asked for 'Advice'—probably the only English word they had learned for the match. They beat us six love and then asked for 'Advice,' which I gave them."

"I bet you did."

"Yes, I'm very good at giving advice. What advice can I give you?"

"Not so much advice—though I would greatly value any you had-—but information."

"About the war?"

"Yes, the war. Where were you in the war, if you feel like saying."

"Oh, I do feel like saying. Manchuria, for the whole of the war. I came back on a special 'repatriation' ship. I remember that. It was a word I had never heard, 'repatriation.' A pretty word actually."

"When did you get back to Japan?"

"I didn't like Manchuria. It was cloudless, without any clouds. Just a very harsh blue sky. I didn't like it there. And very cold. Not at all like Japan. Very cold."

"And what did you do there?"

"I worked in a hospital."

"So you didn't see much combat."

"None. I never fired a rifle. I saw only Chinese patients."

Owen swiveled his coffee cup, then stared at the crust around the finger sweet on the plate between them, then finally plunged ahead: "And one foreigner I guess—maybe a Danish fellow."

"Ah, you've been talking with Mioko," Kawabata said.

"Yes, she didn't think of it much as a hospital."

"We always called it a 'research hospital.' There was a Dane there. A very nice man, very worried about his family in Denmark. He'd lost a finger somehow. That bothered him a lot."

"Which finger?"

"I'm not sure. Perhaps his fourth finger and his wedding ring. He seemed very disturbed about that loss."

"But you enabled him to write his family?"

Kawabata sighed, then put both hands on the cold formica table top, then scratched his forehead. "Yes. I did that. It seemed the only thing he wanted."

"He didn't want to live?"

"Mioko has told you?"

"No. Nothing. She showed me some of his writing. Notes to her, apparently."

"Yes, to her." Kawabata said quietly.

"They weren't much."

"They were enough." Kawabata said. "Certainly much."

"I meant they weren't very descriptive—they wandered a bit."

"Wandered?"

"They weren't orderly. They described a little and then became emotional."

"Most of them were in Danish."

"In Danish? The ones I saw were in English. I didn't see any in Danish."

"Do you read Danish?"

"No. Not at all."

"It's very difficult. Very hard to pronounce. Mogens taught me some words."

The name lingered between them like a cloud, a mirage that seemed to chill the air above the table.

Owen said, "What happened to the Danish ones?"

But Kawabata seemed detached. He smiled insanely. "I think I gave them to the Danish embassy in Tokyo. I didn't give them to Mioko. I didn't think she understood Danish. She didn't you know."

"Of course. You gave her the English ones."

"That's what he wanted. And Dr. Matsuno said that's what I should do."

"Dr. Matsuno?"

"I worked for him. He was in charge of the research."

"He knew about the letters, the notes?"

"Oh, of course."

"All of them? Even the ones in English?"

"Yes, of course. When the Russians came into the area he told me to keep the notes and take them back to Tokyo. I was supposed to deliver the English ones to Mioko, and I did. One packet I lost on the way back."

"And the Danish ones?"

"Dr. Matsuno said to take them to the Danish embassy. And I did that the second day I was back in Tokyo, although most of the building had been bombed. I gave them to a clerk at the front gate. Dr. Matsuno says I did the right thing."

Owen thought about mixedup verb tenses, "Dr. Matsuno said you did the right thing or Dr. Matsuno says you did the right thing?"

"You tell me, which is it?"

"When did Dr. Matsuno say that to you, what year?"

"He says it every time I run into him, but I don't see him often. He lives in Nagata-ku."

"He's alive?"

"Of course. He's only three years older than me."

"On Mt. Rokko?"

"No, in Nagata-ku. I don't go there much."

"You've been to his home?"

"No. I've seen the map in his office. When they thought I might have stomach cancer, I went to him. He's very *erai*—you know that word? Worthy, well-known, well-thought of, distinguished even. He's a very fine cancer specialist. He never charges me."

"That's incredible. You were together in Manchuria, and now here in Kobe, almost 50 years later. How old would Mogens be, for this reunion?"

"Too old I think and besides he was always very sick in Manchuria. I don't think he could have survived. He was very yellow just before the Russians came into the hospital. And he had a very high fever. I remember him saying just before the Russians arrived that he couldn't believe it, but he was actually looking forward to the winter in Harbin. Just to cool down a bit.

And no one wanted the winter to come. No one."

Owen paused, swallowed to clear his ears which it seemed had filled with phlegm—sound itself seemed to flow down into his throat. He felt himself go dizzy and to cover in a quiet voice he said, "Perhaps we could get something stronger than coffee to drink here. Is that possible?"

"Oh yes, I keep a bottle here, "Kawabata answered. "They will bring it to us, if you'd like."

"A bottle?"

"Yes, Suntory Special Reserve—a nice smoky scotch-like liquor. You know about our custom of keeping a bottle—you get a little silver chain with your name on it, and they put it on the bottle and bring it to you whenever you want. Does it bother you hearing talk about the war?"

"Yeah, I guess so."

"Each man does his duty, and then it's over. And so long ago."

The Special Reserve flavor was smoky and very smooth. They each had two drinks and on his way home Owen stopped at Sannomiya and bought a bottle to take with him back to Nishinomiya.

He sat at the phony wood grained formica table in the huge central room that opened on to wooden floored hallway linking two rooms, one a *tatami* sleeping room, the other a western style carpeted room with a faux leather couch and a large desk. At one end of the hallway was a galley kitchen ; at the other end near the genkan shoe drop at his front door was a bathroom entirely contained in a fiberglass chamber complete to drain in the floor before the toilet adjacent to the deep tub. At mid-hallway there was a narrow stairs to upper rooms kept by the university for now absent foreign instructors.

He quickly finished half the bottle of Suntory Special Reserve. It was as if Mogens sat beside him, yellow, feverish, vaguely smelling of feces and vomit. He seemed to be muttering his children's names, but Owen couldn't catch the low guttural sounds, couldn't differentiate them. Then prompted by the fumes he imagined, perhaps, or the excess of whiskey, or perhaps the information Kawabata had so casually delivered, Owen felt himself beginning to retch and involuntarily he spread a thin film of chocolate cake cocoa and Suntory Special Reserve in black bile across the cool table top. Would it lap to the edge? Owen dropped his head down to stop that possibility. And just before unconsciousness set in he heard Mogens, Mariko, and Jesus saying softly, "Do this in remembrance of me."

6

Owen was mildly hungover for the next adult Sunday school class, having consumed the rest of the Suntory bottle Saturday night . It seemed the church's air conditioning, so strong on the bottom floor, wilted as it climbed to the roof. The room shimmered in the moist heat, and the tall glasses of *mugicha* barley tea that Yasuko had carefully set out formed ellipses of moisture on the table top. In fact Owen hated *mugicha* which tasted suddenly like leftover Suntory Special Reserve out of which the alcohol had evaporated. Owen thought, and what was the topic for this morning's discussion? One lesson blended into another in his mind.

Hesseltine came to his rescue: "We want to talk about justification by faith. We're not sure how that fits your lesson plans, but we've been having difficult discussions about Paul's argument and we'd like to see what others think."

Mariko in a softly blue sundress that displayed her incredibly soft tanned shoulders said, "Difficult discussions?"

"All our discussions are difficult," Jena Hesseltine offered as a mild joke.

"Believe and you are saved—that's not difficult," Mariko added. "If you believe, you are justified. Just a simple statement gets rid of all your sins." She smiled at Owen.

"We're in a class studying Paul's letter to the Romans, and it seems that's not the interpretation of the text."

"Really?" Mariko pressed in. "An what is the better interpretation?"

"That it's Jesus's faith in God that saves us, not our belief in Jesus. His perfect certitude redeems all of us in God's eyes."

"So we need do nothing?" Owen asked, massaging his temples.

"No. We need to act as Jesus acted, so far as we can. Belief has nothing to do with it. Only our actions must accord with Jesus' instructions."

"Faith without works is dead? Is that it?"

"We may have no faith at all, but if we act as Jesus commanded—his belief will justify us."

"So we can believe anything we like about Jesus, so long as we act in accord with his stipulations?"

"Stipulations?" Mariko said. "What are stipulations?"

"Directives," Owen answered. "Maybe commands. Strongly stated suggestions, requiring necessary action. Everyone believes they're Christian, Kierkegaard argued, but nobody acted in a Christian manner. Hence all Christianity was phony."

"So those who believed in Baal, worshiped Baal were also justified by Jesus's perfect faith, so long as they practiced Jesus' ethic of compassion, Love of God, Love of Neighbor as love of oneself? Is that what you are saying?" Jena Hesseltine asked, apparently of her husband or Owen.

"That's an odd position to be asserted at the Kobe Union Church," one of the P & G wives said.

"Good point." Owen said. "So let's put it in another context. A simpler more direct one. A more testing one. Let's pose the question that a parishioner faced here a good while ago. He was in a kind of concentration camp, a medical experimental facility in Manchuria. And every day he watched "scientists" and "doctors" try various diseases, tortures, inflictions on children kept at the camp. Freezing some to death slowly outside. Exposing some to plague, or smallpox, or anthrax germs and recording how they died. Starving some. Water ballooning others until organs burst. Mainly children, but some adults."

"Why would they be doing that?" Jena Hesseltine asked.

"Why indeed? Apparently for 'research purposes' to learn how to live longer, fight better, inflict greater damage on the enemy. And further suppose that this parishioner was entirely innocent, for indeed he was, of any crime. He just happened to land at the camp. Why were they doing it? Maybe it was fun for them. Maybe they did it because they could do it. Perhaps they enjoyed it. Perhaps they felt powerless in their lives and took it out on children. Maybe they thought those children were sub-human anyway. Lesser beings, animals for experimentation. Maybe God or Satan told them to do it. Now let's examine the 'faith' of the hapless parishioner placed in that prison of misery."

"Examine it?" Jena asked.

"It's too extreme to be relevant," someone from P & G said.

"Maybe we need a better more detailed description of the misery," Mariko said, smiling.

Owen answered, "You can fill in the blanks. Isn't it Abraham's situation but later in the cycle—after in fact Isaac has been sacrificed? We are told that Abraham's supreme faith in God, his absolute trust in the Lord, the Lord of Hosts, allowed him to walk up to the supreme madness of butchering his own son, because God asked him to, allowed him to pick up the knife and explain to the boy that God would provide a sacrifice, allowed him to begin the process that then, and only then after initiation, God short circuited the game. That supreme faith saved Abraham, pleased God and sheltered humanity for eventual salvation. But the hapless parishioner picks up the story in mid actual sacrifice, witnesses and permits (though he hardly was able to prevent) the actual butchery. The actual dismemberment, the slow pus filled expirations, the buboes festering, the dysentery constantly spilling out, the inner organs turning to rich black blood and gushing out of the orifices of the not quite adult body. What is the parishioner's faith here? Is it that God's sees the bad with the good, and makes all things right again in some distant future? Or better yet, that God has shown the parishioner the twisted back side of the tapestry and soon enough with legions of angels will flip the coverlet over revealing the stunning peacock designs, the magnificent colors that childrens' blood and offal actually construe in the eventual reversal? What would have been Abraham's faith after he cut out Isaac's organs— kidney, spleen, intestines splayed out on the stone and the child writhing in slow freezing pain?"

"Only our trust that Christ's faith could transcend such a situation," Archie Hesseltine answered.

"So that we should be consoled believing that since someone could encompass this chaos our inability to do so is acceptable?"

"Redeemable" Jena Hesseltine added.

"What does transcend such a situation mean?" the V.P. asked. "And is this what we came here to study? I don't think so."

"I think 'transcend such a situation' means 'find something worthwhile in it' or 'be able to accept it, although it makes little logical sense.'" Hesseltine said, putting two closed fists on the table top in a way that signaled, he wanted to engage the V.P.'s second assertion.

Owen insisted however, "But what about the hapless parishioner in his situation being sick himself? Poisoned himself. With a fever and in constant pain, perhaps from a lopped off limb, perhaps because of the numbing cold, perhaps because of some injection of some bacteria, or some deranging drug, so that, spinning wildly, he has to watch the misery all about and put it into the perfect trust, that Archie talks about. Can that really be done?"

"All things are possible," Mariko said, smiling even more fully.

"It would have been a blessed derangement, it seems to me,"Jena said. "Who would want to see such things? I suggest we read a psalm together."

"Why?" Archie asked, "to make us feel better?"

"Yes, to feel better, "Owen said, "Let's read a verse each around the table, the 88th Psalm." And after a suitable interval while bibles were opened to the correct page, he started off:

"Lord, God of my salvation I have cried out day and night before You."

Yasuko in a voice barely audible: "Let my prayer come before You;

"Incline Your ear to my cry."

Mariko: "For my soul is full of troubles   And my life draws near to the grave."

Archie Hesseltine: "I am counted with those who go down to the pit.

I am like a man who has no strength,"

Jena Hesseltine: "Adrift among the dead.

Like the slain who lie in the grave,

Whom you remember no more.

And who are cut off from Your hand."

V.P. : "You have laid me in the lowest pit, In darkness, in the depths."

V.P. spouse: "Your wrath lies heavy upon me   And You have afflicted me with all Your waves."

Owen: "Selah, You have put away my acquaintances far from me;

You have made me an abomination to them.

I am shut up, and I cannot get out;"

Yasuko: "My eye wastes away because of affliction.

Lord, I have called daily upon You'

I have stretched out my hands to You."

Mariko: "Will You work wonders for the dead?

Shall the dead arise and praise You? Selah"

Archie Hesseltine: "Shall Your loving kindness be declared in the grave?

Or Your faithfulness in the place of destruction?"

Jena Hesseltine: "Shall Your wonders be known in the dark?

And Your righteousness in the land of forgetfulness?"

V.P. : "But to you I have cried out, O Lord, And in the morning my prayer comes beforeYou."

V.P. spouse: "Lord, why do You cast off my soul?

Why do You hide Your face from me?

Owen: "I have been afflicted and ready to die from my youth;

I suffer Your terrors;

I am distraught."

Yasuko: "Your fierce wrath has gone over me;

Your terrors have cut me off."

Mariko: "They came around me all day long like water.

They engulfed me altogether."

Archie Hesseltine: "Loved one and friend,

You have put far from me,

And my acquaintances into darkness."

There was a peculiar silence in the room for a moment and then Owen said, "There, now, don't we feel better now?"

Mariko said, "I don't feel better."

"Hasn't God reached out to us and made us all feel better through his word?" Owen continued. "And the parishioner in Manchuria died slowly seeping in delusion and feverish at the end, and howling wildly at the atrocity spilling all around him. Didn't he feel better? David's infinitely gentle psalms spread over him like spring rain, softening the earth of his despair. Shall we read it again?"

"You want it all to make sense, is that it? But what does God want?" Archie Hesseltine said.

"God wants us to act like adults and help others and believe his word and follow his commandments," the V.P. said. "That's what God wants. Not this treacherous doubt and this stupid bleating. God wants an organized lesson and clear directives and measures of success in meeting his aims. That's what God wants. Not stupid self-immolating whining. Anybody can see that."

Part Three

1

"It might be that Proctor & Gamble is indeed the voice of God," Father Bonneau remarked when Owen recounted the Sunday school class. "Marketing clarity serves God's purposes, doesn't it?"

"If you say so."

The priest started to speak but stopped himself, looking longer at Owen. Through the curving windows ravens could be seen circling out over the mountain side. The priest worked his tongue along the inside edge of his lower lip, bulging outward back and forth , running the back of his tongue along the top of his lower teeth. Scrunching his face a bit Bonneau squinted as if to underscore the seriousness of what he was about to say, but at length said nothing. Merely cocked his head to one side and regarded Owen as if he were some kind of antique of not yet correctly evaluated worth.

"Let me tell you about a seaman I knew aboard the U.S.S. Harrison off Okinawa. We'd taken a kamikaze strike—did a lot of damage to that tincan. One more strike and we'd have gone under. Fire everywhere. You could see bodies jumping from overhead into the water, and a piece of the plane sliced right into the seaman's stomach, protruding as if it were a serving tray and you have expected to see his intestines slide out on to the tray. Pretty good size piece wedged right into him. Splayed him out on the deck pinioning him against the bulkhead. I reached for the edge of the piece to pull it out, but he shook his head at me, smiling and shaking his head. 'It's not important,' he said, 'not at all important. I'm elsewhere and it's lovely. Don't move it.' That phrase, 'I'm elsewhere,' has stayed with me. Sometimes before I go to bed I hear it, 'I'm elsewhere. And it's lovely.' A surgeon explained to me that when the body dies, blood pressure drops dramatically, releasing a mad torrent of endorphins that gather you up in ecstasy so that you are indeed 'elsewhere' and it truly is lovely. It's the way the body eases you into dissolution. Some call it salvation."

"So I should realize Nielsen enjoyed his torture, his fever, his dissolution? Is that it?"

"No. But you should understand there is an accounting at the end and eternal respite from what seems terrible to you and to me. It may be there is compensation for what seems uncompensatable, a way to wash over the misery like those soft waters David keeps mentioning in the psalms. A way to wash everything clean again."

"Bio-chemical redemption...a nifty thought."

"My boy, the psalms are full of nifty thoughts."

Owen watched him, thinking, this fat idiot, this saturnine fool imagines some remembered war movie of his youth actually helped him walk among the wounded during the war and even now. An imagined good humor truck dispensing "elsewhere pleasure" keeps him humming through the well-heeled life of the Kobe Union Church. Peace be upon him, for he knows not what has done or is doing or ever will do. "I do feel better hearing you," Owen said with slow conviction.

"Of course, my boy. It's just rephrased biblical wisdom. Now let's walk down the mountain and I'll tell you something I know about the Danish resistance movement and about Peder Nielsen, Mogens' brother."

"Before you do that, tell me about Dr. Matsuno in Nagata-ku."

"Matsuno?"

"Yes."

"I don't know the name, common though it is. At least he's not part of the church."

"I didn't expect so."

"Who is he?"

"One of the doctors who tortured Mogens."

"And when you say 'of Nagata-ku' you mean a cemetery there?"

"No I mean probably a lovely home there, currently a resident of Nagata-ku."

"My boy, Nagata-ku isn't a lovely neighborhood. An *Etta* and Korean neighborhood in fact. I do know my Japanese and my Spanish." the priest laughed. "And I know my chronology. I very much doubt any of Mogens' torturers are still alive."

"But Matsuno is. I was told so by a fellow, also very much alive, who worked for him in Harbin."

"Ah, a nest of ancient eagles, come home to roost," Bonneau said. "I'd heard that Unit 731 personnel were more or less protected by the American occupiers, protected and allowed to continue practicing after the war. Some got quite high in Japanese medical circles. Respected fellows, venerated in fact. But not I suspect Dr. Matsuno from Nagata-ku. Why on earth would a successful doctor live in such a neighborhood?"

When they got to Rokko station, rather than get on the Hankyu line and continue to Sannomiya they went into a second floor Chinese restaurant that Bonneau insisted had the best lemon chicken in Kobe. They took a back table overlooking the harbor far below, lights now twinkling through the haze of T.V. attennas. Bonneau pointed out the monorail that took passengers out to the filled-in island where P & G personnel tended to live.

"Do you know when the Rokko liner passes near apartment buildings, the windows on the train automatically fog over so you can't see what might be going on in the flats, and when the train passes beyond the buildings and is over the sea heading out, the windows clear. That's how these people manage to live quietly on top of each other—they fog their minds over what's going on right next to them, and wait for open water. You notice how in the mornings when you're rammed right into the pack on the trains, you don't hear anything. Not a word. Not a comment. Nothing—even the trains run on rubber wheels, noise-free. Just 300 people crammed into one train car and no sound at all. It's perfect mind-fogging. The fellow about an inch from your face, and pressed against your chest and legs suddenly doesn't exist. You don't see or feel him. It's a Zen experience. In Europe people talk, argue, shout. People smell and comment on what's next to them. In Japan, nothing. No commenting. Even in places like Kobe, hardly overcrowded. Still mind-fogging: perfect mind fogging."

"I'm waiting for the windows to clear," Owen said.

"Ah, my boy we all are. That's what living means. Waiting for the windows to clear. And they will, they will indeed."

"It might be better to be fogged over," Owen said. "It's a trick Mogens surely would have wanted. Anyone would."

"It's really a matter of perception isn't it? For example you and I know that the average Japanese media depiction of America focuses on the latest murder in downtown Detroit. For all the average Japanese knows, there's a killing every 40 seconds in the great United States of Slaughter. And you and I know that the American depiction of Japan focuses on car-building robots and geisha chicks and double-dealing and back-stabbing, or alternatively mangled earthquake corpses. But when you live here, you know, just as you know living in the states, the media view of things is really quite skewed."

"And therefore Mogens really didn't see atrocities? Is that your point?"

"My boy I'm merely saying 'mind-fogging' cuts both ways. You're as right to think of it as a blessed state as a self-deceiving one. And how did we get on to this anyway, when the Kirin is so cold and the lemon chicken so delicious."

So Owen did indeed desist. He watched the narrow Rokko liner ease out into the Inland sea The stops were metronome perfect, the recorded announcements he imagined timed to six seconds before the doors opened. Everything, he knew, was computerized.

Not an attendant on, or near, the line—ever. Owen wondered but knew immediately his answer, whether the windows fogged over if there were no one on the train. Was it a filament that turned water to steam in a trice? Or was there a bag of phony fog that could be piped in and vacuumed away, recyclable, and majestic? He wondered if Mioko sold bags of the stuff.

But Father Bonneau interrupted this reverie. "I keep a bottle here. Don't tell the parish. It's the custom, you know. A nice bottle of Suntory Special Reserve, a nice liter bottle with instructions to keep a second one in reserve—the reserve for the Reserve," Bonneau laughed, "when the main bottle falls below a line marked on the side." He waved to the waiter, holding his thumb and forefinger in a way suggesting a shot glass. The waiter nodded and brought the bottle with its silver medallion, on which was embossed a cross.

"That's a nice touch," Owen said.

"Ecumenical," Bonneau said, pouring two neat glasses. "Peder Nielsen was killed in the war in Copenhagen. He was a prisoner of the Nazis, held in a building the Brits bombed in '45. Gestapo headquarters, and the clever fiends deliberately placed the leaders of the Danish resistance as prisoners on the top floor of the building. Used them as shields so HQ wouldn't get bombed. But the Brits did it anyway. Peder Nielsen never made it out. He'd been an effective leader in Jutland operating out of his parents summer place on the coast. He received British paratroopers, set up cells, oriented anti-Nazi propaganda."

"Is that what you were going to tell me."

"There's lots more," Bonneau went on. He motioned for two more Kirins, and leaned in across the table. "Rielmann told me that the Germans learned from Mogens where Peder might be in Jutland. They did it subtly enough. Over drinks the ambassador began talking about summer retreats, listing off favorite German spots and asked Mogens, casually enough, if he knew of any in Denmark. Mogens described his parents place on the coast, giving the actual address, Rielmann said. And nothing seemed awry since neither Mogens nor Rielmann knew Peder was setting up cells. Letters from Denmark were always innocuous indeed. The assumption, doubtless true, was that they were read at both fascist ends, by the Nazis running Denmark and by the, what shall we say, the Shintoists, the militarists, running Japan. So a little summer reminiscing led directly to Peder's capture and the destruction of most of the Jutland operation. Rielmann thought that was more than enough compensation for allowing the church its autonomy."

"Whatever's truly irrelevant is always autonomous," Owen said after they had received the second Kirin.

"A calculated wisdom, my boy, nifty sentiment, but a bit cynical don't you think?"

"Rielmann thought he had traded Peder for the Union Church's survival?"

"Oh not at the time. He parsed that out later, much later. He was worried much more immediately over what befell Mogens. His Gestapo saviors insisted that Mogens remain in Tokyo for what they said was only a week or two. That time would be needed to work out the paperwork that could return Mogens to Denmark since, in fact, repatriation was what Mogens had been requesting. He missed his family who had returned home right after Pearl Harbor. But Maersk correctly surmised that fascist and free orders would triple in war time, and Maersk wanted Mogens to stay on top of the burgeoning Asian war needs. All sides needed shipping. The economic expansion was truly dizzying. Things are so much more interesting when a war's going on, don't you agree? The helterskelter of war allows all sorts of adventures to go on, and lots of men thrive on that. It's not boring. Shipboard life is generally boring. You pray for action and when it comes you're handed somebody's intestines on a metal tray. 'I'm elsewhere and it's lovely.'"

"I imagine Mogens was very worried about, very lonely for his boys," Owen said, to see if Bonneau's nostalgia could be interrupted and perhaps hammered into a tray for his disembowelment.

"Ah yes, he was very close to his boys. That happens in expatriate life—you'll know that some day I suspect. I have a very tight bond with my Phillip."

It was the first time Owen had heard the rector mention his son. "I suppose you wouldn't like to see him freeze to death. Maybe with one arm hacked off. In a salt solution submerged outside in minus 30 Celsius, with a wind near typhoon scale. I suppose you'd grieve about that."

"What are you talking about?"

"Mogens wrote Mioko that's what he witnessed everyday."

"Oh I doubt that. Mioko was just testing you, spinning out a story to see how it played on your sensibility. She's quite adept at that, you know. A marvelous story teller, in her cute, coiled, coy way. But really quite round the bend."

"I don't think so."

"Of course you don't. That's her gift."

"You've seen the stuff on Unit 731. It's all confirmed. Independently verified. The American records are devastating."

"And locked away. Not printed."

"Wrong, published in various forms. Even Dr. Matsuno, resident butcher is chronicled. The beast of Nagata-ku."

"This is taking a dark turn. I'm not sure I'm up to it."

"Yeah, dark enough I suppose," Owen said. "Rielmann turned Mogens over to the Gestapo, is that it? And got your church as payoff?"

"Oh it's better than that. Rielmann was told. After a suitable interval—doubtless enough time for them to find his brother, and 'take down' (is that the term?) the Jutland resistance, then they told Mogens he was going home via Harbin, Moscow, and Berlin to Copenhagen. But they didn't let him past Harbin. They took him there and cut off his fourth finger and wedding ring,sending that digit along to Copenhagen for the Gestapo there to use against Peder Nielsen. Doubtless as evidence for Peder that they had his brother and would continue the de-digitizing unless he cooperated. I thought as Rielmann explained it that it was the first truly global movement I knew about. But Rielmann only cried about it."

Bonneau poured another shot of the Suntory Special Reserve for Owen and then one for himself. "Rielmann told me these truths," he lingered over the phrase, "right after the war when I was just a twenty year old swabbie on leave from Yokosuka, looking in at his old church to see if it made it through the war. And I made the mistake of telling the most Reverend, most revered pastor Rielmann that his God was just a stupid figment of his own fear. I surely knew that, the way twenty-year olds know, really know things. And that's what made me such a perfect set-up for Rielmann. The perfect receptacle for his bleating confessions—a twenty-year old absolute atheist, in full denial, but still able to receive the most dreadful news and discount it, dismiss it absolutely. Rielmann knew he was talking, telling all to a deaf mute." Bonneau looked at Owen, motioned to the shot glass and offered a brief *kampai*, to get the Suntory down. And continued to look at Owen in a way conveying he saw him as a naive receptacle worthy of himself just after the bombast of the war.

2

"When the ship sinks, even the rats make it into Officer's Country." Bonneau stopped to see if Owen grasped the statement. He didn't. Bonneau washed the Suntory down with Kirin, and motioned for Owen to do likewise.

"Rielmann was a supreme rat and when the church was sinking he ended up in command and he knew that responsibility was more than he wanted. Some people wilt in command, do you know that Mathias?" Again, weirdly eyeing Owen.

"If you say so, Pastor."

"I do say so, and Rielmann wilted, caved in, utterly collapsed. The savior of the church was utterly hollow and a betrayer. He begged forgiveness from me, knowing I'd dismiss him totally, as fried by his stupid convictions. He wanted absolution from me—a twenty-year old arch atheist, arch hater of all things Christian, in full flight from my missionary parents. We were standing in the shell of the downtown church, roof blown away, the altar rain splattered and split in two magnificent shards, with a chaplice lying over the broken fissures, seared timbers partially overhead. It was a helluva fire-bombing. GI's in the corners, chewing gum and watching past the broken altar to the empty harbor. You could see right down to the Inland Sea. All the way down from Tokyo to Kobe—not a building obstructing the view. In that wonderful wreckage—we pasted the living crap out of them, didn't we? In that wreckage he sipped tea after the service, tea from heavy white Navy mugs, like 3rd class petty officers carry around. Somebody at Yokosuka liked Rielmann, liked the Kobe Union Church. It was divine intervention, those mugs, or so he said to me. 'And I don't deserve it, don't deserve it at all.' 'But of course you do, father,' I said, supreme naif of the moment. 'You saved the church from a government takeover—from the fiends of the *kempeitai*.' 'Oh, I traded survival for life,' he said. 'Meaning what? I asked, supreme naif again. 'I gave them Nielsen. Brought him to them, delivered him. Hands off Kobe Union Church. Hands on Mogens Nielsen.' 'I don't understand.' 'That's why I've told you,' he said smiling. 'I told Mioko to tell Mogens I was afraid. I needed support, company—especially foreign company. I needed bolstering. They wanted to talk to him. I made that possible in return for autonomy in Kobe. The Danish Option, they called it. Such a double meaning —the Danish option for a Dane. And I confess it to you, since you hardly care, hardly grasp what I'm saying, or grasping it, ignore it, belittle it, dismiss it utterly. What do you know of soul's endangerment, since you already know the soul is soulless?' It was a bit dizzying for a twenty year old swabbie—the preacher of his youth confessing some dark mysterious violation in the bombed out shards of the kid's only church, now rejected. Jesus, how I longed to get away from the soul-sacking certainties my parents endlessly parroted. You detest the smug P & G saints, don't you?"

"Detest?" Owen said.

"Oh, don't play pious tolerant with me. I see your hostility to their utter certainty, their Max Lucado spewing righteousness. Their *homat* heresy, their sickening condescension their supremely sweet, teeth-whitening convictions. Think about your own displeasure with them and raise that to the nth power and you have how I felt about my missionary beginnings. Of course I was as perfect a receptacle as Rielmann could find; he could confess everything to this kid who rejected the whole construction. He could claim as he did over and over again, 'Full culpability,' confident that the dimwit he told would comprehend little of it, accept none of it as worthy of his consideration. I didn't know Mogens. Oh, I had heard his name when I was an acolyte for Rielmann, but I only knew it as a name with a funny pronunciation: Moans. That actually interested me—what would life be like for a man people called 'Moans?'"

Owen thought, "the *maruta* that moaned."

"Mioko explained later that on another visit. The second flunkie at the Consulate spelled it out clearly: The Kobe Union church could have the Danish option—i.e. independence from government control, but only in return for something. That something was a man named 'Moans' whose brother was more than a little active in the Danish resistance movement somewhere out in Jutland. Peder Nielsen was the target, Mogens, just the navigator. The necessary navigator—a small price for the Danish Option. One Dane for another plus the Danish Option for the good pastor's church. A small thing. Bring along next time a modest possible conduit for troublemakers elsewhere in the empire. The interrogation would be so subtle as to be undetectable, and once sufficient information had been gleaned, then Mogens would be reunited with his family in Copenhagen, and with his beloved brothers. The second in the Consultate would guarantee German passage to Denmark via Harbin, and Almaty, Tehran, Berlin and home. In Harbin something happened. Only Mioko knows what, and presumably why. Ours is not to question. We have only to listen to Pastor Rielmann explain his complicity and watch him weep for atonement. But of course atonement seemed insane to this swabbie of twenty years. Here was Rielmann lugging an oxygen tank on wheels behind him, dabbing his eyes with a thick Japanese summer towel handkerchief, Rielmann confiding in the dumb sailor who had come back to see if the church of his miserable pious youth was still standing. It was, but barely. Tarps everywhere, since the rainy season was already underway, then Rielmann stopped his teary confession. 'This,' he motioned backwards with his left arm pointing toward the broken church roof, 'this will be reconstructed, this will flourish, but this,' he patted his chest, 'this won't.'"

For a moment Owen imagined that Bonneau would join Rielmann in weeping, holding his shot glass out, but the rector only sighed briefly and then resumed his pedogogical stance. "A lot for you to digest, isn't it. But you will, I'm sure. I'm up to three quarters of it now, almost nothing at the time. Almost nothing then. Rielmann knew I'd be a slow learner. He counted on that. It took me forever to figure it out and only partially. Not that I care for clarity on the issue. Nor does old Mioko, I gather."

"Sometimes she seems very focused. Sometimes not."

"Prerogative of age, my boy. Prerogative of age. After seventy you can turn to anyone for any reason and end the conversation by saying 'Can't talk now. Bowel disorder,' and scurry off."

"She never said so."

"We're both slow learners it seems," the rector observed.

Later Owen wondered why the rector had told him about Rielmann's confession. It must have been a planned revelation, but one layered with so much aleatory circumstance as to seem haphazard. It must have been festering in Bonneau's consciousness and suddenly burst out uncontainable. Owen might have inquired about that but initially he had always assumed adequate strictures on expression were equally distributed among his friends. Surely they understood limits. Nothing religious was ever broached after church, for example. It was as if the clouds of T.V. antennas seemed infinitely more concrete on the lower slopes of Rokko, than any religious ambivalence. If you sought absolution from a pagan misfit did that make your repentance bogus? A mere joke to be handed around to non-comprehending saps who laughed mutually to cover their ignorance? We could all have a quick chuckle that old Rielmann sent Nielsen to his tortured doom, was that it? Extravagant distancing was the first defense of *gaijin* in Japan. You looked quite consciously for a situation that tossed a double perspective on whatever you were doing—the floundering foreigner in a landscape totally misperceived—a cloudless sky that was always raining, for example. You could not quite grasp what bus passengers were saying to you, so you speculated on their intentions, even as they became more frantic in their gesturing to you, all the while you were riding the bus in a direction totally opposite to your plans. And soon enough you discovered your silly error—you had been heading west instead of east. Suddenly what the passengers had been trying to communicate to you became clear and laughable; meanwhile, the passengers had long since exited the vehicle. This bus was going into errant country and you recognized you'd have to get off, crossover the roadway and recover all that lost ground, but the days were softly warm, the nights mucid, cool, the *sake* clear and thirst-quenching, the camaraderie overwhelming, so that one could not be truly separated. In precisely understood rituals everyone was in fact not disconnected, but enclosed. Among allies favors were returned—in a perfectly balanced universe, one salvation occasioned another's loss. Perhaps Rielmann understood that the weighing of conscience in Japan had nothing to do with the rightness of a decision. Outside structure enfolded all before it, and inner voices were all social, not individual. Mutual gift-giving carried all before it. And what, if not a gift of wondrous wealth, was Nielsen? Easily worthy another other parishioner and among them all, perhaps the most appropriate for them all. There was, perhaps in Rielmann's mind, a certain equivalence of future autonomy balanced against Nielsen's deprivation. Did Rielmann content himself that the asymmetry of the offer was nonetheless appropriate because after all, *gaijin* did not really understand or accept the rules of the game? Just as the Japanese did really understand or accept the tenets of Christianity?

Owen imagined that Rielmann may even have believed the ambassador's assurances that Nielsen would be safely transported back to Denmark, to join his family, his friends, his anti-Nazi sympathizers. More likely Rielmann contented himself that Nielsen's fervent grasp of the Danish option, his stupid belief that the Kobe Union church would, like Denmark itself, exist autonomously beyond Nazi surveillance, beyond fascist control, beyond violence, would cloud his grasp of the enemy his brother had already engaged in killing. Still, Rielmann needed to discuss it, so that none of the poison leaked out. He could show the wound, acknowledge the strangulation, and know his audience would only shrug and wonder why such information had been shared. Such redemptive suffering would occur, per force, in another country.

3

PERHAPS IT WAS THE Suntory softness in the evening air or the Suntory wobblyness of his walking gait or the Suntory silliness of the hazel tinged darkness amid sudden porch lights that sent Owen imagining he was not in Kansai but in the suburbs of Tokyo. In Setagaya-ku where he taken seminary preparation and where he remembered with absolute vividness the raven crows suddenly flocked up on one tile roof, only to burst off that and onto another. There were ravens in Kansai but not nearly so many. He heard them skittering across the roof of the western style house he occupied on campus, but nothing like the fierce flocking of the ravens in Setagaya-ku. He imagined them in torrents, and it was those memories that later should have tipped him off something was going to happen. For, there were no ravens, not singly or in pairs, much less in flocks, anywhere to be seen on his walk home.

Owen trudged past houses with no illumination past silenced cars, and empty bus-stop rain shelters, and looked to the sky in search of any sort of bird. But there were none. Instead, a thick wavy silence —he expected to hear cat clicking across the asphalt or an assaultive barking of dogs on the way. And most of all he looked forward to hearing the brilliant, caustic moaning of the dog belonging to the house behind his residence. Apparently the dog spent the nights outside, but never accepted that assignment. Each evening when the dog was pushed out of the tiny house, it set about yowling protest. The tone was so strident, so human-sounding, that every evening Owen imagined a six year old boy had been sent outside and his arm simply pulled out its socket, ripped away at the shoulder. The screaming was so pitched that it seemed the boy (the dog) was retarded and utterly incapable of shutting down the pain. The dog's high pitched mordant moaning went on for about twenty minutes and then, exhausted, the animal gave up the ghost. The blessed silence was only interrupted if an errant family member went outside to check on the benighted creature.

But this night the dog was dead silent, inert, even though Owen walked by at the precise time of the dog's usual maximal complaint. Perhaps, Owen thought, they've let the animal stay longer inside tonight. But no, the dog eyed him from a slumped, almost frightened position. Eyed him and whined nothing at all. Owen lingered at the house's gate, thought about prodding the dog into some commentary but decided against it.

So neither the birds nor the dog were bellowing predictably. That should have suggested something to him, Owen decided later. But at the time he was merely thankful he didn't have to imagine some way to assuage the dog, didn't have to decide once again that the skittering across the tile roof was not that of a thief or murderer, but only bored ravens looking endlessly, as they did, for something to eat.

Owen in his house, put on his slippers and went upstairs to watch T.V. He was just in time to see the daily showing of "The Wonder Years" the only program in Kansai that broadcast in English. There was something deeply reassuring about young Fred Savage's interactions with his overbearing father. A good husband Owen had heard in Japan was "healthy and absent"— the breadwinner totally alien in his own home, a place chosen by his wife in accord with her strict rules for the success of their children. The father of "the Wonder Years" was extravagantly present, tangible, influential in an Archie Hesseltine way without the Suntory and without direct knowledge of the long suffering Dane. So cavalierly mentioned-—a mere translation obstacle— a set of different data to be cracked open for the upset ambassador to ponder and any seminarian to turn over and over in his mind.

There was no reason for Archie to connect Mogens to the Kobe Union Church. Surely Archie knew of Mioko and presumably she had slipped into her "silver housing" before the Hesseltines came to the near top of Rokko mountain. But still Archie had mentioned the Dane. Could that just be a peculiarity? A coincidence? Why not?

The birds and the dog were silent and Archie mentioned Mogens. No connection there. The petulant father orchestrated young Savage's life. The petulant father convened Owen and Archie in a in a Chinese restaurant at Rokko station on the Hankyu line. What of it? The petulant father lifted the veil to reveal one aspect of the issue, simultaneously keeping it from others who may have been unwittingly involved. Jesus spit on some dirt, rolled the mixture to hardening mud and pressed into the eyes of the blind and presumably their faith saved them. Saved them and, as a byproduct, restored their sight. Of course he could believe that. God was always a healer, but he did not restore the sawed-away arm of the child log *maruta* in Harbin—or relieve the swelling black armpits of plague-ridden Mogens, did he? Indeed, the immediate inflictor of that misery returned to raise his family and live a rich, full life of adulation, respect, admiration among his occupied people. Occupation soon enough ended so that riches, honor, might be more fully bestowed upon the inflictor. The birds, the dogs were silent in awe before such exoneration. The unsocketed, semi armless children simply froze to death and were tossed after sufficient examining evisceration into the chill lime pits of Harbin. They receded into the frozen earth across two or three summers and their bones or chips of bones may have turned up in the ice sculptures Harbin showed to the tourist world in January/February 1995.

And in Kobe the MD inflictor consoled his patients and at home slipped into a warm *yukata*, and after a long soak in a doubtless giant deep bath, he might even be taking one now as Owen imagined himself soaking in such a tub in his own western style home—kept for *gaijin* instructors at the college. But he did not take a bath. Instead he sat at the *kotatsu* table in his one *tatami* room, legs warming under the blanket attached to the electric heater in the table's center, and wondered why the depressed, exiled dog did not whine and bark as usual.

Did the miserable logs call out to Jesus? Did Mogens? Or in the haze of infection (cholera? anthrax? plague?) did Mogens imagine Christ walked over frozen water to him, each step lessening the vast slide-away Mogens experienced as part of this treatment? The slide-away from understanding each moment toward a dull acknowledgment of some throbbing, some sobbing discomfort moving swiftly toward explosive collapse. How paltry was crucifixion compared to witnessing the dismemberment of your children! Christ had none. How could his suffering force salvation? It was too little and much too early and over too quickly, as if God had no stomach to contemplate Harbin. The dog didn't whine. The ravens didn't flock. And the Suntory-soaked night was as silent as steel. And as coldly unyielding and Owen thought: "Consider the ravens, for they neither sow nor reap, with neither storehouse nor barn, and God feeds them. Of how much more value are you than the birds?"

Why had the ravens fled? Why had they disappeared? What did they know? Or were they endlessly searching for food? They may have been fully socketed, but continuously looking for sustenance. Worried about their next bite, and their children's next bites. Nobody tore their wings off. Why were they not around?

No matter. One should be thankful for the silence and the Suntory-soaked sleep. Owen decided . Good enough and not to be questioned. He turned off the *kotatsu,* spread out the trifold rubber mattress beneath his futon. Then drew his bath and watched bemused by the drizzle sound as the deep tub filled. More bemused by the slow mist wafting off the rising surface. He showered and sat on his plastic stool outside the tub and then eased into the scalding sea.

He wondered in the encasing heat whether a moment arrived for Mogens in which after questioning, or complaint, or howling derision, he just slipped away. A collective numbness that announced simply and easily— you have passed beyond commentary on this experience. Time separates to second-by-second recognition that what is going on, is simply going on, unrelated to before or after.

This, that, this, that, this that. New hat, old hat. Better to unplug the mechanism that connects this to that and sit deep in heat watching one part unrelated to any other part. Sit bemused and imagine his children with arms fully socketed, elbows unsawed, livers uninfected. Watching endless Danish windmills dissolving against the greying sky. Surely Mogen sobbed remembering his family, but what of Chinese parents outside of his hell worrying about their children? And the good doctor itemizing their agony and above, beyond, over—the supreme good doctor supervising these desecrations. Would that Grand Inflictor stop the butchery if Mogens could persuade the deity that at least 40 Logs in Harbin were in fact honest good citizens, guilty of nothing? And if for 40, then perhaps for just one? Why worship anything that could encompass such systematic atrocity? Imagine being forced to translate the journals, lab books, data collections of engineered slow slaughter. No wonder Hesseltine retreated to Suntory soaked irony and bitter commentary. No wonder Owen listened to Archie so carefully. For Archie knew the way out of hammering care and into moral slumber.

So Owen drained the tub, took the minute, thin towel Japan prescribed, dried off enough to get into his giant heavy futon, yank the covers enough to bunch his light *yukata* up around his stomach and then drill his hard head into the harder bean pillow. The bath's heat would carry him through the rest of the night.

But, unfortunately, he began conjuring images as he drifted away, images of the little nasty Japanese scorpion-like centipede called, in Kansai at least, *mukade.* The *gaijin* house had been infested with them, apparently coming down from the shrubbery on the hillside and finding some warmth in crevices near the gas heaters. They were almost impossible to kill. Stomping on them only energized them. They squirmed out from under your heaviest stomp, pincers furiously snapping. You cut them into pieces, each of which would scurry off presumably to grow new pincers. Japanese colleagues claimed the only sure killing was to pick them up with tongs and hold them over a gas burner until they burned up. They tended to travel in mating pairs. The worse thing was to find only one and kill it. The other would eventually find you.

Owen had purchased and regularly set off special bug bombs that after filling the house with unbreathable fumes did manage to kill the youngest *mukade*. He made the bombings a monthly ritual, confident that he was keeping the creature population down, even as he was sure his own chromosomes were deracinating. Everything in the house was scented with the killing fog, but even when breathing was heaviest he felt blessedly safe. Except for the dreams. After each bombing, after a six hour wait for full dispersal of the deadly fumes, he found the baby *mukade* in clusters of death near the space heaters. The littlest ones did not grow stronger from the fumes. Their elders apparently find some way to survive. They would live to terrify him at a later date. But the future he had incised.. The shards were before him and he delightedly swept them up. Exaltation came with each collection.

But in the dreams that night it seemed even the baby *mukade* revived. It seemed their elders pushed them into massive formations, piled them together and somehow got them clicking their pincers in unison so that the floor of the house was beginning to sound first in a mass crackling clicking sound, and then a fiercely growing, crackling roar—a jet engine aimed from the center of the earth directly at his *futon*, which suddenly began bouncing up and down. Lifting off the spongy *tatami*, falling back, lifting again, as the jet engine roar notched up toward unbearable decibels. The sliding glass doors of the room in the latest catapult off the house's foundation, splintered into falling sheets of panes, spraying outward and slicing into the *tatami*.

Owen and the futon were flung upwards toward the ceiling, then resettling as if to gather torque from the suddenly stabilized *tatami*—only to be tossed up again. More clattering, roaring. Anger of a billion *mukade* summoned toward, then lurching away, from some fire in the earth's center, roaring their way upward, screaming his name and pledging: "We're com-ing to get you!"

In a moment of upward, then downward then upward lurchings Owen realized it was not a dream. The earth was pulsating and he remembered Japanese colleagues warning him that damage and death came from earth-quakes that moved up and down. "If it moves up and down, look out! Big Trouble! Get to a doorway. Cover your head. Pray. Up and down means toppled buildings. Side-to-side? No Trouble. Up and Down? Death." It did seem God was dribbling the house like some spongy basketball, explor-ing in escalating frenzy just how quickly he could unpinion the building, explode it upward, drive it downward, pushing the pilings, the foundation, back toward the source of the energy hurtling everything upwards. "Up and down" —howled the Japanese mentors of his memory, "Up and Down— you die! The buildings topple, the fire spreads everywhere, and you die, you die. YOU DIE!"

Side-to-side earthquakes always ended within ten seconds—they dis-oriented you just long enough to work their eerie magic that indeed the earth would end in rubble and slaughter then eased off their terror, so that it was almost laughable how fearful you had been. But this up and down whirlwind didn't end in ten seconds, didn't end in twenty seconds. No, it seemed Owen had been appointed to ride the building up and down like some crazy carnival ride far out into the night, up among stars, above the sparkling Inland Sea, off into the firmament, up and down, up and down so that for an instant he thought his hands were actually controlling the throb-bing. He could settle the house and lift it simply by relaxing his grasp of the *tatami* rupturing beneath him. He cut fingers in the rush matting, his arms lacerated by the splintered glass could nonetheless guide the building back down toward its cement disks holding the porch pillars, down toward the cement slab on which they rested so perfectly before the tumult. He heard the kitchen cupboards empty spewing flour and liquor and dishes out onto to the wood floor, heard the refrigerator wobble walk across that floor until it spun over rupturing vegetables, leftovers, sauces from parties or partially eaten meals. The refrigerator joined the *mukade* chorus announcing jointly, "We're coming to get you!"

Owen felt the whole house shifting, dancing toward the edges of its foundation. When it came off that poured edging the walls, he under-stood, walls couldn't hold up the heavy tile roofing. He saw flashes from the toppling and yanked-up space heaters, and still the roar continued, escalated, buffeting the house. Books flew off the shelving which suddenly was wrenched free from the studs. The grand piano in the living room seemed air pressured upward and down. Soon enough the legs snapped, left and right, and the soundboard and strings dumped over, pinging wildly as the walls rattled applause. When would it stop? Never! It was determined to shatter the house, pulverize it so the *mukade* from the hillside could march across the broken tiles. And there was the scent of oil. Oil fumes saturated the building, the open night air pouring through the smashed glass panels—a weirdly clean petroleum smell. Did the gas lines belch the smell out? Had the house's semi-collapse somehow triggered a geyser of oil somewhere? Then just as suddenly the jet engine roar dropped off to absolute silence. The house stopped bouncing. The walls were still in tact. The roof had not come down. There was a chance to get out. Owen took it.

He staggered across lamps, books, glass shards and in his underwear made his way to the long narrow hallway toward the front door. The darkness was impossible. Pictures had fallen in his path and near the entrance he smelled beyond the pervasive petroleum scent the odor of sewage. He imagined there were broken lines in the suddenly cracked-open earth. He struggled into his shoes, grabbed a black pea jacket from the hook in the *genkan* and started running away from the house.

At the gate the guardhouse was entirely dark. And then Owen noticed a small pen light picking its way inside. "*Daijobu*?" Owen shouted at the light through the window but there was no answer. "*Daijobu*?" he asked again. "Are you okay?" he shouted in English.

No answer, but the light threading its way inside the tiny shack, now moving back and forth in the window, then retreating to an interior room. Owen remembered the Japanese in danger stay inside. Inside was always preferable to outside. He passed through the gate and noted candles appearing in the windows of some houses down from the college. When he reached the intersection of the lane to the college and the main road to Nishnomiya Owen realized he had no reason choosing the route he did. "What am I doing?" he thought. "Where am I going? Why am I going anywhere?" He wanted to discuss the event with anyone. Why did no one come out to say anything about the noise, the shattering houses, the pervasive oil scent? And if they had come out, what would they have thought about him? In his pantless legs, sockless shoes and pea jacket, jockey briefs visible from the edge of the coat. Who would risk talking to this deranged *gaijin*?

What am I doing out here? He peered down the road. It seemed three hundred yards down a truck had overturned and beyond the truck over the crest of its upturned side a rose-colored plume, doubtless from downtown Kobe. A rose plume that grew more orange at its base, disappearing behind the toppled truck.

Owen thought, so I'm here in my skivvies waiting for what? Traffic? Pedestrians? Looters? Someone to embrace in celebration of mutual survival? But only darkness. Mephitic darkness and shame at wandering outside (in the dreaded outside) from a known shattered place to a lonely, apparently crippled other place. Better to go back. Better to be inside. Better to dress if one could, and if not then better to sit quietly and wait for daylight in order to pick around the ruins.

Owen leaned toward the college and shouted suddenly, *"Daijobu?"* Would not someone answer? He thought he heard an answer from somewhere down the road. *"Abunai desu neh!"*

Abunai! Dangerous! So it's dangerous, Owen thought. What a revelation. It's dangerous.

Better stay inside. Better get crushed in your own rubble, than be clobbered in someone else's.

Was that the key? Safety is always inside.

Owen went back up the lane to the college and in that trudge he began to turn over in his mind the directives he'd seen about earthquakes and their aftermath. Get water. Eat perishables first. Stop any bleeding. Yes, there were superficial cuts on his lower legs and hands—glass shards, but nothing deep. Get water, Owen said to himself. Yes, water would be the first essential. I need to fill the bath tub. Yes, that should be my first priority. Fill the tub. Fill the tub, get dressed and consume the food before it spoils. Yes, there could a specified order to the next hours. A careful, stipulated plan. Fill the tub. Get dressed. Eat. That was how to live. Make the plan and follow the steps. Ignore the damage. Focus immediately. Solve the first issue. Then, the second. Then, the third. Yes, order, sequence, mastery. He felt power flowing into him, fear draining out. Fear slipping on the lane, spilling behind him, fear seeking out the drain pipes protruding from distant highways. Of course! Sequence carried all before it. He passed the gatehouse and was about to turn into his yard when the first aftershock hit. The earth jiggled again, the roar started again. He watched his house shift off the concrete disks that held the second floor porch supports. Those supports splintered; the porch tilted down but didn't separate from the rest of the house. The heaviest tiles from the roof began a tearing separation from their bamboo underlay. Good God the whole house is coming down, Owen thought, as the porch tiles wrenched free and slid toward the yard, dumping on the thick moss sod of the yard. Thunk! Thunk! Then everything held again, suspended. The porch roof was tilted but still connected; the tiles stopped sliding. Owen sat on a massive imported granite rock at the edge of the lane, a safe distance from the house, should it collapse entirely. The granite felt wet through his thin underwear; he tried unsuccessfully to tuck a portion of the pea jacket under him. The darkness will lift in another hour, maybe sooner, and then someone will come. Someone will come and tell him what to do. The main thing now was to wait patiently, silently—no more screaming inquiries about the health of the universe. Someone would come. Someone would come and instructions would be forthcoming too. Owen thought, well I'm alive, and it's cold. And if no one comes, still I have a plan. I'll go in carefully and fill the tub, as soon as I can see a path inside. I need only wait until I can see where I'm going.

4

WITH SUNLIGHT IT SEEMED the oil fume dissipated, and Owen picked his way into the leaning house. He had difficulty sliding the door open to the tub compartment; pressure he figured from the slow easing down of the second story. When he opened the bath faucet nothing came out. Perhaps there would be water further up the campus. He changed his clothes, shaking the broken glass out of his trousers on the *tatami*, then he packed a small duffle bag with changes of underwear, shirts, and one pair of pants. He assumed he would have to go elsewhere, a thought confirmed by the shout, "Come out! Come out! Now, Come out!"

At the edge of the college lane, a guard was standing on the sod near the granite boulder and shouting at Owen. He motioned with his hand and seemed quite afraid Owen would not respond to his shouting. To reassure him Owen bellowed back, "*Wakarimashita*. I understand. Okay. Okay. I'm coming out." He picked up the duffle, looked across the crippled piano, the smashed dishes and the broken bottles of wine and liquor, the sprawling refrigerator, the flung books, toppled pictures, the leaning-down porch and the rearrangement of the expected room seemed to saying to him, "Ah, here, now is a situation most unplanned—what is important now is that you act in a way you won't regret. Certainly you wouldn't wish to add to these wrongs, would you? In memory you would want others, wouldn't you, to say," Owen Mathias showed great compassion, courage, solidity in casting aside his own needs and tending to others." The guard, for example, needed tending to, didn't he? Time to put aside self and in this catastrophe show what was noblest, truest, bravest, most edifying in human nature. Wasn't that it? So Owen picked his way slowly back through the hall and outside to hurry to the anxious guard, the first human being who seemed concerned about his welfare, and while he did that striding in nobility and sweet graciousness, he listened to Archie chiding voice: "Okay fop, you plan your appearance, but they do it automatically. You think yourself grandly compassionate, but notice the broken shops aren't studded with looters, the broken pipes belching out necessary water have developed long, orderly lines of patient Japanese, orderly seeking their share and no more—no gangs, no strife, no tearing selfishness in disaster, no pushing self forward, no wallowing in suffering and demanding relief, just simple patient, quiet, seeking. And done automatically."

One might wonder why? Maybe because they didn't understand redemption?

Nobody died for their sins. That's it. Nobody died for their sins. No resurrection. No new life.

No enlightenment either. All that avoided, and cooperation emerges. Even the damn prices don't increase. Water will be the precious commodity and broken shops will sell what bottles they have at the exact given price, until the supply is gone, and without supplication or prayer.

Think about it, seeker. Dwell on it. Adopt it. Get a Mongolian flap to your eyes and chuck the Gospels—things will work better.

The guard interrupted Owen's reverie. "Follow up!" Doubtless he'd practiced that small English phrase the whole time Owen picked his way to him.

"Follow up?" Owen repeated to elicit clarification.

The guard didn't speak, only pointed up the hill and started walking. Together they passed the main administration building, already leaning to the right, parts of the second and third floor having pushed down the archway entrance to the first floor. It didn't look safe. The main Junior High building beyond the administration offices had collapsed entirely. Dust filled the air around the shards. Fortunately no one should have been in the building during the quake. But there were crushed cars scattered around the ruins. Beyond the crushed Junior High they took a narrow path through a calculated garden—everything in precise placement so as to appear entirely unplanned and natural. Yet even here they stopped and the guard pointed to the collapsed tea house that had been the garden's natural center attraction. At length they came out onto the central quad of the campus, at the very top of the hill, leafless cherry trees surrounding the muddy green space. They crossed the lawn. The giant gymnasium beckoned across the quad. "Go there!" the guard demanded, pointing to the entrance. And as he got closer Owen heard hubbub as if a game were being played in the well lit gym. But it was a game only a few might have understood—about three hundred Junior High school girls in pajamas seated on the floor of the gymnasium, chattering to each other and passing around a gallon jug of what looked to be orange juice, and large plastic bags filled with rolls. Owen heard someone say, "The dorms collapsed but no one was killed. It's a miracle. No one was killed."

No, Owen, thought, the real miracle is this pajama party—shared orange juice and rolls. He wondered if the plastic roll bag spontaneously regenerated new rolls as old ones were taken out. The juice jug was ever filling, was that it? Maybe the earthquake hadn't happened. All this was a reverie designed to initiate him into something he didn't grasp, didn't want to grasp.

He thought, if this is to be my residence, my designated place ("Follow up!"), then getting something to lean against might be required. Wall space seemed already claimed, except for a spot just beyond the unfolded bleachers. He eased to that opening and sat down so that his back had a piece of the wall for support. When the roll bag arrived he pulled out two, then felt ashamed and put one back. The girls went on chatting. And in a sudden terrific aftershock. the whole building shook, lifted momentarily. Chatter ceased. Glances sped toward terror. Abruptly in the shaking, the overhead windows abutting the ceiling simply splintered and shards poured down on students along the walls, on Owen who covered his head and imagined a sheet of glass coming down as he'd seen in the movie "The Omen". But no blessed decapitation occurred. He'd still have to account for, plan around, his collapsed house, his crumpled college, his evident extraneousness to the whole miserable experience.

Better go home, foreigner, things will be very tough for a good long while, and you don't really mesh in the revival possibility. We must set about dealing with our atrocities, and having you around is not only inconvenient, but also quite annoying. You seem to have other expectations about how to behave and more importantly how to be treated. In a crisis who needs foreigners about? Disaster is our mother language—we are inured to it. You seem upset, puzzled you're alive. You shouldn't be. One lives, another dies, and the wheel keeps spinning, surely you understand that. If you don't, why pay more attention to the friendly chatting going on, now that the shards have been brushed off.

Owen thought, "And what about the next aftershock?" But the chatting ruled that out. Owen felt acutely tired, suddenly very sleepy. Had the rolls been tinctured with something? And he did doze off, only to be awakened by the chaplain shouting through a bull horn. He understood several buildings had collapsed, that the roof of the Literature Building had been torn off, that the Tea House in the special herb garden had collapsed, that faculty housing had collapsed too. The long archway connecting the main administration building to the classroom hall had pitched over. No students had been killed, but the collapse of housing off campus had killed at least four faculty members. Downtown Kobe was burning, and the Dean lived near there. The slums in Nagata-ku home to *Etta* outcasts and Korean immigrants, were an actual inferno now. No fire services were available to them. But some school yards had become refugee camps. The trains and highways were out. It would be a long, long time before classes were held. The litany of destruction droned on, with Owen only intermittently grasping the Japanese phrases. The bag of rolls came back, filled again. This time he took two and put one in his pocket. He heard a reference to at least one faculty member being in the gym now. Then there were instructions for some students to take pails to the nearby swimming pool and fill them for use in the bathrooms of the gymnasium. So flushing would happen manually then, and he wondered where the pipes, presumably broken or inert, led?

And drinking water? The chaplain explained that in the later afternoon, when presumably the biggest aftershocks would have finished, everyone should make their way home—to their parents' house. There, of course, would be no transportation. Fortunately Osaka and Kyoto had been unaffected. So too the mountain suburbs had been undisturbed. Some of the churches were providing safe haven for those whose homes had collapsed or burned. The man-made islands had suffered some erosion, some liquefying——some high rises were tilting, but the islands were in tact, but now unlinked to the Kobe mainland. Perhaps two thousand people had been killed, but the chaplain expected that number to rise. In areas where television worked, names were being scrolled across the screen on two channels. We all should, concluded the chaplain, thank God that we survived and eventually the college would re-open. For now just wait for further instructions. Owen thought, await instructions and pray for the repose of the souls who perished, shouldn't the chaplain mention that? But the chaplain only lauded the general courage and urged all to try harder in the coming travail. Did the chaplain doubt prayer? How did one thank God for catastrophe?

Through the afternoon, aftershocks roused Owen from his dozing, half slumped against the concrete wall. By four o'clock most of the gym was empty, faithful to instructions. Owen decided going home to his shifted house made as much sense as slumping in the gym. Outside grey clouds had replaced sunshine, like grey lacquering beyond the leafless trees. The air was colder. A hot bath would have been nice. Owen smiled at the impossibility. Light was fading at his house and he managed to find some candles and there was one bottle of water that hadn't broken in the tumult. He wasn't hungry but the water tasted wonderful, and soon enough he had cleared the *tatami* of pieces of glass and spread out his *futon*. Fully clothed he lay down and pulled the top comforter momentarily over his head. Why was he so tired? He put the candle out. I should say sturdily enough now, "Things will look better in the morning. Yes, things surely would look better in the morning." Some time after 9 p.m. a very gentle, very straight down rain began to fall. So the kind deity paid close attention to the blown in windows of his minions, was that it? Surely a sign of divine consolation. However, the orange glowing of burning downtown Kobe seemed to grow stronger as thickening darkness painted the sky.

"*Mathias-san! Mathias-san. Gomen, kudasai. Gomen, kudasi.*" The chaplain's voice came harshly from the front door.

"*Hi dozo,*" Owen answered. "But walk carefully. I didn't pick anything up yet."

"I can feel that," the chaplain answered. "You had better do so soon."

Owen understood that the English sharpened the sentiment, tossed unconscious rudeness into the expression. It was normal enough in Japanese to suggest, 'you had better' do something. Still Owen knew the chaplain disapproved of him and had done so the minute he learned that Owen was in clerical training. He was not just the English instructor the chaplain and the college hired every two years. An actual Christian in a nominally Christian college. It was discommoding, disturbing to the natural order of language learning. A *gaijin* with extra baggage. And perhaps judgmental in some strange ways.

"I'm checking the buildings still standing. I may need to put others in here—your roof is still on."

"Of course," Owen answered. "I could probably go elsewhere, if you need the whole premises. That's the least I could do."

"It's an idea," the chaplain said. "There are beds in the rooms upstairs?"

"Yes, three total. Never used. I've always been embarrassed to occupy so much space."

"We like to keep instructors on campus. And westerners expect so much space," the chaplain said, just a voice in the darkness.

"Japan is a small narrow island, used to disasters," Owen said, aping Hesseltine's sarcasm. "And Americans especially like to walk on our *tatami* in their heavy boots."

"Of course, of course," the chaplain said. "I will move in only Brits, they know how to maximize space."

"I'm worried about the foundation and the porch coming down. I don't think the building is safe."

"But it is standing."

"Yes. Whatever you think is best."

"Well, for now I'd stay out of the western parts of the house. Something's likely to come down. In the *tatami* room you don't have an upper storey to worry about."

"I noticed at the gym you didn't ask us to pray for the dead in this earthquake. Why was that?" Something about the absolute darkness emboldened Owen.

"The dead are all good," the chaplain answered. "I will come back tomorrow with engineers, and if they clear the building I'll put many more in. Stay in the *tatami* room tonight. Good night. Sleep well."

Owen heard the chaplain's footsteps going back down the hallway. But then he stopped and said, "One thing more. You should try your lights periodically. Some parts of the campus have electricity. It's quite inexplicable. But there it is. And there is a broken water main in the highway nearest the college's road. You can't live without water, I'm sure you know."

"Yes," Owen answered suddenly regretting the chaplain's departure.

"See you tomorrow."

"Unless an aftershock brings the house down," Owen said.

"Pray that that doesn't happen. Pray for that," the chaplain answered, and closed the door.

5

In the morning Owen found two yellow buckets and carried them down to the highway.

Already a long line of patient Japanese had formed, holding buckets, and with robotic slowness filling each from the protruding pipe, in the middle of the roadway. God's fountain, Owen thought. A single black pipe thoughtfully shoved up from beneath the asphalt. In halting, very slowly articulated Japanese Owen asked the stooped elderly woman in front of him whether she thought the water was safe to drink. She sighed, and said , "*Tabun. Tabun,*" A cagey answer that he took to mean "perhaps..." It seemed perfect to Owen. One paused on the edge of an abyss and when asked whether the pendulum was headed out into the void or back toward solid earth, one answered, didn't one? "Perhaps." Certain answers had been swept away. The tower at Siloam toppled for no reason anyone could fathom, Owen remembered, and Christ made some pertinent remark about that catastrophe, but Owen couldn't recall what it was. And that failure of recollection was itself the most profound signal about something or other, wasn't it? Perhaps these Japanese were not patient long suffering, focused individuals. Perhaps they were just zombies as stunned as he was that the earth could so arbitrarily erupt, so capriciously silence the ever-present ravens. In twenty more minutes he had his two buckets and walked back up toward the college gate.

The electricity came back on. In dizzy celebration he cooked in his electric *sukiyaki* maker scrambled eggs with softened cheese and spoiling mushrooms. And the T.V. worked showing spectacular helicopter shots of areas of Kobe burning, soft smoke spiraling up toward Rokko mountain. It seemed Nagata-ku had been incinerated. There was no auxiliary water system in that poor section of the city, and the houses were mostly wood, and over fifty years old—dried lumber better than kindling for the flames. NHK periodically showed a listing of names scrolling down the screen, and the death toll continued to mount—from estimates of 1,500 to 3,500, and by evening reaching 5,000. At no point during the day did the estimates recede. Shots of turned over highways, collapsed buildings, rubble before smashed train stations, tilted high rise buildings, some sheared away revealing a neat doll house view of living rooms, *tatami* rooms, even bathrooms, an endless slide show of destruction spread out through the day. When he wasn't cooking up refrigerator remnants, Owen boiled water in the *sukiyaki* skillet, pouring the "sanitized" liquid (complete with bits of egg and over cooked mushroom) into a large vase—his drinking fountain. And then apparently exhausted by the chore of boiling water, he slumped in front of the television in the upstairs *tatam*i room and dozed watching fires, streaming refugees, tent cities in school yards. and always overhead the flash of helicopters, even as their constant noise directly over his house carried him into the screen, and above the swirling smoke, wafted him up Rokko mountain so that the vaunted views of the Inland Sea disappeared into the smudge below and he imagined the Kobe Union church standing sentinel over the toppled city.

Just before sunset voices outside his front door roused him from his sleepy reverie of destruction. Then he heard Archie calling his name. "Yes," he shouted from the second floor window.

"It is you!" Archie answered. "We called the embassy and I asked if they had information about Owen Mathias and after the longest pause the fellow said, I swear to God, this is actually what he said: 'I think I saw that name on the scroll a while ago.'"

"Well, he didn't" Owen said.

"We've brought you something. Can we come in?"

Jena added, "Or are you waiting for a proper '*gomen kudasai*?'"

"It's open. I was asleep."

Coming down the stairs Owen noticed that cracks along the wall were widening.

In the living room Jena said, "*Tokyu Departo* has been dispensing essentials and we've brought you two of their best offerings."

Archie added,"Yeah, long underwear—packets for free. And *natto*, your favorite."

Owen laughed—his abhorrence of Japanese *natto* a kind of thick black fermented soybean paste that was unfailingly nauseating to him—was a standing joke with the Hesseltines.

"Given your tender proclivities, I also managed to find these," Archie brought up a bag of McDonald's egg McMuffins. "Yes, manna from McGod."

Jena added, "Yes, McGod who sends us earthquakes to keep us honest."

"Honest?" Archie asked.

"Why yes, honest and alert to our vulnerabilities. Have some *natto*. I'm starved."

"He won't stop us," Archie said pointing to Owen. And they began spooning out the vile paste.

"It's the Japanese equivalent of Stilton cheese," Jena said. "An acquired taste. We've been here quite long enough to love it, especially when we're hungry."

"It took a couple hours walk to reach you, but in stumbling overland we came upon a better way out. And we're here to take you out."

"Why would I want to go out."

"Maybe for water, maybe for food. Maybe for safety. "

"Certainly for health. Conditions here can only deteriorate. God knows where sewage is going now." Jena said.

"At least this house is still standing." Archie said between mouthfuls. "But the foundation's giving way. I can see it in the cracks along the stucco outside."

"You can see it?" Owen asked.

"Yeah, I can see it all right.—"

"Because the chaplain is thinking of moving others in here. The roof still works."

"Better not do it,"Archie said, "you'll die together. Who'd he want to move in?"

"Other foreign faculty. Their houses collapsed, but somehow they weren't killed."

"That's fortunate indeed," Jena said. "When a house collapses that's mostly curtains for occupants. The tile roofs weigh a ton you know. And when the roof comes down, why then it's the end. Isn't it Archie?"

"The absolute bitter end. Nothing left but *natto* and fresh underwear."

"And maybe absolution in a public *sentoh* in Osaka—is that right, Archie?"

"But I suppose," said Hesseltine, ignoring the Osaka option,"I suppose having the *gaijin* faculty all in one place and then having the roof collapse would have its attractions to any Japanese administration. Don't you think so, love?"

"Oh yes, Archie, so much less shame than directly poisoning people. God sent the roof down."

"Not the roof," Owen interrupted, "the tower."

"The fire rids Japan of *Etta* and Korean immigrants, what could be better than that? Blessed earthquake, blessed flames."

"Better not make light of the dead," Owen said.

"Such a proper fellow. No wonder you flourish here," Archie answered. "But it's time you bathed, isn't it, love? I mean what does he smell like?"

Jena answered, "Earthquake musk. Come with us to Osaka. We can pick our way to Nishinomyia station. I always need a bath after *natto*. A long hot soak will make everything clarify."

"Things are too clear already," Owen said.

"No they aren't," Archie said. "You'd like to think they are, but believe me they aren't clear. The weather will clear in a day or so, brilliant sky blue days and crystalline sunshine all about, as if the earth had shaken off a dirty cloak. But nothing will be clearer. We'll still be here, eating *natto* and wondering what the hell happened, won't we, love?"

"But we'll be more relaxed and far cleaner and so will Owen. Besides, you learn the best gossip at the *sentoh*, and isn't this a supreme occasion for gossip?"

"Hot water can't fill emptiness," Archie said, smiling and finishing his cup of natto.

"Oh yes it can," Jena answered, "if you let it. That's their secret, you know, what they're willing to let fill up the space inside you."

"What space?" Owen asked.

"Yeah," Archie echoed, "what space?"

"The space where God comes to rest." Jena answered smiling insanely.

"Oh that space," Archie answered.

Owen thought but didn't say, the space where you get to watch a boy with a sawn off arm bleed/freeze to death. That special chamber where the all-knowing, all-loving Lord pauses and looks back to summon you on. "I need a soak," Owen finally said.

6

THE SEARING HEAT OF the *sentoh* quite dissolved Owen's puzzled resentment. He lay back in the sizzling water, folded towel on his forehead, and felt the tentacles of temperature slowly disassemble first his legs, his torso, his back, neck and arms. Any movement made the heat worse, so his consciousness focused on stillness and paralysis. Where were you, Job, when I churned up the universe and created all life?

Just don't move the water; speak as harshly as you want, but don't stir the sea.

I appointed you witness to my fondest atrocities so I could test the extent of your resilience, and you have disappointed me. So let me stir the waters further.

—Not that. Just stillness. I will lift my head a bit and then be brought beyond the churning.

I will cook you until you are done.

—I am a dull frog in your wet hands, Lord.

Archie said, "Takes the ache away doesn't it? They're onto something really civilized aren't they? These silly, pernicious people are on to something. Or do you hear me, Mathias? Do I need to reach for my folded paper fan and beat you on the head?"

"I hear you, but you don't say anything pertinent. Nothing to wake me up."

"Well, let me wake you with the following. This morning I remembered something I read about your favorite Mogens. There was a listing of *maruta* in mid August, 1945. I remember M. Nielsen midway down the list of *gaijin* followed by the phrase, 'taken by Russians'. Can you imagine it, liberated by Russians—how's that for irony? "Archie stood up in the bath, apparently to relieve some of the boiling sensation in his upper arms. "The whole time we did the translating I kept thinking of Lear's line: 'It's not the worst, when you can still say it's the worst.' It's never the worst so long as you can say it's the worst. Words to live by."

"So live by them, quietly," Owen answered. He did not imagine the Russians were supportive liberators.

"Doubtless the Russians knew about Harbin, far more extensively than the Americans did. Right on their border after all. And their own interest in biological warfare had to be thicker and more desperate than Truman's. The klutz probably couldn't pronounce the term." Archie said, sounding surprisingly academic.

"So Mogens simply went from one harsh laboratory to another?" Owen asked.

"The data didn't say." Archie answered. "Often the case with data, don't you think? Maybe you could inquire of your Japanese contacts. I mean, of course, once the trains get running again—maybe next summer?" Archie laughed. "But we both know Mogens is only a distraction. Neither one of us cares what happened to him."

"Yes," Owen answered. "He's just a witness—a bystander, a choleric bystander. And maybe no more confused than we are."

"Are we confused?" Archie said. "I'm dreadfully clear."

"Dreadful anyway."

"And clear. A byproduct of aging is, after all, clarification. Count on it."

"Does pontificating expand after an earthquake?"

Archie said, "You better believe it. And listen carefully to me."

Owen decided to submerge entirely, letting the mini towel float free. Beneath the surface the heat escalated or so it seemed, his eyes burned, his forehead seemed to exfoliate in invisible strips and when finally he popped his head out, he could scarcely breathe. Archie was saying something, repeating something, but Owen struggled toward the edge of the tub. He wanted to slither away from the fiery enervation of the bath. He was aware of Archie's mockery, his sarcastic tones, but oblivious to actual sentiments expressed. He wanted only to lie on the cool tiles and button off the subtle rumbling of his stomach and the weird spasms passing through his lower legs. He thought he heard Archie shouting, "Behold, the King of the *Gaijin*," as vaguely embarrassed Japanese made their way around Owen's sprawled body.

Later, after they had collected Jena from her side of the *sentoh* Archie said, "That little epileptic moment on the tiles, Mathias, was disappointing, to say the least. Especially since you'd displayed such perfect *sentoh* manners. Still, what seemed perfect to me was the way the locals exchanged glances about your twitching—acknowledging that, after all, *gaijin* were nutty. It was to be expected."

They had walked back to Umeda station and thence into the underground multi-tiered mall called San Ban Gai. They went underground, down three floors, and found the open atrium area with its 3 storey water fall. The noisy falling water had generated a chill breeze in the open area with its plastic tables and chairs.

"It's a kind of mini Niagara Falls," Jena said. "And in the summer it's a wonderful place to come to cool off."

Owen imagined the water re-circulated somehow, setting aside any extravagance that might be implicit in an underground cascade within a shopping complex. Beyond the waterfalls was Archie's favorite *tonkatsu* restaurant, some place called YKK where the sliver-disks of pork were breaded with the lightest batter and fried crisply, then re-assembled in a long roll and placed on a bed of shredded cabbage. A burnt barbeque sauce sat in a separate jar on the table. Archie said, "This is one delicacy the Japanese keep entirely to themselves. It won't turn up in your country," he nodded toward Owen.

"You travel, do you, on a Japanese passport?" Owen asked.

"Touche," Archie answered.

"It's your country too," Owen continued.

"Well, either way, the Americans won't get *tonkatsu*, will they love?"

"No, Archie. Never. It's kept special here for us."

"Consider the wider irony," Archie said between sucking bites on his pork. "Our brethren in Kobe are shivering against the cold and wondering how far tomorrow they'll have to walk to find water. And food will be dropped to them from the air, and it won't be manna. Probably cans of stuff and no can openers. And a hot bath such as we've accomplished is only a dream for them. And it will go on that way for maybe three months. Twenty minutes to modernity, and twenty minutes back to subsistence. Has there ever been a clearer demarcation between haves and have nots? Better yet——there was discussion on NHK this morning that temporary housing will be built on Rokko Island, amid the high rise *homats*. Just imagine, tin roofed shacks, or attached endless one room housing for refugees right beneath the buildings with doormen and entrance recommendation requirements, and huge, huge flats. So that the V.P.s can go out on their 37th floor balconies and watch the displaced *Etta* and Korean immigrants doing their laundry in buckets outside their tiny 'temporary' digs. And best of all, the housing erected so quickly in the name of staying warm will endure twenty years on the most expensive property in Kansai. Presto, you thought you were in safe Japan, but actually look around, you're in Manila."

"You're getting too excited, Archie," Jena said.

"Yes," Owen agreed. "I'm going back to what you describe, if you don't remember."

"And who brought you underwear and *natto*, sustenance itself? And Egg McMuffin. Of course I remember your terrible suffering, all alone in Harbin with your fingernails pulled out and plague in your kidneys."

"We should pray for those dispossessed." Jena said, without guile.

Archie smiled at her. "A noble sentiment. How many Hail Marys?"

"We're not Catholic," Jena answered unswayed.

"Okay, some Lutheran ejaculation then, is that okay?"

Owen emptied a spoonful of the barbeque sauce on the shards of his chopped cabbage.

"Why do you still attend church, given how you feel."

"And how do I feel?"

"Disillusioned. Atheistic. Sneering and maybe frightened."

"Who wouldn't want to hear what Father Bob Bonneau will say about the great catastrophe? Reason enough to attend church tomorrow. Let's go together. I'll get a car and pick you up at Nishinomiya station, south exit."

"Why attend at all?" Owen pressed.

Archie smiled, "Have you seen the Mission Retirement Center outside of San Francisco?"

Owen nodded and ate more cabbage.

They took him upstairs and put him on the train back to Nishinomiya. He picked his way past broken street lights and toppled tile roofed houses, through the little village of Mondo Yakujin and thence up the hill to the college. There was a flashlight at his door and he made his way to the open air *tatami* room downstairs. He might have wanted to read but electricity was off again. Still fully clothed, he got back into his *futon*; the bath warmth still lingered with him and, absent any shimmying aftershocks he felt reasonably safe and cozy in the *futon*, even closer to nature now that the sliding windows were smashed and the trickle of soft rain which began after midnight reminded him of tent-camping a thousand years ago in another segment of the planet. If Archie worked up a lather concerning the indifferent God, what did Archie know of soft nature and big American skies? Rice farmers ought to feel adrift in the Sinai or in Oklahoma. Rice farmers longed for total community. American Archie knew better.

Christ himself said two or three would suffice.

At 3:00 a.m. Owen awoke to the first three bites. *Mukade* had gotten under the *futon* and seized on his plump forearm. He came screaming standing, shaking them off, then smashing them with the flashlight, breaking the glass. God, how many of them were in the room? He sprinted to the front *genkan* struggled into his outside slippers and burst through the door, out into the center of the mcadam road up to the college. Oddly there was a streetlight on and a lantern at the guardhouse. There was an ellipse of light spread on the roadway and he sat in the middle of it, light rain pelting him as if to caress the swelling arm.

But at least he could see enough of the surface to know, no *mukade* were on the road. Of course a swarm of them, disrupted by the quake had come out of the shrubbery and trees up the side of the college's hill. A swarm coming like fire ants down the side of the hill and through the open house, a billion clicking across his consciousness and all set to snack on his forearm, which grew redder and fuller by the minute. He remembered a woman telling him at church that *mukade* shouldn't kill an adult, but children were vulnerable and had been butchered by the sickening blackish saliva the creatures excreted. Owen remembered once staying with an uncle in California in the hills some place beyond San Diego, and in the mornings sometimes he'd accompany the fellow as he kicked over small rocks and pointed to scurrying spiders.

"Tarantulas. That's a 10 packer," he'd say, smiling. "And that, that's a 15 packer." And Owen asked: "What's a 10 packer?" "He bites you. You go to bed with ten packs of cigarettes and when they're done, you feel like you're gonna live. Ten packs gets you through the pain."

Owen imagined the cigarette vending machines were probably still working despite the quake.

After ten minutes sitting on the roadway, and before the forearm began to throb, Owen decided to go back inside, get tougher shoes, a sweater and jacket and then return through the multi-legged darkness back to Nishinomiya station. Sleep was gone entirely anyway. It was better to keep moving.

7

"WHEN DID THE SWELLING start?" Jena asked from the back seat of the Toyota Archie drove.

"Right after the bite. Around 3:00 a.m."

"And you've been up since then?"

"I had to get out of the house. *Mukade* were everywhere. So I just started walking to the station. There are candles and flowers near collapsed houses."

"That means someone died in the collapse," Jena said.

Archie said, "Wolfe got it right. You can't go home again. He thought it was the past, but we know it was the Goddam *mukade*. He'd probably love the fucking *mukade*."

"When the home's collapsed you can't go home again," Owen said. "When the roof has crushed you, you can tell you're home again."

"True enough," Archie said, "you have to wait for someone to bring you underwear and *natto*."

"Or better yet, Egg McMuffins," Owen said.

"Those were her idea," Archie nodded toward the back seat.

"Well they were wonderful. And I thank you. As was the bath, and the *tonkatsu*."

"And now Father Bonneau's Sermon on the Mount." Jena said, "such a wise man, I mean with all that Navy experience—all those smart men, maybe five thousand of them, on one ship altogether, day after day, month after month, always thinking of each other."

"And what did those fellows do with each other's socks, eh Jena?" Archie asked.

"You said they beat off into them, but I never believed you. Maybe Owen knows for sure."

Owen said, "Owen doesn't know for sure."

"That's a disappointment," Jena said, "maybe Father Bonneau knows for sure."

"He's always sure," Archie said. "We'll drive half way to Kyoto and then circle in from behind Rokko Mountain."

"The backside's wonderfully rural," Jena said.

"And full of *mukade*," Archie added. "And crusty socks."

Owen focused on his swelling forearm, listening for those under-the-skin murmurings sending dull screeches to the brain. Would they clarify? Voices of children freezing ? Would buboes in the armpits and groin duplicate the *mukade* swelling? Might Archie be able to answer that? Check the Harbin data—surely something on getting the lymph system to inflame; did instant freezing slow arterial spewing? If so, would it follow then that spraying liquid nitrogen on an open wound would save life? Tomorrow could we not try that for an experiment? Identify a Log and tear him open, and let us spray his fiery innards to put them out. Surely he'd last long enough to know that freezing was or was not the preferred coagulation method. Medicine marches on. Over the rows and rows of Logs. *Murata* refute *mukade*. Or perhaps set them free to come down the hillside.

There was a funny lisp to Jesus's pronunciation. He called out over the empty traffic on the empty lane, past the rushing pine trees, past the litter on the highway—"Watch carefully now for it is now that I will topple the tower, thus clarifying for all to see whether in fact the residents drawing water in Siloam were more guilty than, say, your own forearm. What do you think? Surely your forearm is not guilty of anything. Unless of course it's connected somehow to those crusty socks on the USS Indianapolis—is it? If sin is the water we swim in, dwell in, then how is the minnow or the whale, the floating sock or the hapless *mukade* shrieking for its mate more or less sinful than anything else? Topple the tower."

To begin his homily, Father Bonneau said to the five persons in the church (Archie, Jena, and Owen were in one pew). There was a sailor in the back pew, Owen noticed, and Mariko came in some time later: "You don't serve 27 years as a Navy chaplain and not get acquainted with catastrophe. Not only from war, but from all sorts of crazy accidents, weather screwups, homegrown explosions, you name it. You see it all. And you get used to it coming at you when you least expect it."

Owen noticed that Archie rolled his eyes after turning slightly toward him.

"So I turned to scripture last night as I watched the names scrolling across the television, using my trusty topical guide to the Bible. I checked every reference to earthquake listed in that compilation. Earthquakes have something to do with God glancing, or grimacing, or pointing, shouting, or expressing dismay somehow. And from that lengthy review of all the listings—I'm always a thorough researcher—I came to the following conclusions: 1) Earthquakes are listed as manifestations of God's anger; 2) Earthquakes are referenced as emblems of God's majesty; 3) Earthquakes are metaphors for the end time of life—the utter unpredictability, randomness of that moment. In the Old Testament in particular earthquakes seem a part of God's command and skin, if that makes any sense. He shrugs his shoulders and the earth splits open; he glances and the rams go skipping off in terror; he points and the earth shudders. You get the picture. So in its first use, earthquakes are agents of anger, retribution, compensation for some perceived slight or error or sin. And that's kind of comforting. About what, five thousand, maybe six, maybe more, people perished in the earthquake a few days ago. It is comforting, is it not, to think most of those who perished deserved to die. They were, after all, filled with sin and doubtless less than perfect in all their human relations. They had to be worse than us, because we're here listening to me explain how God judged them. So you should feel good that those losers got swallowed up or burned up or got crushed in debris. Even the so called innocent ones, the littlest children perished as they ought to, because, after all, they shared in the general sin and that's our condition. And presumably at the moment of the first sustained shudder their sins had been weighed and found more severe than ours, isn't that so? Well it is sure nice to think that. That's the 'suffering is deserved and just' rationale and it's only partially gratifying. When you think a bit more about it, the obliteration of innocent seamen, innocent children, the random destruction of what apparently are rather guiltless people, when you think about that, you grow a little uneasy, don't you? And pretty soon what the shrinks call 'survivor guilt' sets in and you brood that they died for no good reason while you lived for no good reason. Sometimes near death is a conversion experience, but in the Navy at least most survivors forgot about their close call after a couple of months—or at least it didn't affect their behavior in a way I could see. They were still the boozing, whoring jokers afterwards as before. And that's of course what the Navy wanted them to be. So 'just- suffering' arguments are stupid and unconvincing . So you look around for something better.

"At seminary my mentor—we all get one, you know—a superior who has anticipated and dealt with your questions, or so it's argued. My mentor insisted that by sending catastrophes God was actually providing human beings with experiences that brought them closer to his holy presence. Since most people turn to a supreme being as they are about to incinerate, it follows that God is munificent and supremely caring by sending us earthly disasters. In such extremes he draws us closer to him, we anguish and ask for his comfort and invariably the argument goes, he gives us succor."

Archie mouthed "succor" to Owen.

"But I don't like it much. I can't accept it. God makes us suffer so he can console us and share our misery? I don't believe it. So my mentor suggested the tapestry argument."

Archie said softly, "Ah, of course, the tapestry argument. It's surefire."

"He said, suffering is like the knots on the back of tapestry—bristling, ugly, full of pain, but in heaven we get to turn the tapestry over and we realize that those tangled knots, all that painful tying up, had a purpose of great beauty once you get the flip the fabric over. We can't do that tossing over, but God can and He does when it suits him to reveal the full majesty of what we go through. It's a nice idea. But I can't accept it either. What's the flip side of an earthquake? Is something magnificent shining out from the other side of the fault line? What might that be? A lake of calm water in the center of the earth? "

"No," Archie said softly, "it's no tapestry at all—just a portrait of Jesus on velvet and iridescent."

"I'd like to believe the tapestry argument. I'd like to think dying sailors heaving around in dark, near-freezing seas get to see the better picture of our miserable life. I want to think there's a clarification somewhere near at hand. I'd like to believe that, but after you've looked at absolute puzzlement, mystification that such suffering should exist, should continue, and even grow, you don't believe in the tapestry stuff. You just don't believe in it. Of the tragedy at Siloam Jesus asked the only question: 'Or those eighteen who died when the tower in Siloam fell on them—do you think they were more guilty than all the others living in Jerusalem? I tell you, no! But unless you repent, you too will all perish.' And that statement comes between his broader question: 'Do you think these Galileans were worse sinners than all the other Galileans because they suffered this way? I tell you, no! Unless you repent, you too will all perish.'

And right afterwards Jesus talks of the fig tree with no fruit for three years that should be cut down and thrown into the fire, although the gardener argues for another year—another lost year. Our standard response isn't it? We'll rebuild, start a new, everything will return to joy."

And the rector slowed down, as if imagining something would right itself with time. Owen wondered whether that was a calculated contrivance (improbable enough for Bonneau) or loss of rhetorical direction, or maybe just a movement acknowledging that what was going on, was less a sermon than a peculiar monologue with acceptable long pauses. Instead Owen thought about how Harbin and repentance fit together. Medical experimentation as the path to repentance? Was that any screwier than a flipped tapestry? Was Mogens being shown the path to salvation by dragging himself through the anthrax chute? Lose a finger, gain a soul? Was that it? Did Mogens imagine that his life in Harbin was nothing more than anyone's spreading a blanket before the tower at Siloam and taking the consequences. Was there no more reason for his discomfort, his tenuous explorations of the mica edges of survival, than the Siloamites innocent presence before inexplicable judgment. And what should repentance consist of at Siloam or Harbin? What was the message? Get your mind right before the ax falls? The folly of imagining life consisted of anything other than random inexplicable suffering? To repent was to accept and relish puniness. To utterly embrace the bamboo cane that drew endless blood from your backside, was that it? To know God was to ask for and receive purest anguish. How could you forward your misery against my utter omnipotence voluntarily nailed to a cross? Stick work suspending the Almighty deliberately crippled with your moaning complaining, sharing your despair. And showing you the deliciousness of its inexplicability. Was Jesus, adrift from the cross and floating, beckoning Mogens at the end?

"Well, he stumped himself, didn't he?" Archie said. "The practical man squatting and excreting among abstractions. Won't wash, will it? Shouldn't wash, and truly doesn't." Archie was holding his tea cup, vapor of Earl Grey curling off the surface, then dunking a biscuit in the tan liquid. "Some things never change. Down the slopes about six thousand dead and half of Kobe burning, but some rituals must go on. This tea is delicious. Too bad the view is soiled with charring bodies. Thank the Lord we had the endowment to build this nifty church on the upper most levels away from the earth's sliding plates. For perfect salvation always rely on P & G. Old Bonneau really lost the thread didn't he? You bump up against the felt header and you realize too late that the air in the vehicle is slowly being replaced by water. You lean your head sideways desperate for a last gulp of oxygen and then, zip. The flush fills your nose, your lungs."

Jena said, "But not yours, Archie."

Archie smiled at her, "My little puncturist. Do you think we can be happy in Mission Retirement, Pilgrim Place."

"As soon as you stop pontificating," Jena answered.

Part Four

1

OWEN THOUGHT, ARCHIE WITHOUT pontificating might not be Archie at all, but he said nothing.

Instead, they all stood watching as Mariko came into the empty room brilliant sunlight now in long bars from the curved windows. Mariko poured herself some tea from the push thermos and stood with the group for a moment watching the vapor off her cup. Owen remembered that Japanese were quite comfortable in group silence, as if the deepest communication was circulating from heart to heart or belly to belly entirely without words. But Owen did not believe in *"haragei"*—Japanese belly silent communication. He thought it smacked of Japanese narcissism. Still, it was interesting to him that Mariko stood easily, imbibing the silence as well as the tea, content in quietude, apparently awaiting no revelation, expecting only that the quietness would continue to suffuse the atmosphere. Owen remembered once sitting at a very long low table with an American poet at his side. Across from them were two Japanese professors of French literature; the table was only twenty inches wide and so it seemed you could not avoid cross-cultural staring. No talk was permitted or even assumed since the banquet had not officially begun. There was a kind of tortured mutual nodding acknowledgment of dinner partners, but not a word. Finally the poet said quietly to Owen, "So now we know the origin of the expression: 'Here's looking at you.'"

But then Mariko identically whispered to him, "Mr. Bannerjee died in his restaurant when the Tokyu building collapsed. I just learned that last night."

"But the building collapsed in the early morning," Owen answered. "Right when the quake hit. What was he doing there?"

"Always he opened the restaurant for produce and fish at sunrise."

"Thirty stories coming straight down." Owen said, as if to comprehend it.

"Yes, I doubt they will find him."

"You mean what's left of him."

"Of course," she answered, smiling.

Owen felt foolish to have added such a stupid, gratuitous bit of speculation, but pleased that Mariko had hardly chided him.

"Well, it seems the disaster has not increased church attendance," Bonneau said, speaking toward them but to no one in particular.

Archie said, "When disaster strikes people naturally turn not to their ministers but to their televisions, which are full of survival grace."

"So disaster doesn't bring out the best in us?" Bonneau said.

"Some survivor guilt feels like repentance," Archie answered.

"Spoken from longevity," Jena said. Archie looked at her admiringly.

"So here's an option to test your instincts, "Bonneau said, "all our instincts. Mioko wants to know if the church survived. I propose we drive out to tell her. The van is here and Hiromi too. He can take us by the back route since it will be months before the shore line will run again. To call upon the shut-ins and the infirm, what could be more Christian?"

"We'll go," Jena said. "And Owen since he's with us. He has to go where we go."

"Always," Archie added.

"Ah, consensus—the Japanese way, by fiat," Owen said.

"No one cares about your maundering observations about Japan," Archie said.

Mariko stifled a laugh, covering her mouth with her left hand.

Some minutes later, after Bonneau had changed into light blue slacks and a white guayabera shirt yanked taut across his bulging stomach,and a grey cotton cardigan, they assembled at the narrow church van, a Mitsubishi. Hiromi was apparently unhappy with the prospect of driving to Suma. Jena had handled the initial instructions in Japanese but quickly it became apparent that greater finesse in the language would be needed. Mariko interposed and the conversation became quieter, lengthier, eventually a near-whisper, as if the natives needed to share some final truth that made capitulation acceptable. Bonneau stood shifting his weight back and forth while Mariko plied Hiromi with aphorisms Owen vaguely sensed had something to do with dealing with *gaijin* and Mr. Bannerjee's recent demise. Apparently a promise of Daimaru Department Store's most fluffy towels carried the day and Hiromi got in behind the wheel. "Tell you later," Mariko said to Owen as they got in.

It did seem the van could tilt over easily as it cleared the empty parking lot and started toward the crest of Rokko mountain.

"This van," Archie said, "could in fact pass through the eye of a needle."

"Or so we hope," said Jena.

"Our faith will svelte us," Bonneau offered.

But soon enough the thick wooded beauteous descent at the back of mountain overcame the banter. The occasional precipitousness of the roadway enhanced the van's instability.

To cover Jena said, "Mrs. Ward said Tokyo looked like 'one long Elizabeth New Jersey,' but she never got to this part of Japan—the real Japan, bucolic, verdant, utterly unspoiled."

"Shut up," Archie said.

In the third seat Mariko slid her hand up Owen's thigh, softly nudging his crotch.

He drew a breath and whispered. "Bannerjee was killed. All his tissue, all his fluids pulverized."

Mariko looked into his eyes, and stopped her stroking, "Pulverized?" she said. "What is pulverized?"

"It's what I'm going to do to you."

"Here?"

"Not here. In Suma."

"That's good," Mariko said. "Pulverize me."

"Yes, pulverize. Pulverize, but not now. We'll wait until the van crashes."

"Crashes?"

"You have to be dead before you get pulverized."

"It's a joke," Mariko answered, "I see. It's a joke. But I don't follow it. You cannot joke in a different language."

"No jokes, then," Owen said.

"Yes, thank you. No jokes."

"We might find a way to pulverize live bodies. We might, you know." Owen smiled.

"No jokes."

"You press them together very hard, one on top of the other, pushing down. So the flesh dissolves. Mutual dissolving flesh."

"No jokes please."

"Who's joking?" Owen said, suddenly aware as the van swerved down the backside of mountain, past eddies of snow droppings at the highway's edge, that nothing could compete with pressing harder on Mariko. The dropaway views swirled through him but they were nothing compared to his sudden loin surge demanding resolution—a braying, unstopped tumbling that mirrored the van's lurching—crested, unsettling swimming everywhere in the heat of the vehicle. "Don't play with me, Mariko-chan," he whispered to her when Father Bonneau's voice saturninely interrupted his swelling reverie.

"Mioko," Bonneau shouted from the front seat, "wants us to all hear something she has to say about the history of the church."

"God spare us historians," Archie said.

"And complaints about historians," Jena added.

"An addendum to the yellow book, is that it?" Archie said.

"Something like that, "Bonneau answered. "Something that's been bothering her."

"Maybe only complaints about her 'silver housing.'" Jena said.

"But the church has nothing to do with her housing." Bonneau said. "She needs to be reassured the church came through the quake. We can do that, can't we?"

"The church, yes. Attendance, not for a long time. What will the P & G veeps do without their chauffeurs?" Archie said.

"Just the walk-in congregation," Jena said.

"When only two or three are gathered in my name," Bonneau said.

"Originally churches were in homes, weren't they?" Mariko asked. "I mean they could be any place."

"And without priests," Archie added. "The parasitic class. And without the Vatican's endless resources."

"Careful," Bonneau said, "Hiromi's a Catholic."

"I rescind my thoughts," Archie said.

But as if reaction to a perceived slur, Hiromi slammed on the brakes sending all lurching forward into seat backs or dashboard. The van skidded a bit, slurried toward the guard rail, clanged off of it, and recovered on the sandy roadway.

"More than rescind, abjectly apologize," Archie said. "More than apologize, beg for forgiveness."

"Repent," Bonneau said, "Do you think these other passengers were more guilty than you are?"

"He's the guiltiest." Jena asserted. "Abolutely he's the guiltiest. Hiromi take him."

"Thanks dearest love," Archie said.

"We're playing, "Owen said, "but around six thousand actually died."

"And at least four thousand deserved to. God told me so," Archie said.

"Which four?" Jena asked.

"Those who knew and liked you, darling," Archie answered.

Mariko whispered to Owen, "Do American couples often discuss like this?"

Owen shook his head, then drifted into a reverie imagining Mogens suddenly aware he was going to die, die in some experimental hideous fashion with a smiling Dr. Matsuno and an attentive Kawabata holding his hand. Everywhere chill winds blowing through the cement building with howling freezing children in salt solutions outside as the nifty cloudless Manchurian sky ice blue as if made of some lucite mounted off of the horizon, arced up and filled the black heavens, as indeed the curvature of his skull, with pure cold, chill blueness swelling inside his brain, inside his rib cage, exploding outwards in some contained way that kept him conscious and supremely frightened, breath tightening, rancid thick arctic oil filling his lungs. "I'm choking," Mogens said. "I'm choking. Please stop the choking." Kawabata's grip tightened soothingly. The oil seemed to level off, even as the van moved into the flatland near the Suma coast.

"We should reassure Mioko that the church is fine. And then we should see if we can get her to talk about her role in saving the church in 1942." Father Bonneau said.

Jena said, "No one has trouble getting Mioko to talk."

"Unkind," Archie said. "You should not speak ill of the silver-housed."

"Especially those outside of San Francisco," Jena added.

Archie laughed. "Is my longing so evident?"

"Yes,"Owen laughed. "It's your recurring theme."

"It does renew my faith," Archie conceded. "It re-warms my faith. It's the final incubator to get me hatching safely into eternity, toward that final retirement community in the sky."

"For your blessed wood carving," Jena said.

"You ought not to mock my phallic shavings," Archie answered. "They might sell in Castro if we ever go in from the farm."

"There's no farm."

"I was just being metaphorical." Archie said.

"I believe Mioko wants our absolution somehow."

"Ours or yours?" Archie said.

"The church's and the community's. The congregation's. It's little enough we can do for someone half way through the exit door."

Mariko asked, "Is she sick?"

"No," Bonneau replied blandly. "Just old and increasingly infirm. Such people want to reminisce I find, seeking to right something that happened so long ago no one could quite remember it, but which is bothering them. Absolution is necessary near death, you know."

"What if you're being butchered? Does absolution help then?" Owen asked. "I mean while you're being butchered."

"An odd question," Bonneau replied.

"And one to extend the pastor's limited perspective," Archie said.

"You get no absolution." Bonneau answered.

"But I still feel butchered," Archie said.

"Who is being butchered?" Bonneau asked.

"Oh no one that I know," Owen said. "But I was wondering if at the moment it becomes clear you're going to die, does that prompt you even in the last seconds to think about absolution?"

"Of course it does, my boy." Bonneau said quickly.

"Absolved from an unjust, butcherous death?"

"Again, who is being butchered? It's true I suppose that I've never absolved someone being butchered, while the butchering was going on, but I've absolved plenty of fellows who were dying unexpectedly, from explosions, shellings, torpedoes. Scores of them, guts spilling out on the decks and life leaking in great gushes. Plenty of them."

"Ah, the old salt emerges once again." Archie said.

"You're right. I am an old salt. And I'm proud of it."

"You should be. Attending all those dying sailors." Archie said.

Bonneau turned back and stared out the front.

Jena said, "Archie, you go too far."

Banterless silence fell across the van. As if to fill in, views of the Inland Sea crowded through the front windshield. Steel grey water dotted with small cones of tree/islands. It was as if the placidity had totally submerged the recent quake, a rippleless absorption of all threat. While he softly stroked Mariko's small breast through her cashmere sweater, Owen imagined Mogens swimming through that dark sea, a widening V streaming behind him, two separate tiny logs of evidence trailing away, ever diminishing. Could Harbin diminish a fever? The chill heightening the fear and the ecstasy. Swimming out into the Inland Sea, pulling back gray oily waters, parting steel sheets to see what below the surface? Blackened rotting feet? Ropes of lost excrement? Ligaments slowly pulled away from their attachments? Joints slowly turned inside out, and a skull leaking bloody mucus.

2

It was dark when the van finally got to the Suma residence. Mioko was sitting in a red metal chair in the foyer. She had wrapped herself in a maroon blanket but quickly rose as they came in, tightening the blanket around her shoulders.

"Such a delegation," she said, apparently delighted at the company. "It might be a standoff. Your five against my three."

"Three?" Bonneau asked, following her down the long hallway toward a reception room.

"Perhaps another concert," Owen said quietly to Mariko.

'Yes, I have three other callers. I'm very popular after a natural disaster," Mioko said.

"Everyone wants to check in to see if the old lady is still viable."

"And are you?" Archie said.

"At least so, I suppose," Mioko answered. "You'll have to be the judge."

"I've already heard you're around the bend." Archie said.

"With salvation and tea sweets," Mioko answered, leading them into the reception room with its chrome and beige chairs arranged in a circle. On the low table in the center of the circle was a tall thermos dispenser, doubtless full of green tea. And, as promised, a plate of leaf-shaped tea sweets.

Jena said, "Are they from Kiyomizudera?"

"Of course," Archie answered. "We've all taken the leap to get here."

"And were the roads treacherous?" Mioko asked.

"No. Not at all," Bonneau answered.

"He means the guardrails proved strong enough in several instances," Jena said.

"I know Owen has met Kawabata-san," Mioko said pointing to the far side of the circle where Kawabata sat between two women. "But I bet he doesn't know Kawabata's daughter, Keiko. Yes, my dear it's proper to stand, since you don't know any of these people, and you're the youngest. Except maybe for Owen."

"I'm older." Owen replied, eyeing Keiko for the first time and finding her attractive.

"And this," Mioko pointed to the other much older woman on Kawabata's left, "is Sanae, daughter of Dr. Matsuno. Here with rather sad news."

"I'm sorry," Father Bonneau said, picking up a tea sweet.

"Dr. Matsuno died in the quake, "Mioko continued. "Under his house, a lovely old home in Nagata-ku. Perhaps you know that area suffered most. Collapsed roofs and then fire. Horrific fire." Mioko looked around, as if to celebrate her expertise.

Father Bonneau nodded between mouthfuls. "I'm terribly sorry. Such a shock. Were you in the house at the time?" He asked Sanae, who merely smiled in return, then looked down. "Such a shock," Bonneau repeated.

"She got the defense force to pull apart the tiles. They found the body, crushed and burned."

Owen watched Sanae as that news was fed to the group but she betrayed no emotion. Could it be she spoke no English? Owen fantasized she had been born elsewhere, perhaps in Manchuria under watchful Russian eyes, or some place in colonial Korea after the war. Or perhaps she did comprehend but was still in some kind of shock. Why come to silver housing to nurse your shock? Then Owen began to understand that this might not be the Dr. Matsuno of his ruminations. Matsuno was a common enough name. Why had he assumed so automatically that Manchuria had been her home. The timing was hardly right, she looked scarcely fifty years old. Of course Kawabata would know precisely, but Owen understood whatever Kawabata was, careful, considerate, thoughtful, above all, slow, characterized his approach to everything. Mioko invariably liked to lift corners of the tablecloth to reveal portions of the meal, or in a sudden delight whip the cloth off to reveal a feast; Kawabata wanted most to set heavy dishes down on the corners to keep the repast hidden.

"Perhaps, Father Robert, you could say some blessing for her loss."

Owen wondered if there weren't some not too distant opprobrium in Mioko's careful articulation of 'Father Robert,' as if Mioko preferred not to recognize 'Father Bob,' that most parishioners used.

Bonneau smiled saturninely and swallowed the last of his bean paste sweet. "The Lord be with us, let us pray," he said, with rather too much immediacy. "We thank you, Lord, that we may be all together during this difficult time, to share our grief and bewilderment at the workings of your will," and Archie winked at Owen . "Our grievous sense of loss and in particular for Sanae's loss of her father, a wise and good man serving the poorest and most needy of our community. We thank you, father, for gathering him and bringing closer to your radiance, your all forgiving presence, in Christ's name. Amen."

There was a general hush and silence, while Bonneau picked up another sweet. Then Owen said, "Kawabata-san, was Sanae's father the Dr. Matsuno you worked with in China?"

"Of course," Kawabata answered.

"In Harbin?"

"Yes, in Harbin," Kawabata replied easily.

"And his wife?"

"Yes." Kawabata said.

"Where is she?"

"In Kobe attending to the funereal details—at her sister's . The home burned out. Is that the right word?"

"Burned up might be more usual." Owen answered.

"Burned up. I see. Burned up."

"She'd have every right to be burned up, all right," Archie said. But Kawabata only smiled through his confusion at the phrase.

"Dr. Matsuno served the *Etta* community and the Korean immigrants. He lived among them in Nagata-ku, died with them in the quake and the fires. Perhaps, Father Robert, we'd call him a saint, although he was no Christian, I do believe," Mioko said.

Father Bonneau said, "I heard he came to the Kobe Union church once, after the war. But I don't know if it's true or not."

"I asked him once to come," Mioko said. "And he came once. You're right. He was very busy with his practice."

"Not in my time," Bonneau said.

"He'll have a Buddhist funeral." Mioko said.

"Doubtless his serving the poor in Nagata-ku will leverage him to a better new life—perhaps a pastor at a well heeled ex-pat church," Archie added.

Mioko laughed, "And a church that can survive earthquakes."

"Yes, we can," Bonneau said. "And we did. We did indeed."

"We did, "Archie continued, "Nagata-ku didn't. The good doctor didn't. What's the lesson Owen?"

"Stay out of Kobe."

"And on the mountain top," Jena said, and then turned to Sanae, "Your father served the *Etta* and Korean immigrants, is that right?"

"Yes," Sanae answered softly.

"Did he say why?" Jena continued.

Owen thought, only an American would press in with such a question.

"He knew they did not have many doctors. And there were many such people in Kobe."

"Far fewer since the quake," Archie said.

"Such people don't have much money to pay and sometimes national health omits them. That's why my father helped them."

Sanae's answer seemed to silence the exploration. One of those weird silences settled over the group; each moment seemed to prop up the ease with which the Japanese endured the extended non-commentary.

Finally Father Bonneau interrupted private reverie, "It seems we have here a living saint who strode among us unrecognized —someone to emulate, someone to study, someone to follow carefully. That it does." He took another leaf sweet, chewed a bit and then continued,"I've come to believe these disasters have their impacts for a reason. Some of them tear things up so that we see clearly what kind of people we truly are. What we really want. What we can really adopt, follow, embrace."

"And what would that be, father?" Owen asked.

"Sanae's father. Humbly working for the poor, the rejected of this society. Living among them working for them. Not profiting. Not in smug satisfaction, but in silence and obscurity. Tirelessly helping them. Isn't that admirable? Who wouldn't want to emulate such a person.?"

Owen turned to Sanae, "Did your father talk about his work in Manchuria?"

"No."

"Do you know what that work was?"

"Medical research."

Mioko said, "Japanese doctors found new ways to stop plagues, new ways to treat water so that cholera could be avoided, new ways to preserve infants from disease. They did important, difficult work in Manchuria."

"The *maruta* denied it." Archie said.

"What did you say? "Mioko asked.

"He didn't say anything," Jena answered. "We came here to tell Mioko how the church survived. Undamaged. In tact. God watched over the Kobe

Union church. Watched over us all. We're here to show that He did care for us, did preserve us to do the work he has planned for us."

"And what work would that be, darling?" Archie said.

"The work that Dr. Matsuno demonstrated to us all. Caring for those less fortunate."

"How less fortunate?" Archie asked. "Most days I feel less fortunate."

"Deservedly," Jena said.

Archie smiled at her.

Owen said to Sanae, "Did you father speak of being forgiven?"

Mioko said loudly, "There was nothing to forgive."

Owen continued turning to Kawabata, "Is that true, Kawabata-san?" But the old man did not answer, merely smiled insipidly at Owen, smiled and smiled more broadly. More silence fell on the group. Owen in the lock of something he didn't quite grasp but could not shut down simply pressed ahead, "Terrible things—"

"There were no terrible things," Mioko cut him off. "None whatsoever. I don't know what you are talking about. Dr. Matsuno was an exemplary person. Moreover, the dead are all good. Surely you know that."

"I know that's a Japanese belief," Owen answered.

"And a true one. Death is absolution."

"So there was something to absolve?"

"Absolutely not. Death simply empties all the record. The dead are all good. New soldiers for the new cause."

"New cause?" Archie asked. "What the hell are you talking about? More medical experimentation? Plague injections? Freezing children? Then hacking them up? New soldiers for a new cause. You sound like some cult figure."

"Perhaps he was."

"Who was? "Owen asked.

"Dr. Matsuno," Mioko answered. "Not that he knew it or cared about it. He didn't. But he understood the new cult of Christianity well enough."

"He didn't happen to believe in it." Archie said.

"That's your argument, and you are welcome to it."

"So we're not talking about a new cult at all." Owen said.

"Right." Archie answered. "We're talking about why and how you get up each morning."

"He's a light sleeper," Jena said.

"Who is?" Owen asked again.

"Jesus," Archie answered. "Always weeping late at night in the garden."

"No mockery, none what so ever." Father Bonneau shouted.

And there was silence in the room, while Bonneau picked up another leaf sweet. "Mockery only undercuts itself. It does, you know."

"There's no mockery in hacking children up," Archie said. "There's no mockery in translating the detailed record of atrocity after atrocity, by a new solider in a new cause, is there?"

"My father was incredibly tender to all children. Especially to me." Sanae said.

Archie sighed, looked to the ceiling and said finally, "Well, maybe it was the chill in Manchuria."

Sanae picked up the cool tea cup, put both hands around it, stared at the surface, avoiding looking anywhere else. She seemed to be measuring her breaths, staring and staring at the teacup top.

Mioko said, "He was gentle with everyone. Gentle and kind. Kind and concerned."

"A kind, loving cauterizer," Archie muttered.

But Sanae continued staring, and after a minute, Mioko said, "I thank you so much for coming to let me know the church survived. I thought as much, at the top of the mountain, but I know you all had better things to do than worry about some old lady's grasp of her church. Sanae has suffered enough, losing her beloved father."

Owen thought, she's going to stare at the tea until we leave her. It's a amazing, such anger He wondered if she could vaporize the tea, or at least set it boiling again with her fixed gaze. We don't exist. We're not here. Did the daughter have the father's focus? Perhaps the *maruta* were not there in Harbin, dismissed there, as here—stupid, extraneous elements incapable of understanding her hurt, causing greater hurt by our presence. Greater anger by their moaning. Fury ginned up by our pain.

Suddenly Sanae said, "My father became a Christian, a baptized Christian. Not at the Kobe Union church. Never there."

"Never?" Owen asked, "Why never?"

Sanae did not answer.

"Perhaps he felt uncomfortable among so many *gaijin*," Bonneau said. "It's difficult being an outsider."

"Like a chaplain aboard ship, in war time," Archie said.

"You have no idea of what you speak," Bonneau answered.

"Oh but I do, having been in myself you know. As indeed you do know. Spending months translating documents about Sanae's father's activities."

"What activities?" Sanae asked.

"You don't want to know. Neither does he. Neither does Mioko, and for that matter; neither does little Owen here, the newest disciple in this miserable gang of four."

"Archie," Jena cautioned.

"When you butcher children, you damn well better get right with God. Damn well better be a Christian, a fucking baptized Christian."

Father Bonneau stood up, put down his napkin with the traces of leaf sweet on it, nodded toward the staring woman. "The Lord grant us a safe evening, safe return," he said in a kurt, quiet voice. And then he led the five of them back down the hallway to the front genkan.

3

Hiromi steered the van past the shops of Suma and into the hill country. An increasing rain sloshed against the windshield, rivulets so thick occasionally that it seemed he was driving blind.

"The quake has upset us all. All of us." Father Bonneau said to the oddly silent passengers.

Owen wondered if Mariko was interested in resuming pulverization, but she sat almost primly, as if to keep proper distance from his left thigh.

Bonneau's observation seemed to fall into the rain, as more meaningless dribble, but at the last moment it was rescued by Archie's "I don't think it was the quake."

Jena said, "You specialize in not thinking."

"Ah, love, you simply don't want the truths of this world pointed out, do you?" Archie answered.

"The quake is truth enough," Bonneau said. "Or it will have to do. Mioko didn't share with us what she really wanted to say."

"We hardly let her," Jena said.

Archie continued, "But now the good priest of the P & G Union church will tell us what she wanted to say."

"Yes, I will, especially if you can get P & G to up the endowment." Bonneau laughed.

But then he did not continue and the rain took a vault into greater velocity, smearing the side view and rendering the van suddenly very rattle-ridden and vulnerable.

"What was Mioko going to tell us? "Mariko asked.

"About a trade in the middle of the war." Bonneau said. "A deal that actually preserved the church, kept Kobe Union out of the hands of the so called Japanese Christian church."

"A trade? You mean like cash?" Owen said.

"No. Flesh. "Bonneau answered, sighing.

"Exotic, "Archie said, "Human slavery. More than just Korean forced laborers? More than Chinese comfort women? More than Filipino house servants? More than Iranian ditch diggers?"

"What can be more than those?" Jena said.

"Obviously whatever Mioko participated in. Isn't that so Father Bonneau?"

"She said she felt guilty over something in the war," Bonneau continued. He turned more fully toward the back seats. "Something she evidently wanted to tell us. But it's true, we didn't give her a chance. I think she was more cooperative with the *kempeitai* than we thought."

"Wasn't everybody?" Jena said.

"Tough choices," Bonneau answered. "But she and Pastor Rielmann probably had to give something back to keep the church independent. In war time the deals are never one-way."

Archie shrugged. He seemed more interested in the guardrail looming across Bonneau's shoulders. "Water over the dam, over the van." Archie said. "Guard rail over all!" Archie shouted as the van hydroplaned toward the edge of the road. "Don't brake! Get off the brake," Archie pushed at Hiromi's back. But the car still drifted sideways, nudged the guardrail screeched along the metal, shooting sparks (immediately extinguished), ringing along over the rivets, and then, as Hiromi eased off the brake, hydroplaning across into the descending lane.

There was no one coming down and it seemed the van might bounce over the blasted rocks on the other side and right itself going up the mountain. Pailfulls of water slammed into the windshield and just when it seemed to Owen that magically they would sluice to the proper lane and avoid absolute disaster, he was aware of light coming through the torrents, headlights like glowing meteors coming directly at them. But so slowly as to be avoidable. He had only to shift a little to the left in his seat, shove Mariko over, and then the meteors would whosh on by. If only he could just push sideways, but it seemed he couldn't move quite fast enough. There was time, but not enough energy. It seemed a gluey molasses had spread on the seat in the rainwashed air inside the van, solidifying so that he couldn't quite generate enough torque to push Mariko over, couldn't quite lift his thighs off the adhesive seat. With wondrous slowness the meteors advanced toward the windshield ahead, climbed slowly over the van's sloping hood and then clattered into seats in front of him. The engine between the meteor lights appeared breathing and ratcheting, throbbing at his knees, grinding up Hiromi and Father Bonneau, churning through the Hesseltines devouring the upholstery. A chewing spining, spewing, spitting creature that seemed intent on getting into his lap. Was it a joyously ener- getic cougar with a laughing, lapping playful sentiment trashing everything in its way toward some perch beyond the rain? Caress me father, for I may have sinned, wasn't it speaking to him, even as its jaws tossed blood, limbs, bones about the accordian van? Speaking playfully in a gruff, high pitch. I may have sinned and you wanted to feel redemption, so here tis, spinning wildly through spark-soaked rain. Ultimate inexplicable redemption, the grace of God bounding into your open lap, scrunching up in your curled arms, overflowing your tear filled, blood-saturated eyes. Pass through the stretched elastic of end of life, listen to the clatter as it distances itself from the crowning meteors beaming their broad energy sweep through the utter blackness of the bounding cougar landing so effortlessly on your forehead, claws locked into your ears,temples, and cheekbones.

"No damage done," said Father Bonneau. "We're in tact. Immovable but in tact."

Hiromi was screaming, apparently some part of the firewall had buck- led in on his left kneecap.

"We're all okay," Bonneau repeated, a little louder than Hiromi's howl. "God has watched over us."

"Oh, horseshit!" Archie said. "Ask Hiromi if he's okay. Is he?"

"No paramount damage, we're in tact and underway with full weigh on."

"Spare us the nautical crap." Archie continued. "We've had an accident. We're lucky to be alive, and if we don't get out of this van we're going to die."

"My boy that's nonsense, this vehicle is safe. We're safe," Bonneau said.

It did seem Owen had crushed Mariko against the side of the van, an unprovoked pulverization. She pushed him away. "Someone help Hiromi," she said, loud enough to be heard in the front seat.

Bonneau leaned over his driver, pushed at the buckled firewall, raising it enough to get Hiromi's knee freed. He stopped screaming. The wind- shield had caved in toward the center and large gaps in the frame let heavy rain come into the van.

"I can't open my door," Jena said. "Should I kick out the window?"

"You want more rain to come in?" Bonneau answered.

"What if gas is flowing now all through the bottom? What if we ex- plode in a fire ball?" Archie asked.

"We're not going to explode in a fireball. It won't happen. I can tell you that authoritatively. I've seen fire balls and we're nowhere near one. Not a chance. We're safe, sound, dry here. We should be thankful."

"Yes, we are thankful. That is the proper expression. We are profoundly thankful," Mariko said. "And we can go out the back way if Hiromi will release the back gate." She repeated her request in Japanese and miraculously the gate unfastened, and then slowly swung upward as the hydraulic lifts kicked in. Rain that was becoming sleet came around the edges of the lifting back gate.

"Tilt the seat all the way back and we'll climb out."

"Climb out? Why climb out?" Father Bonneau said, "it's safe in here, out of the rain."

"Sleet," Archie said.

"Whatever it is, it's out there. It shouldn't be coming in here. Close the back gate."

"I smell gas," Archie said. "And I'm going out." He turned and pushed Owen across out toward the back, off his almost-level seatback. Mariko followed. Then Archie plunged rearward, spilling out onto the highway. "Come on, Jena." Archie called out, then reached in and pulled her across the sloping seat onto the roadway. The four of them stood huddled under the lifted gate of the van.

"It's really wet, Archie," Jena said. "Maybe we should get back in."

"I don't see any gas," Mariko said.

"Yes, get back in," Bonneau called from the front seat. "At least we'll be dry."

"Not very," Archie answered. He hoisted Mariko up over the sloping seat. Then Jena.

"Owen, my boy. To you goes the task of saving us." Bonneau said. He threw a set of keys the length of the van. "Take these and start off alone. Up the hill. There's an umbrella under the rear seat. Go back to the church. Get my car and come back down to pick us up. It's a good hike but it's not too bad. We'll be safe here. And, who knows, maybe somebody will come along and offer us a ride. Hiromi can't walk."

Owen probed under the back seat and pulled out the black umbrella. "The road goes to the church directly?" he asked.

"Directly. You can't miss it. Just past the top of the mountain, a little on the downside. It's on the left. You can't miss it."

"And your car?"

"It's in the side lot, cream colored. You can't miss it."

"He can't miss it," Archie echoed. "It may be too windy toward the top to use the bumper shoot." Archie smiled at Owen, acknowledging his coming dilemma.

"I'm afraid you'll get very wet, my boy," Bonneau said. "Think of it as absolution, and a joyous suffering for others."

"Especially the joyous part," Archie added.

"I will think of it that way," Owen said, opening the umbrella so that momentarily one of the spires caught in the van's overhead gate. He motioned Archie back in and slowly closed the gate after him.

"Should take less than an hour," Bonneau shouted. "You'll save us, my boy."

"Yes, I'll save you all," Owen shouted, holding the open umbrella tight against his head and stepping away from the crumpled van. He nodded to them as he passed ahead and started up the mountain.

It wasn't long before his shoes were sopping wet, and the heavy rain turned to thicker sleet as he proceeded. It was tough going. The grade was such that even the clever Japanese hadn't found a way to exploit the land. He felt his calf muscles tightening in the grey exertion and he remembered a Kendo class he'd been forced to take when he first came to Japan. A theology professor was also a Kendo fanatic and had his own club, 30 university sophomores who apparently delighted in his lengthy inscrutable lectures about the mystery and sanctity of Kendo, even as they lived to try their luck against the American novice, hoping to whack any arrogance out of him. The professor told him loudly in front of the others that he needed to learn how to walk all over again, or rather glide the Kendo glide was the key to great sword-fighting. He'd have to learn how to walk again, glide again, and to do so he must hold a large bowl of water and glide across the floor toward the full length mirror. No water must spill. How would they know in this sleet, Owen wondered. One gliding foot, one catching-up other foot, glide, glide, step, glide, water motionless and content in the bowl before us. It played similar havoc with his calf muscles. And there was the gloating mirror wall reflecting his awkward motions beneath the billowy *hakama* pants. And always at the end of the class Owen, the invited *gaijin*, had to kneel in the Japanese position not in the line with the other novices, but separately to the right so they could glance at him, as the professor intoned and intoned on the joys and mysteries of Kendo. He usually spoke for ten minutes. Owen's pain from slumping back on his calves seared along from toes to hips, contorting his legs into a pressed iron shape, unmovable.

He believed that reliving that anguish made the sleet bearable, made the exertion of pushing upwards on the icy hillside easier. He held the umbrella clamped against his head, covering his shoulders like an immense bat, but still the sleet flew in, splashed in, unimpressed by his protection.

Near the top of the hill the walled houses appeared just as he remembered them from the other side of the hill. Tile roofs with ice and snow dapplings. Would the elderly gentlemen in winter yukatas be strolling the surprisingly long driveways? Evidently not. Doubtless fur- laden and huddled around *kotatsu* and incomparably warm, they were unaware of his gliding past their residences, oblivious of his sloppy shuffling, or the sleet-caressed perspiration streaming down his face and sides. Should he knock on doors and beckon them to follow him? Lay aside your fleece blankets, your fur wraps, your Panasonic speakers spewing Mozart, and come out to save the children from freezing, or at least the grown ups muttering to themselves in a van two miles below? If you could watch the 12 year old's arm slowly being sawed off, could you then genuflect before the crucified Lord? And would your genuflection count for much against his crucifixion, or his sawed off limb? The questions, Owen understood well enough, could not substitute for worship—were, in fact, signs of worship's erosion. In precisely the same way the child's bleeding arm stump eroded any inclination toward worship.

4

Near the summit the sleet/rain turned harder and whiter, spreading before him like white faience tossed on the tile drains and the black macadam—almost bits of white cloth left somehow on the roadway. Owen's breath grew noisier and occasionally he slipped, skidding his shoes out beneath him. Bolting forward and at the last second regaining his footing. The motion jarred his right knee, snapping it backwards in a sudden crisp ache that pitched him forward again and again.

It was silly, he knew, this ungainly gait, this spastic walk. He reached the apex opposite the entry way to the Oxford manqué, St. Mary's of Fuji Steel. He wondered if the dons were sipping port and watching a small wood fire? He would have to ask Kawabata about the heat in Harbin. Sure, there had to be some—no one could have survived without it. Yet how hard it was to kill a human being. Deprivation was never enough. There had to be time—acres of it. Some strains of flu might kill in a day but Unit 731 never dealt with them. Owen wondered why they were overlooked. Surely Dr. Matsuno and company knew of the decimation of 1918-1919. How the doctor could have advised them, and it was clear the opportunity of controlled decimation, experiments in atrocity, had attractiveness. Did Mogens understand that the ability to maim and devour was seductive to any who commanded it?

Satan entered into Judas, says Luke's gospel. The only one mentioning that particular explanation. God's plan required it. At the end, as the Russians carted him away for further experimentation, did Mogens grasp God's plan? Satan entered Judas. There was comfort at the thought. Satan had entered those who sawed the limbs of children and left them to bleed/freeze in the night. A simple explanation. Part of God's plan.

Owen remembered Luke's gospel before atrocity: "Then they will begin to say to the mountains—fall on us, and to the hills—cover us. For if they do these things in the green wood, what will be done in the dry?"

Was that Mogens' comfort? He could still imagine far worse acts? "It's not the worst said Lear, when you can still say, This is the worst." Was that Mogens' mantra? Owen doubted it.

Mogens had children. He knew what axing them up meant, he knew the worst as the worst, knew the full limited space of the pit—the 19 sides of it. Felt all the corners, dismissed all the exit toe holds. Listened carefully to its endless screaming. He doubtless prayed to God, to Jesus, to the Holy Spirit, and imagined their intercession, awaiting their deliverance and collapsed at their neglect. Mogens may have imagined, as sometimes Owen did, whether the soft visage of Jesus, winnowing out of the darkness, beckoned toward some new deliverance, a new soldier for a new age.

Was choking on your own vomit the best relief—the most transcendent exit from the howling agony, lapping up the concrete hallways? Even the heaviest, thickest, if most sporadic (as now) snow was quite unable to envelope the screams of children. Their torrent-scream came through cloudless chill Manchurian Lucite-like platinum light, electrifying everything.

Satan entered Judas, then exited, paused just long enough for a kiss. Dr. Matsuno glistened, imagining he'd found a way to coagulate blood under artic conditions, paused long enough to seal off plague for separate, targeted delivery, and then departed—leaving the vessel empty and longing for interior volume, something as all-consuming once again. And he found it: in this daughter and among outcasts; until God's plan dumped his house down on him, crushing the eighty year old's ribcage like a bicycle running over a styrofoam cup.

Satan entered and then left. Human shards all around—a limbless boy in a frozen bathing suit, or a pancaked 80 year old physician's fluids drying in the soft Japanese snow and sporadic sunlight. Satan entered and then left.

Starting down the long side of the hill Owen finally saw the church's parking lot. Yes, there was the cream-colored Toyota, the Rector's overlarge model, marked "Presidente," just beyond the church.

Part Five

1

MIOKO BEGAN, "SO IT could not be exactly said you saved Hiromi's life?"

"Hardly," Owen answered.

"He wasn't bleeding?"

"Hardly. We drove him to Awagi, to a hospital there. It took quite a long time.

He would have died if he'd been bleeding. Oh, there may have been some internal bleeding. His leg turned a funny blue color."

"That must have been Yodogawa Kirisutokyo Byoin. Father Bonneau knows it well. Even though it's Seventh Day Adventist."

"It's not. It's Presbyterian. It's near porn theaters," Owen said.

"Yes, that would be properly Christian wouldn't it?" Mioko said. "Our Lord hung out with prostitutes and derelicts."

"I didn't see any," Owen added, "but I did see a number of retarded attendants in the hospital, doing janitorial work."

"Some people are suited to some kinds of work. Would that we had more around here. Did you get to read what I sent you?"

"It's in Danish, and I haven't found a translator in Kobe just yet."

"And doubtless you won't be able to, will you?"

"Kobe's very cosmopolitan," Owen responded.

"But somehow you won't find the energy or connections to get the words into English, will you?"

"Maybe not. Maybe it will be too sad, too discouraging, too awful."

"I suspect it will be awful enough. And that's been my solution, too. I couldn't find a translator. Time and again I'd go to a party and I'd be making small talk with someone from Denmark, say Copenhagen, or maybe Jutland and it would be delightful, filled with good humor. And later I'd suddenly remember, I should have asked them to look at Mogens' writings. Surely they could have quickly told me what they said, and then I'd have known. But that's the issue isn't it? Knowing what they said. We don't really want to know what they said, do we?"

"I can guess."

"So can I. Full of remorse and longing to see his children. That was his least attractive trait, wanting to see his children. Pining away for them. I'd often ask him if his career at Maersk wasn't so important, then why not just go home and be with them. It was unseemly to whine about their absence and do nothing about it, don't you agree?"

"I don't know."

"You're most blessed condition, and one you cultivate even more fervently than do I."

"I'm not sending out personal writings I can't read," Owen answered.

Mioko smiled and paused to pour them green tea from the heavy orange tea pot. The handless cups seem very old, very rough. "It's true enough. I send out feelers from this silver lair and I hope to snare some hapless *gaijin* into my net of concern, my little reticule of care."

"Care?"

"Yes, certainly a kind of care?"

"But what kind? It seems more like spearing an old boil to see if you can get the corpse to twitch."

"You think Mogens is dead then?"

"Of course I do. No one lived after experiments in Harbin. Even if the Russians carried him away. What condition could he have been? Kawabata certainly thought he died."

"Did he say so?"

"Not in so many words."

"So you filled in the sentiments? Is that it?"

"Don't be ridiculous. Of course he perished."

"But you thought the same of Matsuno and Kawabata himself."

"They were perpetrators not victims. Victims don't live."

"What if the documents prove he lived?"

"Well, when you find a translator then you'll know."

"So you're not interested?" she asked.

"You've said it. Didn't you? Neither one of us is interested. Me because it seems like mucking around in someone's horrible tragedy, for no reason but a search for what? Explanation? Some piece of perception that makes the inexplicable horribleness explicable? I don't have the time, the stomach, the savage inclination." He paused, then added, "But you do, don't you? Why? Was Mogens something more to you?"

"Oh, I'd like to know what you've conjured up in your very limited imagination."

"I could conjure up lots of possibilities, if I wanted for you."

"But it would be like trying to find a Danish translator, wouldn't it?"

"Let's talk about something else." Owen said.

"Perhaps the tea?" Mioko answered. "It's not first rate, is it?"

"Tell me about Pastor Rielmann."

"Oh, that is something else. But I thought you actually wanted something else. How is that something else?"

"Bonneau says Rielmann felt guilty. Why?"

"I'm not good a guessing what was in the mind of German pastors."

"Especially if you share it with him."

Mioko smiled that wondrously vacant all-covering Japanese smile. "I don't believe any of us shared much with Pastor Rielmann. He was more than a little detached, remote, solemn, removed. Just like you."

Owen grasped the tea cup feeling the healing warmth through his fingers and palms. The scent of the hot tea seemed suddenly like the fumes of cut lawn in hot summer in the states. He'd made pocket money during the summer cutting lawns. Mown grass was infinitely tranquilizing; he worked alone, sometimes cutting half paths rather than full reels to make the sentiments of quietude and groundedness last longer. At such times he knew, actually knew, what "vocation" meant, as if God had cupped and pressed him to a particular place full of shade and clear markings of what he had done.

"And guilty?" Owen continued.

"I suppose we're all guilty, aren't we? Or at least ashamed. Besides Pastor Rielmann had no family, so he hardly sinned in that way."

"Sinned?"

"Oh you know. Carried on about how he missed his children. How he wanted to be with them as the war spread and spread."

"It was the experiments on children that most anguished Mogens, wasn't it?"

Mioko looked aside, smiled again. "We might imagine as much, mightn't we?"

"It takes no imagination." Owen answered. "But I'd like to know how Mogens imposed Christ on what he saw-—but maybe he wasn't a Christian."

"A nominal Lutheran. I understand all Danes are, or at least their taxes for the church say so."

"Like Rielmann?"

"Yes. Exactly like Rielmann." Mioko said. "Oh, it's true enough Pastor Rielmann thought he was somehow implicated in what happened to Mogens. He sometimes thought if he hadn't taken him to Tokyo, it would not have happened. But in fact we both knew it would."

"You and the pastor?"

"Of course. He knew and I knew. We both knew the *Kempeitai* wanted Mogens for some reason—for a particular reason. His brother Peder was very active in the resistance in Copenhagen or nearby. We knew that."

"You knew that? And you delivered Mogens to them?"

"Oh, I suppose if I were very Lutheran I might brood over that in some fashion." Mioko answered. "And I suspect Pastor Rielmann understood if he were to save his beloved church some exchange might be required. Or maybe he just imagined that, so he could brood about Mogens' delivery and that brooding would fulfill his destiny of unhappiness and gloom. There are people who feast on their own misery, I suppose. And I might have been one of them, I suppose, but I had my music and lots of good memories of my time with Mogens."

"Your time with Mogens?" Owen asked, putting the tea cup down.

Mioko smiled broadly again and cocked her head a bit. "We did enjoy each other's company. He was a wonderfully kind man. He had no meanness. No anger."

"Unless the Danish diary reveals otherwise," Owen said, aware of his own meanness.

"So we won't get it translated will we? Instead we'll debate what it might have said. I say it's full of sentiments for his children, and sorrow about the children confined with him."

"Maybe rage against God," Owen said.

"Yes, rage against the Lord. That would be appropriate, as would the feeling that by suffering he was fulfilling God's plan. Wouldn't that be it too? Of course it would. God's plan saves us all. Saves Pastor Rielmann and even Mioko Tanaka, and maybe even Owen Mathias with one 'T'. 'Thy will be done,' we should all say it, all the time. I will say it, all the time."

"Yes, it could echo down the hallways of Harbin; it could be the motto over every door in Unit 731's many buildings. 'Thy Will Be Done!' 'Plague be done!' 'Frozen hearts be done! Eviscerated children be done!'" Owen said.

"I can see it's going to be difficult for me to get absolution from you. Very difficult." Mioko smiled.

"Harder still from Mogens."

"Oh no, that would be easy. The dead are all good. We Japanese believe that passionately. Death cleanses everything, especially memory. I would only have to glance toward him. He would sense my request. I'd never have to speak it. He'd grant it silently. I would grasp that instantly and quietly. No word need be spoken. It would be done and would glide into infinity like a shot."

"What a fantasy," Owen said. "I'd still know. So would Bonneau. Probably Archie and Jena too. And Kawabata."

"He'd never speak of it. Nor would they, I do believe. When the sin is substantial recognizing it makes everything impossible. Isn't that so? When the burden is incredible, you simply bear it, and helping hands simply deny it. We Japanese track everything in mutual dependence. Kawabata and I count on each other totally. Besides, Mogens' only wrote something like: 'cries absent and my piss is less muddy—a very good day!'"

Owen picked up the teacup again. So in fact she had found a translator. Maybe she read Danish. He felt manipulated and oddly that feeling seemed liberating. Since she held all the knowledge and direction of the game, he escaped responsibility. Mogens' method of survival retreated into some figment of her imagination. Perhaps she had concocted everything, and if she had, then all could be dismissed, ignored, even laughed at. Owen could almost hear Archie's sarcasm cascading through the empty canyons of care, now pushed back down into flatlands—arid, deserted, fissured. He could walk over the parched land in hot flip-flops, could conjure mirages up ahead, instant bushes by temporary springs, spreading shade before they died in the scorching sunlight. Yes, here was Mogens the phantom of frozen children, delimbed and with blood coagulating as it froze. And then poof! gone, gone before grasped or believed, while the lady strummed Chopin and served tepid tea. If that weren't true, only a translator of Danish scribbling could tell. And wouldn't that be perfect? You have until tomorrow to find a translator of Danish who might unlock the perfect set of atrocities before they receded into after-death memory— a place of total exoneration. Such translators didn't hang around Shinjuku Station in Tokyo waiting for work, nor Sannomiya in Kobe. So then let the lady have her reverie, especially since her reverie restored the throne of heaven, unblemished, omnipotent and just. It was as if the metal plate pinioning the sailor to the bulkhead was only a figment; the twins in arctic tanks, only an old lady's dark imaginings, compensating for some slight too swift or benign as to be unrecognizable by Mathias. In any event Owen could end his fretting and get about the serious business of identifying a true vocation. Would that be something along the lines of Dr. Matsuno's post Harbin focus? Owen thought: if only the tile roof would collapse. Come crushing down you harsh, heavy tiles, come crushing down.

Mioko called him back, "You seem a thousand miles away," she said, smiling.

"What do you want from me? Why am I here?"

"Only a little news about the church," she answered, smiling even more. "You seemed to want to open the past a bit, and that surely suited my needs too. If sin isn't shared, it isn't sin. Don't you believe that?"

When Owen didn't answer, Mioko said: "You replace me, but I imagine you have trouble accepting that. It's the lack of a second 'T' in your name, I do believe. Originally I'm sure there were two 'T's'. But in replacing me it's important that you realize and acknowledge God's plan and my role in it, and Pastor Rielmann's. You have trouble with that, don't you?"

"I don't have trouble with something I don't believe makes any sense."

"Good, you can just dismiss me then, and everything else. Just dismiss it. That's good for you and for everyone. Mogens' complaints eventually wither away like the cries he constantly heard. You can't hear them now. We can't and we shouldn't. I understand in Harbin the current concern is whether the Ice Carving Festival will be well attended. Have you heard any projected numbers? I understand they use chain saws for the initial carving, getting the blocks of ice into human form. Chain saws."

2

Kawabata's serve was slow and arched and incredibly spinning, and Owen delighted watching their infinitely younger opponents gyrate awkwardly trying to guess how far the serve would jump away from them; each time they failed to anticipate where the ball would be. Invariably Kawabata's mesmerizing twist serve either jammed or escaped their flailing returns, so that their poachable miss-hits floated to Owen at net. Crisply he put them away at their feet, or between them, or past one of them, or occasionally just rifled directly at a stomach crouching opposite him.. Here at last was what Kawabata's soft artistry could do—gin up rifle shot put-aways. The crack of Owen's racket strings echoed across the 32 courts. Distant players turned to see who might have been crippled. The big American surely played aggressively, unJapanesely. Owen was certain that the enthralled audience spoke to itself: we need more of such aggression, such creativity, such sudden, wonderful anger. Champions are constructed of such convictions; Japan needs to learn from this *gaijin*. After each put-away, Kawabata gently remarked to Owen, "Ah, you have played a lot of tennis." The refrain eventually seemed tinged with disapproval.

On a changeover Owen said, "It's the mix of your soft stuff and my bullets that keeps them off balance."

"Only for this first set," Kawabata replied. "They'll learn quickly. Watch, they'll start taking the ball on the rise. Then we're done."

"That's a losing mentality," Owen said, smiling.

"You sound like Mioko," Kawabata replied, startling Owen. "It's a phrase she uses."

"I've never heard her use it."

"Perhaps with you she never uses it. Now let's get ready to receive."

But as points passed, Owen could not avoid coming back to the issue. "What is 'losing mentality' in Japanese?"

"Maybe, *chotto kanashii*" Kawabata answered, apparently irritated at having been asked. "Now we must concentrate and trick them out of this set. Do you understand that?"

"Oh sure. We're not going to wear them down."

"Our condition does not permit it." Kawabata reinforced Owen's conclusion.

But the tide did in fact seem to turn. At four-all the younger opponents seemed to gather strength, gain focus and apply their superior running ability their stronger arms and joyous clubbing against Owen and the old man.

"We must break their rhythm and set them against each other. It's our only hope," Kawabata said. "Take time getting the balls for them to serve. Hit at the smaller one, every time. Hit at him always. Do it! Make him go back from the net. Make him the target so that his partner will worry."

So this was the plotter Kawabata, the strategist unseen, unimagined in fact. Owen couldn't quite believe the old man cared so intensely. Is this what growing old meant? Investing everything in swindles and trickery? His glow of strategy perfectly matched their slick superb resilience, their passionate embrace of competitive struggle. Kawabata and the youths understood each other, recognized each other's gifts; only Owen floated around between unsure, trying to figure out the rules of combat. It was clear their opponents were afraid of Kawabata's guile and it may have been the *gaijin's* sudden power crossed their minds, but that could be handled with reflexes and stamina. The old man was far more ominous-—he could throw up lobs all day, and his smiling Buddha presence was only a reminder that the run up might be in fact the beginning of the run back. He could set them scurrying, like young deer in the sunlit fields while he watched pleased by the prospect of their eventual mental collapse.

Dutifully Owen returned every serve directly at the smaller of the two opponents, a lithe 22 year old named apparently Nagata, who ducked, crouched, flailed, and even, once caught one of Owen's drives with his left hand. If Owen's shot passed him by, Nagata shouted to the backcourt (perhaps to the seven fans who had gathered to watch this generational contest)

"*Onegai! Onegai!*—Help! Please."

And just as Kawabata had stipulated, soon enough Nagata's partner began talking to him, pulling him back from the net, counseling and encouraging him. After six shots directly at Nagata, Kawabata suddenly tossed an easy forehand to the other, who dumped a simple shot into the bottom of the net. Soon enough the partners began a more extended colloquy. Apparently they reassured each other, but Owen could see the swindle unfolding.

"Keep hitting at him," Kawabata instructed. "Don't let up. Six at him, and then one to the other, and see him miss."

"I get it. He's too cold, too out of it, off his rhythm. And he'll have a scapegoat."

"Scapegoat?" Kawabata asked.

"Someone to blame. A victim. Like Mogens Nielsen."

But Kawabata had gone into the backcourt, oblivious to the remark. The old man walked painfully slowly after a loose ball. The young opponents waited, and waited, even though Nagata's partner hardly needed the extra ball to serve. Kawabata hit a slow looping shot into the opponents' backcourt and the ricochet from the fence of course had to be picked up and pocketed before play could resume. Kawabata smiled, nodding and then slowly moved into the forecourt position to receive serve. Owen admired the old man's tenacious implementation of his stalling plan. The serve came wide to the forecourt drawing Kawabata beyond the doubles lines. He had Owen thought two options, a blazing forehand in the alley near Nagata, or perhaps a driving topspin cross court shot out of reach of the partner who had sprinted to net, but the old man found a third alternative. He tossed up a medium speed shallow topspin lob directly over Nagata's head reversing everything. Both opponents spun wildly backwards. Nagata actually managed by turning his back on them to get to the back line and construct an off speed desperate backhand return of the lob. His ball fell short and Owen and Kawabata had already closed toward the net. Owen anticipated a direct overhead smash angled short away from Nagata righting himself in the backcourt, but Kawabata muscled into the net first, showing astonishing speed from beyond the alley, and smashed the ball himself, pounding it directly down with such velocity that the short bounce literally flew over the hapless opponents' heads.

"Nifty power," Owen said.

"Nifty—I don't know 'nifty'. What means nifty?"

"It means you hit harder than I do, and that's surprising."

"Perhaps it surprises them," Kawabata smiled.

Amid their bickering and disconsolate double-faulting, the set closed out easily.

"An easy win," Owen said, "once you unnerved them."

"A swindle. I like that word. A real swindle."

When Kawabata declined a second set, Nagata insisted he and his partner stand before them for 'instruction.' Owen did not follow the Japanese Kawabata poured out, beyond an occasional *"Chotto matte yoh,"* which stopped their attempts to disengage from yet more delivered wisdom.

Later as they drank draft beers at the rooftop beer garden of Tokyu department store near the station, Owen asked him what he said, but the old man grew silent, as if letting the swell chill of the beer render him inert. He paused only to pinch some edamame beans into his mouth between swallows.

"Had you played them before so you knew out to psych them out?" Owen asked.

"No. I knew only that they were young and arrogant and would be amazed even to lose a point."

"So you improvised the plan as we played."

"Improvised?"

"Made the plan up, from scratch."

"Scratch?"

"Oh, I see. We should talk about something else."

"We should let *nama biru* do its work, don't you think?"

"Of course."

"After victory, *nama biru* tastes exceedingly excellent, don't you think?"

"I surely do. And I'll buy us another pitcher."

"Do that. That will be very nice."

The sunlight was soft, enveloping, filled with a calm distant moistness, peculiar Owen thought to Japan—the blue overhead silken in its effect, slipping over their shoulders and surrounding the muted buzzing conversation of the patrons on the roof. The thick dry cold of the draft beer almost seemed to add spice to the soft atmosphere. At such times, and in such beer gardens, always after the second pitcher, it seemed to Owen that Japan was the sweetest, most welcoming, most softly embracing place on the planet. It was the dizziest mix of clear social expectation mollifying any longing for individual distinction. A place that simply opened to the world, reshaped any individual thrust into some kind of generalized fellow feeling. There could be no greater relaxation than post physical exhaustion tinged with alcoholic bon-homie.

"You said Mogens Nielsen was taken by the Russians, didn't you?"

Kawabata eased back in his chair, rested his hands on the small paunch beneath his immaculate Fred Perry tennis shirt. "Did I?"

"Yes."

"I don't think that is so."

"You didn't say it, or the Russians didn't take him?"

"Both."

"What happened to him then?"

"He died in Harbin."

"So, he died in Harbin," Owen said thoughtfully. Then after a long, and for him remarkably calculated pause, added, "And you helped him die, didn't you?"

"I don't understand your sentence."

"It's clear enough."

"We Japanese don't value clarity, do we?" Kawabata answered, smiling.

"Your instructions are always very clear. Hit at the younger one. And like that." Owen poured beer first into Kawabata's glass and then his own. "I got a document Mogens wrote which said you promised to help him die. And he was greatly relieved by your promise."

"I don't know of such a document."

"At least that's what the document's translator said."

"Translator? A Japanese document?"

"Danish, a Danish one."

"Ah so. So Mioko gave you one."

"There's more than one?"

"One, apparently, is enough." Kawabata said.

Owen took a long swallow of the draft beer and then said, "I wondered how you did it."

"It's a very difficult thing to make someone die, even someone very sick."

"I could see it as the very kindest of acts. The kindest thing to do."

"Yes, a certain kindness. But still difficult."

"I imagine there was all kinds of monitoring going on."

"Monitoring?" Kawabata seemed puzzled by the term.

"People watching. Taking readings of heart rate, recovery rate, blood composition. And always guards around. It wouldn't be easy. You'd have to make it look natural. That would be tricky, a real swindle. Constant monitoring."

"Maybe not as much monitoring as you say."

"No, I'm sure enough monitoring to make things difficult. I imagined you could have reduced medicine and let the disease take its course. But you'd have to show that you didn't reduce it, wouldn't you? And I thought, as the translator gave me a copy of the document that maybe you could use a pillow to suffocate poor Mogens. Is that what you did? I suspect in the end no one actually wants to die, isn't that right? So it would be difficult."

Speaking softly Kawabata said, "*Maruta* were dying everyday, everywhere in the camp."

"But he wasn't a *maruta*. He was something special, wasn't he? So you'd have to be very clever to disguise his death. Very clever indeed."

Kawabata didn't answer. And finally to fill the silence that Owen found agonizing, Owen said, "So what was it? A pillow? An overdose? Or a reduction? Or something else?"

Not looking up from lap, Kawabata said, "Something else."

"Something else? A knife? Denial of oxygen? A forced swallow of his tongue? Poison? An accident? Falling downstairs?"

"Do you know the medical term, 'embolism'?" Kawabata asked.

"Yes." Owen said loudly with surprising enthusiasm.

"Dr. Matsuno told me how." Kawabata said.

3

"Frankly I don't care how he died or when or where," Archie Hesseltine said just in front of Rokko station on the Hankyu line. There was a celebratory atmosphere at the station, since the line after four months had finally opened again, making a direct connection between Osaka and Kobe for the first time since the earthquake.

Jena said, "Don't be too hard on him. He's learning very difficult lessons."

"Oh right! There's evil in the world. Sigh...Little Mathias is getting his nose rubbed in it. And that's hard for the young American. Sigh. .. Maybe we should get the restaurant upstairs to open early for some Suntory Special Reserve and water. Maybe a 750 ml of it. How about it Owen? I bet I could negotiate it."

"You'd think his children might care to know what actually happened." Owen said.

"Sure," Archie answered, "just have them pop over and let Kawabata explain it to them in his best English. Maybe he could ask them if they ever half ran over an animal in the road, and as they watched the little fellow writhe around, hemorrhaging on the black asphalt, and finally they decided to complete the job by running over it again?"

"Danes don't drive that much," Jena said. "They use bicycles I hear."

"It's metaphorical, "Archie answered. "Mathias needs the big picture, don't you Owen? Broad brush strokes. Plain speaking. My forte. Maybe Kawabata's too. He seems to have upset you."

"He didn't upset me. I can understand what he did."

Jena said, "If in fact he did it."

"You think he made it up?"

"These Japanese often want things not to be discussed and they're quite clever dreaming up ways to say things so conversation stops." Jena said.

"Ah such social anthropology. My dear, you miss the point. Owen fundamentally doesn't care about old Mogens, a fellow he never knew. He's after the bigger picture, the logical tapestry, as if there is one. The puzzle that fits together on his vinyl table top, and becomes before his loving eyes, the Matterhorn of faith. Isn't that it, Owen? You want a narrative that says, what happened to Mogens makes perfect sense somehow. So much sense you can stop thinking about it." Archie paused to draw extra breath as they worked toward the top of an initial crest on the way to the Kobe Union Church. "So much sense that you don't have to care about it any longer. You can file it away."

Archie paused to take in the view down to the Inland Sea. "Without the traffic you can see the coast, can't you? It's surprising. A thousand years ago it must have been striking here on the mountain." Archie hooked his thumbs on his belt, seemed to draw a breath or a perception from the view. "For a long, long time, Owen, a long, very long time I believed if I read all the documents in 1946 about 731, about experimentation, all the lab reports, all the meticulous documentation, I believed I could see how everything hung together, made perfect unfolding sense. I really believed that. It turned out to be a pisser that every bit of new knowledge led in a different direction, toward a different set of answers, different set of villains, different collection of victims. One *maruta* led to another to another and another until I understood I was actually in the lime pit with them, lifting their limbs, pumping my sick blood into their desiccated veins. And none of it made any sense, nor could it. Nor should it."

"That's your answer, not mine." Owen said.

"Oh well phrased," Jena said.

"You little unsettling bitch," Archie chided.

"You over- weight fool," she answered.

"Eighty kilograms for a man of my height and frame is just about right." Archie answered.

"A one hundred centimeter waist is not about right for anyone," Jena said.

"I have, moreover, a near-perfect triglyceride count."

"That's largely genetic, or maybe a function of the rice and soy diet we have here. And the fish. Let's not forget the fish."

"Snake fish filet," Owen said, "Charcoal grilled."

"That's the spirit, the true Christian spirit," Archie said. "You've caught the message Christ spread. Not that everything would fall into place, reason triumphant, explicability clear, but that rather nothing would fall into place, because the whole notion of place and relationship was not compatible with true faith. True faith meant that nothing had validity much less explicability. Everything was silly, everything was 'snake fish filet charcoal grilled.' Room after laughable room to the very edge of the horizon. See, even my silly wife agrees."

In the climb they came at last into the upper, elite division. An elderly Japanese fellow in a long blue and white *yukata* stood in his glistening driveway and watched them pass by.

He was wearing wooden *gata* on his feet, and in the flowing robe it seemed momentarily he might be an aging *sumo* wrestler, but clearly he was far too thin, far too fragile. Archie greeted him in robust Japanese, but the old man merely watched, briefly nodded, then came further out on his driveway as if to make sure they all passed safely beyond his property.

"He don't care for *gaijin* pollution," Archie said. "Absolutely no fear of the Lord."

"Are we the Lord's, Archie?" Jena asked, a line of perspiration across her forehead.

Owen felt the sweat down his sides. He suddenly wondered if the strain of reaching the church would not be the precise signal that it was time to leave Japan. If the walk could be made in twenty five minutes, would thirty-five signal an end of his commitment? He liked the idea of delivering the exit decision to an outside measure.

Owen said, "Kawabata keeps talking about the lack of clouds in Harbin. About the harsh sky. Nothing of the warmth of Japanese blue soft sky."

"It's true enough, the wind here is coddling," Jena said.

"Everything about Japan is coddling, enfolding, strangling," Archie added. "As old Mogens found out, didn't he? And with perfect documentation."

"You think there are documents about him?"

"Of course there are. But it's a question of where, and that, Owen, is utterly beyond our poor purview. Utterly. No one from outside could fathom where these gifted bureaucrats stuck their endless records. Believe me, I've plowed through thousands, millions, billions."

"You were, Archie, so much more industrious in your youth. Whatever happened to that?"

"I got married. And exhausted."

"You got married and lazy, oh my *gokiburi teishu* (cockroach husband), my *nure ochiba teishu* (wet leaf husband)," Jena answered.

Owen said, "Do you often discuss like this?"

"Only before church," Archie said. "But notice how the little lady sprints up the inclines. A darting elf in tennis shoes. How I treasure her acid tongue, her Rubenesque body, those swollen thighs."

"I, too, love your chins, Archie."

"Always the last word. But not the last laugh. Only God gets that, as old Mogens found out, didn't he Owen?"

Owen paused long enough to take off his poplin blazer and flip over his left sweating shoulder. Owen was disappointed that a second wind did not take hold. He took out a handkerchief and mopped his forehead, still keeping a fairly steady pace of climb. He longed for a surge of energy, some renewal that would make the last five hundred yards a lark, but none came. It seemed the distance lengthened, became more sticky and softer to the tread. Yes, there was soft, mucid sunlight in Kobe, as if the harbor tossed moisture first to the solid sunlight and then back to the mountain top in the most tenuous billows. Had the ingenious and tireless Japanese found a way to pipe the inland sea directly beyond the clouds and suffuse it back to Mt. Rokko invisibly to be mopped away with towel handkerchiefs?

As they entered the church's back parking lot, utterly empty of cars, Archie said, "This is what I know of Mogens. The Russians carried him off, amused at first that this distinctive blond westerner turned up among so many oriental corpses or near corpses. Some indication they felt he was a find, an important figure who should be brought to their superior's attention. So even as they brutalized the *maruta*, they tended to treat old Mogens with a certain tenderness, a certain solicitation. And in his hot feverish state, amid his myriad bowel evacuations, some bloody, some filled with green/whitish pus, he was profoundly grateful for their kindness. They put him on a palate and in dark truck and sent him off toward Vladivostok or wherever. And in the truck was a dumpy but exceptionally kind young nurse who offered him a canteen of water. He took it furiously, promptly vomiting afterwards. She mopped that away, smiling at him, forgiving him. She took his hand and lingered over the missing ring finger, looking puzzled at him. He couldn't quite remember himself, swimming in and out of a fever why the finger was gone. Perhaps there had been a ring and someone coveted that? Did someone need the finger? Was it part of a game he might have understood at some previous time but couldn't summon up now? That seemed to be the case. He'd have to relearn that game, but only after he stopped vomiting, and the lesions healed over. He wondered if they would heal. He might have pointed them out to the dumpy nurse, who only smiled at him, and touched the sores with a mild warm solution she produced from somewhere. And the truck drove on through two days and nights of constant bumping up and down. And he expected to find upon arrival another tier of concrete buildings, windowless rooms, cold corridors. But, wonder of wonders, when they hauled him out of the truck, he realized he was not in Vladivostok, nowhere near Siberia, but in some much milder land —he didn't discover until much later that she'd taken him to Kyrgyzstan—And not concrete bunkers but thatched roofs of small houses, with gardens, and low walls like those here, and fresh flowers. They took him inside to a plain room with sliding glass windows half way down the walls, pale green painted walls. They wheeled his stretcher up to the glass and by lifting his head slightly he could see into a small garden with a stone bench at the far end in front of a bank of calla lilies, and a small pink dogwood tree nearby. And he dozed off, suddenly confident that the strains of disease injected into him might in fact subside. Especially if he could sleep in this magical warmth. And he did sleep, at first fitfully as if trying out the luxury of that surrender, then more fully, more confidently aware that internal forces, antibodies galore, were mounting superb counterattacks toward the toxins delivered into him. As he drifted deeper and deeper into healing sleep he heard amazingly cello music, familiar to him—the lilting cello parts of Dvorak's Serenade, as if someone were rehearsing those flowing lines, that long, aching opening. And he remembered hearing a youth orchestra playing the piece in Venice at the Scola of Giovanni Baptiste. He recalled climbing the stairs to the main room in which the orchestra was playing, hearing Dvorak's unbelievably lilting opening phrases as he ascended, soft beguiling strings boiling out through the wood of the hallway and stairs, through muffling doors that only made the longing softer and more enthralling. He'd been to Venice when he was fourteen. Why would he remember that now? He'd periodically lift his head off the salmon colored stretcher and see the dumpy nurse on the bench in the garden and it was she playing the cello. Dvorak over and over again and then later in his sounder, deeper more perfect sleep, Bach's cello suites, especially the lively gigues. She was an extraordinary cellist. He understood that perfectly between his own fevered sleeps. He'd have to find her concerts. He understood that. She was the most magical musician he'd ever heard. Her rather fat arms, jiggling in the sunlight, seemed to blend with Dvorak's kind rhythms—such a goddess, and after a week, a month, a year, maybe two maybe ten he couldn't say, they were together in Copenhagen, at a concert hall, a gleaming immaculate wooden ceramic venue in golden oak and she was playing Dvorak's cello concerto with a decidedly young orchestra, but filled with energy and beguiling piety. Or maybe it was Elgar's concerto. It's hard for me to tell, but she was perfect in playing whatever. So much so that later impresarios came by and offered to sign her up for tours, U.S.A. visits, an Australian tour, and he accompanied her, served as her translator, her advance planner, her hall solicitor, her publicist, and he took to those tasks with the enthusiasm of someone who knows he's been given a third chance at existence, at success. He focused entirely on her career, served her in every need expressed in every favor granted. And all the while in a fever of denial that his life was slipping away in blood maladies too weird for diagnosis. In Paris he came to understand after her most enthralling concert at the opera house that his bones had simply stopped making red blood cells. It would require transfusions every three days just to continue living. And the living would not be gracious, instead it would be the Harbin experience relived. And he fell into despair, and then something remarkable happened. She was offered a second Australian tour, with an extended stay in Melbourne at the tour's end. And he knew she wanted to go and he knew he'd die soon enough en route, but in a weird collection of will he agreed to accompany her, even taking frozen blood with them aboard the Quantas flight. And somewhere near the international date line, he actually felt a seismic shift in his legs—a peculiar loosening of nerves that he thought were forever frozen, inert. They stirred and he sensed something extraordinary was happening. For a moment he imagined he could see his bone marrow beginning to gin up extra red blood cells. And when they got to Sydney he suddenly felt he could delay a day longer before transfusing. And the next morning, he thought he could delay again. He knew the trick was to delay; delay was the key to longevity. Postponement meant extended life, but she doubted. How could he be delaying things? He'd not been able to do so before. But as she practiced he'd repeat to her that it seemed he actually felt better, more alert, more lively, more possible, as if old bones had begun to relearn their tasks. In the pale greens of Victoria, in the very outskirts of Melbourne, in a townhouse with epic lawns about, and weird birds walking in the grass, and a small stagnant lake in the middle of the property, he suddenly felt a healing unimaginable in Harbin. And each morning they

333

33333333333333

consulted and agreed to wait another morning. In the afternoons she practiced, and then they took to riding in their ancient, rusted out Holden, with a back seat that literally rested on the axle, the shocks were that corroded.

They rode up into wine country, the Holden easily taking the sharp hills and they found restaurants on the roadway overlooking the hills with huge awnings that dropped the temperatures beneath them.. 'Look, ' he told her in the Dandenong Hills, 'look, it's clearly paradise. Look at the sweep of the greens and browns, so much frailer, paler, more misted than in Harbin or Jutland. So I want this to be the image on my mind no matter what happens, so no matter what happens, no matter what. No more transfusions. Just this picture. Just this picture.' And two weeks later in a hospital in Melbourne he died, having turned a deliciously yellow color, dotted with blue bruises all over his legs and torso."

Jena said, "And what about his family? His children the ones Owen said he longed for beyond all human anguish?"

"Yes," Archie answered, "we'll have to fashion something about them."

4

MIDWAY THROUGH THE ADULT Sunday school lesson Reverend Bonneau joined Owen's group.

The latest P & G vice president rather ceremoniously got up from his chair at the end of the table, yielding his place to the priest. Owen thought— the Lord must be served. And in the proper place."

At the corner of the table Mariko shifted a bit to the right, as if to give even greater suasion to the servant of the Lord. Or perhaps she didn't care for his odd New Hampshire-accented English, and his shipboard tales.

"It's the rector's prerogative to intervene occasionally so I'm going to exercise that right this morning because, . . . because, well because of a lot of things. And I know I can be like the boatswain's whistle, a pretty intrusive demanding sound, but bear with me." Reverend Bonneau stopped as if to wait for a translator, but of course none spoke. The silence so soothing to a Japanese audience and perhaps, Owen wondered, to Bonneau himself, since in fact he had become after 27 years in country rather Japanese , increasingly became awkward to American ears. Finally Archie said, "What's a lot of things?"

"I've been thinking about the earthquake and God's will, God's plan lately."

"Not knowing is liberating," Jena said, too loudly.

"Of course, my dear. Inscrutability is served to us daily. Of course. But consider how long this community, this church in Kobe has endured, through relocations and bombing, through threatened fascist takeover and now natural disaster."

"We were preserved by Nazis to do the Lord's work," Archie said, smiling at the P & G folks.

"And doing that work has made the community flourish, has made our lives richer and more deeply appreciated."

"And what work was that?" Jena asked. "Pot luck dinners? Crayons and fresh underwear for *Etta* children?"

"All of those things and more," Bonneau answered. "The Lord has led us to partake, really partake of His suffering. His heartache for the way we live." Bonneau stopped speaking again as if to let the silence increase the import of his eventual words. But in the length of time it seemed too, that he had lost the thread of whatever it was he intended.

"Sermon as senior moment," Archie mouthed to Owen who felt compelled to rescue the rector.

"The cross is the substructure of suffering isn't it? "Owen asked the group.

"No, it's the resurrection that points out the natural culmination of all life. Absorption into God means letting love drive out suffering but attending endlessly to it. Devoting yourself to it. Ever ameliorating pain in others. Diminishing pain in the world, in the abstraction of the world, that's God's plan all right."

"So what are we doing now here?" Jena asked.

"What indeed?" Archie echoed. "What beyond getting ready for a long sweet retirement in an alleged 'village' outside of San Francisco? Or getting ready for sushi in the uncrushed bars of Kobe with our sweet parishioners from Rokko Island, who join us from chauffeured Mercedes?"

The vice president interceded, "They're company provided cars. They're not ours. Not ours in any way. You can't chastise us for utilizing them. They're not ours. Not our choice. Besides they provide very lucrative employment for the drivers. Is it Christian to be so judgmental?" It seemed he addressed the question to the Rector.

But Bonneau was caught up in some private reverie.

"Westerners," Mariko said, "are always so judgmental. It comes from English, the language.

It's a judgmental language. Always judging."

"Maybe so, "the Vice-President said, apparently happy to defuse the potential hostility in the room.

"I believe in the resurrection," Bonneau finally said.

"Terrific!" Archie added. "Can we go to lunch now?"

"Always thinking about eating, Archie, aren't you?" Jena said.

"Commemorative cannibalism the essence of our faith, is it not, love?" Archie asked.

"Sacrilege," Bonneau said quietly.

"Indeed," echoed the Vice-President's wife.

Father Bonneau pulled out a folded sheet from his pocket and spread it on the glowing varnish of the thick table top. He pressed out the creases, and then said "Here's what Father Rielmann wrote after the 1923 Tokyo earthquake, when he was just a seminarian: A major earthquake brings immense suffering. Non-believers, pagans—"

"Pagans?" Archie interrupted, "did he mean the Japanese? Pagan Japanese?"

Bonneau ignored the question and went on: "Pagans may try to help if their contact with the suffering does not cause them too much pain. But because they devote most of their efforts in life to avoid pain, to find comfort, to achieve power that keep at a distance those who threaten their security and peaceful happiness, they will, much more quickly than true Christians, turn away in horror from terrible suffering. For one inspired by the spirit of Christ, suffering is seen in a different light. When life at its best, as seen in Jesus, consists in the exercise of loving service of others, in self-giving, in serving rather than having, then suffering—either one's own or that of others—ceases to be a threat. Instead, it becomes the occasion and reason for a close relationship with God and thus to experience genuine life. Without suffering there would be no creative and fruit-bearing love in the world. The condition of isolation from suffering that is most earnestly desired by pagans is actually a condition of utter sterility and death, a condition where love is lacking. So suffering serves God's purpose, which is to help humans grow in love. I dare to suggest this as an answer to the original question— An earthquake is a creative act of our God who loves his whole creation."

"Ah love equals detonation. So American!" Archie observed. "Send in the pagans. We have desperate need of them."

"It does seem," Owen said, "Father Rielmann was struggling with his own capacity to cause harm. Finding some weird way to justify hurting others, isn't that it? Using God and earthquakes to build a case for painful infliction on others."

"A bit harsh, my boy," Bonneau said.

"Suffering as the womb of love," Jena said, cocking her head a bit.

"Precisely pastor Rielmann's argument," Bonneau continued. "Suffering as a kind of salvation."

"Not salvation," Archie said rather loudly, "just salvage for a savagery inflicted on others—done purposely, maliciously, with supreme planned consciousness."

"What are we talking about?" The Vice President asked.

"We're talking about Judas Rielmann, that's what we're talking about," Archie answered.

"I never knew the pastor," the VP went on, "but I can scarcely imagine him guilty of some monstrous savagery. Pastors don't behave that way, or if they do, not for very long."

"Oh, of course!" Archie said, resting both forearms on the gleaming table top. "Pastors don't behave that way. Next question. Jesus!"

Jena said, "Archie, please."

A silence that seemed to warm the room floated out over the polished table top. Owen frantically rehearsed some remarks, but at length said nothing, suddenly excited that a new thoughtfulness had come over the group. At length he did smile at Mariko, delighting in his own recognition that Japanese non-speaking had, apparently, become part of his own artillery of group control.

In silence the VP slowly got up and extended his arm to his flowery wife and together with quick, soft steps they exited the room. Bonneau watched them and nodded at their decision.

The lesson, such as it was, was over. Owen wondered what the lesson actually was. He tried to reconstruct the quoted words Bonneau had tossed out, but Mariko returned his smile and she seemed so much more enticing than Rielmann's musty thoughts. Her upper arms in the sleeveless yellow blouse were far too squeezable, too spongy, and irresistibly pliant.

5

HIS RIGHT HAND DID in fact squeeze her wonderfully malleable shoulder as they walked back down toward Rokko station. His left arm cradled her shoulders, pulled her in close to his side and his right hand just squeezed and squeezed, kneading the soft skin. As they descended past the low walled houses, Owen said to her, "Maybe Mogens died for our sins."

She laughed, "I don't think we piled enough on to justify what happened to him, did we?"

"Maybe his was anticipatory suffering." Owen answered.

"What do you have in mind?"

"Something mind bending, something cleansing, something extravagant, something like nobody has ever experienced before."

"We'll need an extra hour at Tara."

"An extra life," Owen said, "

"No jokes, please."

"On the contrary, jokes all the time. Only in Harbin were there no jokes ever." Owen said and then let the statement stand alone on the descending asphalt. "I never heard Kawabata crack a joke. I bet Dr. Matsuno never laughed either."

"In Japan the jokes aren't verbal. They're centered around things like huge paper fans to beat people on their head. But then Jesus never cracked a joke either. Or so I've been told."

"And who told you that?"

"Someone I translated for, probably an American, maybe a Brit."

"Would you betray the son of Man with a kiss?" Owen said, then nuzzled Mariko's neck.

"I wouldn't," she answered. "But maybe Mioko would."

"Yes, indeed. For less than a kiss I think." Owen said, "Maybe for only stopping talk about his children."

They stopped at the end of a white pebbled driveway. The stones had been cemented in, doubtless in recognition of the steep decline, away from the house with overlarge roof tiles.

Owen wondered if the P & G personnel in their overlarge homats on Rokko Island went to the top of their building and through binoculars looked longingly at the mansions far up the mountain. Were they comparing square footage? How could those without Jesus so prosper?

Owen gestured down toward the island out in the Inland sea. "Those on the high ground naturally command the battlefield. Naturally thrive. With a view like this." He pointed to the gold sheen off the gray-green water, the bits of sparkle radiating through a forest of television antennae on the buildings closest to the water's edge. "Who needs the Lord?"

"We don't," Mariko answered. "But his wrath is so great."

"You believe in his wrath?"

"Of course I do. What else could topple the highways?"

"Good point." Owen said, squeezing her tighter. "To hell with natural processes. All of them. Every one of them," he said kissing her neck again. "Once you start down natural processes you'll never make it to the Hankyu line." He felt her neck get warmer and wetter.

"Unnatural ones, then." She answered softly.

As Owen contemplated what she meant, he was aware that someone was coming toward the driveway, walking along the inside of the wall that bordered the road. Someone walking more quickly, yet with difficulty, and wearing a blue and white summer *yukata*. Someone rushing at them as if they were about to intrude on his land. Owen relaxed his grip, eased off her shoulders, took up a more formal stance, arms dropping to his sides. "Good morning," Owen offered, wondering whether either *ohayo*, or *konichiwa*, would have been preferable.

But the old man in the *yukata* did not answer. He stood in the middle of his driveway and simply stared at them, as if defending his territory, providing an impediment to entry and simultaneously some kind of judgment on their eligibility to trespass.

"We have no intention of intruding on your splendid property," Owen continued, speaking more slowly as if to drive his syllables into the old man's consciousness. Owen was aware he was also talking more loudly than necessary. He recalled the injunction that if your listener doesn't not speak your language, speaking louder won't help. But he couldn't stop himself.

Then Mariko interrupted him using Japanese. She spun out some kind of apologetic introduction that set the old man nodding, if not smiling. He moved closer toward them. Listened intently as she elaborated, so that the old man's face softened in some kind of sympathy and he reached out and took hold of Owen's arm with both his hands. He bowed and pulled at the arm, as if to reel Owen into his consciousness. He yanked Owen into the driveway and along the wall, Mariko following, past three small bonsai trees, and two round foliage bushes Owen had never seen before, until they were all standing in front of a small stone carving, something like a headstone, but far more trellised and terraced although no larger than a basket ball. The old man let go of Owen's arm and gestured toward the carving.

Owen thought, we're supposed to share something, some loss apparently. What had Mariko said to him? The three of them stood there for a moment and then the old man gestured they should leave his premises. Bowing several times they back stepped along the wall. Owen wondered whether to wave to the old man as they walked further down the road. But somehow it didn't seem appropriate.

"What did you say to him?"

"I told him a story?"

"Yes, but what story?"

"What do you think?"

"I have no idea, but it seemed to work. Was that a gravestone?"

"An urn marker."

"For whom?"

"His granddaughter"

"How old?"

"He didn't say. Maybe twelve, maybe ten, I don't really know."

"Yet you came up with an age."

"It seemed important to you."

"And you wanted to please me, is that it?"

"Of course."

"And you told him my daughter had died and we were coming back from the church service. Her funeral?"

"Is that what you imagine?"

"It would fit with his leading us to the urn marker."

"So that's probably what I told him." Mariko smiled.

"Is it?"

"You don't know, do you? How long have you been here and still you don't know."

"I only know what you tell me."

"I told him you spent a lot of time studying horrible things the Japanese did in China and then you came back and your daughter was killed in the earthquake, and that you blamed God for all of it, and he said that was so right, and he took us to his granddaughter's urn and said she had died also during the earthquake —in a school bus that fell over the broken highway."

"I don't think that's exactly what you said."

"I said we admired his bushes, his tortured trees. They're quite striking and perfect for the wall in his garden and he took us back there so we could see the trees better."

"And the urn marker?"

"It's a property marker, the end of his lot, the start of his neighbor's."

"I like that story better." Owen said.

"It's a better story," she answered, taking his arm and aiming him down toward the Hankyu station.

Part Six

1

THREE SATURDAYS LATER REV. Bonneau presided over a memorial service for Dr. Matsuo at the Kobe Union Church. Mioko had proposed the service and Bonneau told Owen he instantly accepted, although Matsuo had never been a parishioner. Yasuko went to Suma to collect Mioko early and together at Sannomiya station they linked with Sanae Matsuo who carried her father's ashes in a cylindrical pewter urn about sixteen inches high. Sanae also carried a tiny oval red lacquer case containing a fragment of her father's umbilical cord which, when Owen saw it, he remembered that the case would be opened and the birth artifact would be dumped into the ashes urn at a point in the service. Owen wondered whether Father Bob would permit such Buddhist shenanigans at a Christian memorial. Not that the good reverend was inclined to adhere to, or even admit, traditional liturgical structures. Bonneau did things the Navy way, by the seat of his burning britches, and it was that looseness that eventually won the hearts of even the P & G princes, or at least their lovely wives.

After the poster size photograph of Dr. Matsuo had been placed at the base of lectern at the altar's right side, and after a very noticeable pausing—before the pewter urn standing as a noble sentinel at a table in the center before the entrance to the altar—the rector moved to the lectern and began in a near whisper. "You can feel it can't you? Feel it in the air and under foot. A new softness, a sudden bursting forth that just lifts you out of where you are and floats you along. Doesn't it? Some sunsets at sea do the same thing—pinks and reds at the horizon swirling up to soft spreading whiteness in the clouds."

Owen thought, Kawabata insisted Manchuria had no clouds, no softness—only a place of ice constructions, indelicate sawings, and death. Mogens must have heard death's sighing every day, little gasps of air, gentle wheezing or tough hacking, and doubtless screams. Juvenile flesh frozen into ice chips hacked away at by guards soured on the enterprise. And God above working their limbs of dismemberment, guiding their drags of frozen corpses across sandy new snow to what? Spring dug graves left empty for the winter's crop? And above a sky absent of puffs of white amid sunglints, just a frozen stretch of pale blue/gray.

"It's on these days we understand that Easter means renewal, means resurrection, that endings are merely beginnings. New starts. Each cherry blossom mirrors creation and destruction, the sudden bursting forth of magnificent beauty and then the shuddering grayness before the blossom drops. Yes, the earth surges upward defying our sorrow. Defying the empty brutality of our entering and exiting, our silly tumbling from the tilting deck into the sea. A billion tsunamis cannot drown a cherry blossom." Bonneau said, smiling, and gesturing toward the crowded narthex in the back of the church. Where have these people come from, Owen wondered, and why so many?

Archie nodded to Jena, and leaned in to mutter, "You got that? A billion tsunamis, not just one tsunami, a billion tsunamis."

Jena whispered, "Archie..."

"I'm here to say this Kobe Union church is just that, a union of Christian faiths, so that everyone can feel welcome here."

"Bring on the *Etta*, bring on the Koreans," Archie muttered.

Owen thought—welcome to my ship, but watch for skittering metal trays.

"Out of the rubble piled all around," Bonneau gestured to the outside world beyond the narrow windows of the church, "you can occasionally see a daffodil, liquid golden light among broken stones. And of course the crocuses..." Bonneau seemed lost contemplating them.

"Little Cardinals in royal purple," Archie whispered. "Little Cardinals—it's what he always wanted, isn't it? But, alas, unionists don't make the hat. Especially in the U.S. Navy." Archie smiled, pleased with his own conceit.

Owen thought—welcome to my ship. Loose the hawsers and bounce off the camel logs guarding the docks. Ease off into the thick dark, greasy sea....

"Our is a good and loving God," Bonneau said as if studying the words as he said them. Was there, Owen wondered, some hesitation in his pronouncement, a kind of holding back for dramatic effect or just careful puzzlement, suddenly recognized as such? "A good and loving God who cares for us, who is beside us in our deepest sorrow, deepest suffering. Who subjected himself to the brokenness of our world for our sake. The God who sits at our end of the table in our deepest despair, who holds us in his strong palms when we are most threatened."

Archie whispered, "Who sits at the other end of the table? Someone wondrously malevolent with terrifically soiled palms."

Owen looked down the pew past Jena, as if to locate the precise whispering of Archie's laments. For a moment they seemed to have materialized out of the heavily shellacked wooden hymnal holders fastened to the backs of the pews in front of them. A wispy breath from the sudden chill in the sanctuary—was that it?

As if responding to that chill breath, Kawabata turned and looked at Owen, smiling that inane Japanese smile that covered so much discomfort; all ill-at-easeness melted into that grin.

Owen nodded to him, as if to sanction Archie's sentiments, but he knew Kawabata was probably just struggling to understand the new word "malevolent" and the new phrase "soiled palms." What on earth could such terms mean to such *gaijin*?

Owen ostentatiously rubbed his palms, for Kawabata and mouthed "bloody" to him, by way of explanation. Kawabata only smiled more obviously.

Mariko squeezed Owen's knee top to signal some inappropriateness in his colloquy with Kawabata. Ah, indecorous, Owen thought, pinning her hand on his knee forcefully and then coaxing her trapped palm up his thigh. She responded with mouthed silent laughter.

Welcome to my ship, Owen thought. At length God gets everything aimed at the crotch.

"God is eternally beside us, enfolding us in his thick embrace so reassuring, so coddling even when we are, as the Psalmist notes, in the deepest pit. There is always a spear of sunlight or moonlight through the darkness—evidence of charity and self-sacrifice in the saddest situations."

Owen remembered, it is not the worst when you can still say, this is the worst. He knew Mogens quoted Shakespeare to his children. Did they hear him now, continents away, decades beyond his phlegm- spewing exit? Was he now in the pews? Was he enviously watching Mariko's sliding hand? More likely he was listening to the howls of freezing boys swiveling wildly to get free of sealing ice.

2

Owen was aware of a certain redundancy in Bonneau's all-caring, all-enfolding God. The nautical references, those sailors perishing in the fires, and the inevitable seaman apprentice pinioned to the bulkhead were dutifully paraded before the tiny congregation. And beyond the boredom Owen saw again the little delighted glint that came into the reverend's eyes as he relived the most indelible moments of his life. And Owen drifted back away from the recitation, preferring the reveries of Harbin and Mogens sad slippage into some squirming, nauseated state before embolic shattering.

Abruptly it seemed, at least to Owen, that Bonneau had switched gears and was now talking about what he called appropriate memory of Dr. Matsuno. Something about speaking for the urn or perhaps from it. Could that be it? Bonneau intoned: the living woman who knew Dr. Matsuno best, who had witnessed as had no others the full scale of his efforts to ease the afflicted of this world, would now tell a little bit of her life with her father. She knew best the extent of his sainthood.

When Sanae came to the altar and eventually side stepped to the front of Bonneau's lectern Owen first thought, she's heavier than I remember her at Mioko's, more substantial and oddly proportioned. Her legs were too heavy for the sylph-like upper torso, her hair blacker and longer, her face over-rouged. Owen imagined Archie saying something like, "Now that daddy's gone the tart has come out to play," a sentiment Owen knew he himself projected onto her, errantly and regretfully.

She began speaking and her Japanese was so soft, so hesitant that Owen almost felt he was understanding what she was saying, quite counter to his expectations. Jena leaned in and supplied a translation: "The night before the quake she and her father discussed Luke's gospel—end of chapter 18 and 19. That was their custom in the evening, going through the gospel."

Owen waved Jena off. "I'm getting it," he said.

"I doubt that," Archie said loud enough to turn Kawabata toward him.

Jena ignored all directives, "The blind beggar, the short guy in the sycamore tree, and then the parable of the ten talents. It's about not seeing, isn't it?"

"Jesus's hymn to investment banking," Archie added.

"Her father said it was not about doubling the money, it was about taking what skill what talent you had and building it substantially. In his case caring for others—making sure that care expanded as widely and fully as possible," Jena said more softly than Sanae, as if to reverence her words.

"Growing the enterprise," Archie added. "Profit through volume. Salvation unfolding like a flower shading more and more children. Curing more and more of the afflicted. Like a balance sheet with greater and greater profit showing."

"Did she say afflicted?" Owen asked Jena.

"Indeed she did," Jena answered. "Indeed, and her father saw more and more of them, extending his hours into the evening in Nagata-ku."

"And what about the guy in the sycamore tree?" Archie asked.

"He was too short to see the Lord through the crowd, so he had to climb the tree," Jena said. "And she says her father thought going to China was like climbing the tree—he got a view of Jesus in Manchuria. He wasn't blinded there. He saw there. The need to help the afflicted. God put him in cloudless Manchuria to see what he needed to do."

"Jesus," Archie said, "that's what he told was going on in Harbin?"

"Not in Harbin," Kawabata said quietly, "back in Japan when he got home."

It amazed them all that Kawabata had been following their conversation in English.

Archie said, "We thought you only knew the stock phrases and the numbers, just like Owen."

Kawabata looked quizzical, apparently wondering if he should laugh——anon, he smiled.

After listening another twenty seconds, Jena said, "She thinks the dead he helped will lift the roof tiles off her father and bear him away to heaven. His goodness will be rewarded, as the scripture promises."

"*So desu neh,*" Kawabata said.

Jena broke off her translation. "Indeed he was a good man," she said affirming Kawabata apparently.

"Except for an occasional, unplanned atrocity," Archie said. "Maybe a gentle evisceration."

"What is evisceration?" Kawabata asked.

"Ask Owen," Archie answered.

Kawabata merely smiled in reply, then turned back staring at Sanae who apparently was reading a passage from scripture.

"Ah, drinking blood again," Archie said.

3

"So Dr. Matsuno was a good man, who, at an early age, committed abominations? "Archie inquired across his coffee fumes to Reverend Bonneau. "Doubtless because the all-knowing God asked him to."

"I doubt that, "Bonneau said.

"Your doubt fills the sanctuary," Archie answered.

"More likely empties it," Owen said.

"Now, my boy, you mustn't be too discouraged. Christianity in this land has risen and fallen in a pattern that can't be predicted."

"We seem to be in a down slide," Jena said quietly.

"Oh, I don't doubt that. The individualism of Christ, the notion of personal salvation may not find fertile ground here presently, but that need not mean the good news has been ignored. Truly it may be gathered in the backs of minds for fulfillment at some future date, when the need arises and extended hand of love can gather more to the Father."

"Good Christ," Archied sighed. "You foist encomiums on a butcher at his memorial and tell us to await Daddy's caress. But Daddy's a pervert, a very sick creature who enjoys eviscerating his children."

Kawabata who had come over to the group that drifted now toward the chrome strapped windows, suddenly said, "Eviscerated," he paused, then repeated, "Eviscerated. What does this word mean.?"

Jena said, "Cut up a body. Knife slice a body so that its guts spill out."

Bonneau interceded, "Jena, please...."

"Can you eviscerate a cat?" Kawabata asked, apparently truly interested.

"No. Only children, little boys and girls, maybe *gaijin,* if they get troublesome." Archie said.

"Dr. Matsuno refused to hurt children." Kawabata said. "He was a kind man."

"How kind?" Owen asked.

"How kind?" Kawabata repeated.

"In what way," Owen continued, "by what process...what is your evidence of Dr. Matsuno's kindness? Please tell us about his kind treatment of children."

"He said their screaming saved the lives of our soldiers." Kawabata spoke with an even tone so flat that he might have been reciting a train station sign.

Owen said, "And you believed him?"

"He was a doctor, a very good doctor. Of course I believed him. I saw how worried he was over the sickest children, how he tried to make them more comfortable."

Owen looked at Archie, expecting him to rush toward rebuttal, hoping in fact, that rebuttal would be coming, but Archie appeared stupefied. His eyes shed any sheen of anger and seemed to fade into some gray tranquility as he stared back at Owen. It was as if something appeared between them that made Archie relive a moment when the broken mirror on the ground rescrambled itself into an image of the Virgin Mary, or when a metal tray pinioned a sailor to the bleeding bulwark . Owen could hear Archie's imagined whisper to him, a thick slow unfolding whisper that said, "Are you listening? Here's something to change how you think. Do you hear it completely? Fully? Do you understand what is being identified here? He made them more comfortable and therefore was a good man. And on that good man God dropped a four ton tile roof. And God saw that as the tile fell, the good man, a doctor, would suffer greatly, so upon the initial impact he dispatched four milliliters of God's best anodyne into the good man's brain, so that as the tiles crushed his chest, his lungs, his heart, liver, intestines, pelvic cavity, he would swoon in sudden elevated delight. Stark screaming turned into laughter and wonderful withdrawal. Do you understand all that now?"

Owen thought, Kawabata had tossed up yet another perfect lob over his and Archie's head deep into the back court and with more than enough top spin to guarantee that the swiftest retriever, the most accomplished back-pedaler, would not get even the edge of the largest racket on the ball. Heart pounding, legs flailing you, sprinted in a supreme burst toward the back lines and the ball jumped away from your hurtling desperate, gasping thwacking. The old man possessed easy omnipotent reserves that glided winners endlessly beyond your comprehension.

"Ah, horseshit," Archie finally said, "he took the dipped bread, swallowed it and Satan entered him. Entered him, and entered you, you scruffy old charlatan. Entered you and no amount of dumped tiles will drive Satan out."

"There is no Satan," Mioko said, cheerily. "Only your tired projections. This Kawabata is incapable of any evil. I have more Satan in my little finger than he does all over."

"Well, get behind me then," Archie said.

Jena spoke crisply, "Archie you're walking a slack rope over a very familiar abyss."

"And I intend to take all these lost souls with me down into the pit."

"You will not," Jena continued. "You and I will go to San Francisco and spend our last years entertaining gay clerics at The Pilgrim's Way."

Mioko laughed heartily then said, "Now that's a future to look forward to—a truly redemptive life."

4

BUT ON THE WALK back down to Rokko Station, Archie rejected quips as a way of transcending Satan's entering Kawabata. "The plan was redemption all right, sacrificial redemption. The special lamb of God spoke Danish and English, didn't he? In the old days just pledging and planning to kill Isaac was sufficient. But the new covenant required the Lamb of God and it required Judas the initiator. So God chose Mioko and Rielmann to get the ball rolling. Satan never came out, did it?" He turned and asked Mioko who was about to answer while still clutching Yasuko's arm, only Archie continued past whatever answer she had summoned. "It turned old Rielmann an ugly grey-green, didn't it? Turned him grey-green and emptied him for another cross somewhere else, didn't it? But it wasn't enough, so God bequeathed the whole century acres of dead. And when the marvelous accumulation of slaughter wasn't enough even after two World Wars, God chose the Americans to escalate the killing. And God chose so well. Maybe 200,000 lost in less than ten seconds. So much more committed than old Abraham—not a moment's hesitation over just one son, instead a steely incineration of 200,000 called, 'the greatest thing in history.' Amazing achievement, but not enough, so God's chosen Americans spread death further in Asia, everywhere the Americans went slaughter followed. G.I. equals 'Genial Incineration.' Never in all history such a talented band of butchers, tenacious technicians of terrible travail. I used to think warfare was a demographic outcropping, but the Americans disabused me of the concept. A society intoxicated by slaughter; no sooner that the war of wars, World War II, was over when the Americans were back at in Korea, and when that paled into truce, they quickly started over in Vietnam—ah, the lure of Asia—and when that became too boring, there were forays into lesser places. Dipped bread and Satan's soft entry. Beside all that what was one Dane, one hapless Dane doubtless wondering why his ring finger was missing and the rest of his body riddled with inexplicable illnesses? Why don't you tell us, Kawabata Sensei why his body was riddled with illnesses. Let me leave out the tough word 'inexplicable.'"

"I know that word." Kawabata said, smiling.

"My unforgivable error, then," Archie answered. "Why the diseases? Please, why the diseases?"

"Dr. Matsuno was a great researcher."

"Jesus." Archie sighed. "Jesus," he repeated.

Mioko from in back, her heels clicking on the cobblestones, "In fact this man was closer to Jesus than you. You have no call to rebuke him. He behaved sweetly, with much care and concern."

Jena said, "The torturer's assistant is always blameless."

"This man saved Mogens from great suffering. I know that. I know that," Mioko said.

"So make him a saint and be done with it," Jena continued.

"If making him a saint would be done with you all, I'd surely do it."

Owen said, "I wonder if Mogens would agree with his sainthood."

"Oh, he surely would, for Kawabata-san brought him past all pain."

"You mean a morphine drip?" Owen said.

"You know what I'm talking about, you know all about it, so don't pretend to something else." Mioko said.

"What the hell are you talking about?" Archie said.

"Ask your accolyte friend, the historian, or so he was introduced to me. Ask him."

Owen stopped and turned back to Mioko, "So Kawabata told you too?"

"Of course, what did you think, I didn't know? I knew right afterwards. I knew. He added a note in Japanese to Mogen's last letter."

"Last letter? In Danish or English?"

"He never wrote to me in Danish. Why would he? I wasn't Danish."

"Good point," Archie said. "I've had my doubts."

"What doubts?" Kawabata asked.

"He means 'troubled fearful questions,'" Owen answered.

"Why fearful?" Kawabata asked.

"Death is fearful," Jena said.

But just then, the old gentleman in his summer *yukata* appeared at the end of his recently watered driveway and stopped the group with a question of his own in Japanese. Mioko and Kawabata stepped into the driveway, apparently in order to answer with some discretion.

Owen asked Mariko, "What's going on? What are they discussing?"

"I can't quite hear, especially with you talking," she answered. "Maybe he wants to show off his garden some more. Or maybe he wants consolation for his dead granddaughter. Should I ask?"

Owen turned away, felt new sweat slowly seep down his left side.

Mariko edged closer to Kawabata and the old gentleman. After a few moments Mariko said, "Still talking about his granddaughter's death. He thinks Kawabata-san has an explanation."

"And does he?"

Mariko broke off listening and came back to Owen. "Kawabata-san keeps asking questions about the girl, how she looked and what she did for her grandfather. He kept asking how she smiled and how he remembers her, how she pronounced words, her favorite foods—things like that. Mostly just soft questions with a lilting voice. A pleasant voice full of soft feeling. I like listening to him. I think the old man does too. But it's private. I shouldn't listen. We should continue down to the station."

She took Owen's arm and edged him back onto the roadway, following Mioko, Sanae, and, further on, Bonneau and the Hesseltines. Owen turned back to watch Kawabata follow the old man into the garden. It seemed their conversation sealed them away from the rest and Owen imagined Kawabata would stay there a long while, listening to the old man. Mariko sped up trying to lessen the distance to Mioko, and the quick walking moistened Owens forehead as the mid-day sun poured down. He brought his slung jacket around and reached into the right pocket. It was awkward as Mariko increased the pace, but he managed to draw out a thick light blue towel handkerchief and sop up the sweat before it stung his eyes.

5

"GETTING ALL TEARY OVER such a saint?" Archie asked, didn't pause for an answer, but went on,"Such a good man, so full of remorse and regret. So charged with restoration. Not many like him in this island world."

Owen nodded and put away his towel handkerchef. "It's just the humidity."

"Ah, the sweet humidity of Japan, the lovely bath of this place," Jena said, settling into her seat at the upstairs Chinese Restaurant overlooking Rokko station. "Soaks everything, mildews all before it, doesn't it, Archie?"

"The laundress speaks, even when not spoken to," Archie answered. "Owen needs to talk about the good doctor, not the weather. Don't you, Owen?"

Kawabata sitting next to Owen and across from Archie said, "The dead are all good."

"Okay," Archie said, "so let's talk about him when he was alive—when you knew him best, over there in cloudless Manchuria. I hear you like reminiscing about the delights of Harbin."

Mioko said, "There were no delights. None. Better not to speak of that horrid place. Nothing good came of it."

"Well, that's a tidy way of summary," Archie said. "But in fact you're wrong—dead *chigau* in fact. I saw all sorts of vital information from that horrid place, and the Americans were terribly anxious to carry it off to D.C. and some place in Maryland. Very useful stuff about killing."

Reverend Bonneau interrupted, "Let's remember who started that war." But then almost seemed to regret the statement. He looked sheepishly at Sanae, Kawabata and Mioko.

"Harbin was functioning well before the big war," Archie said. "Whatever else, the Japanese excel at 'anticipatory data-gathering.' It's their real genius."

"Oh, thank you,"Kawabata said, apparently really pleased by the statement.

"Think nothing of it," Archie said. "I was only trying to buttress your argument that great work was done in Harbin, real research, valuable learning that surely did change the world."

"How was that my argument?" Kawabata asked.

"Maybe it was your advocate's, not yours."

Mioko said, "I said nothing came of it. That's all I said. You seem to think something came beneficial from Harbin. And maybe something did. Maybe Dr. Matsuo himself was the greatest benefit. Certainly his patients in Kobe thought so. Didn't they?"

"I thought so," Kawabata said.

"So we all agree. He was a splendid fellow who, none the less, on occasion, managed to give kids anthrax."

"Is that a toy?" Kawabata asked.

"No, it's not," Mioko said. "It's a disease."

"Often fatal," Jena added.

"Especially for kids under ten," Archie said. "Fatal, meaning it kills them. They die in agony. Their lungs disintegrate."

Kawabata nodded. After a long pause he said, "I have seen that."

"Helped with that, attended to that, "Mioko said.

"Help seems a double-edged word," Jena said.

Kawabata looked puzzled at the term. Owen thought about clarifying it, but knew any explanation would only generate more ambiguity. Thankfully, the Dim Sum cart came by.

The ponzu sauce seemed sweet by comparison. As did Mariko's hand, resting on the top of his left thigh. But that gentle warmth brought an image of the crushed Gaylord's to mind and he imagined both Banerjee and Matsuo flattened by concrete or oxblood tiles. Newly paper thin —people oozing out into Japan's pliant dirt.

Owen said rather forcefully he thought, "The dead are all good."

"Point taken," Archie said. "What can you do with it?"

"It is not necessary to do," Kawabata said softly.

Mariko said, "Mr. Banerjee did not deserve his death."

Owen thought, she follows my mind without my speaking—Japanese *haragei*—God has spoken, and I must marry her.

"You're absolutely right! Banerjee hardly deserved to die." Owen said, rehearsing a marriage proposal in his mind.

"Everyone deserves to die," Kawabata said.

Bonneau added, "No man knows the time or the place. Death comes as a thief in the night or an earthquake in the early morning. We sit thunderstruck at the heavy weaponry of the Almighty."

"Jesus . . ." sighed Archie.

"Yes and Jesus is there before us, offering solace and example, most of all, profound compassion." Bonneau went on.

"The dead are all good," Kawabata re-iterated. "All good!"

"Or at the very least, unable to argue back," Jena said.

"Argue back? What does argue back mean?" Kawabata said, and when he heard no response he said again, "The dead are all good."

The assertion settled into and above them so that for an interval (recognized mutually) only the sound of a arriving or departing train came up from the station. The all-good dead muffled everything else.

Pleased and energized by the quietude, Mioko looked at each member at the round table and then said, "In the words of the poet, 'All things in time grow musical.'"

Archie answered, "By God, you're right! A child's scream, with any luck and solid effort, can achieve high C above G."

Part Seven

1

Mioko said, "Bringing you here. Indeed, summoning you here, because I did not want Hesseltine-san to have the last word."

"Summoning?" Owen said, "I thought my coming was an errand of mercy, a kindness to visit old folks in their slipping away. In their endless rearrangement of the past."

'I'm not slipping away. I'm resonantly still here, and what on earth are you referring to when you say rearranging? I can't rearrange anything."

"So which is it? Resonance, or helpless at rearrangement?"

Mioko smiled and poured more tea into the handleless cups. "When Kawabata comes he'll spank you." She laughed. "And I noticed you didn't bring any *omiyage*. Disenchanted with Japan already?"

"I love Japan."

"You love the feeling you have wandering around Japan. You love being taller in Japan. You love the safety, even when Japan tells you to wear loose clothing during an earthquake."

"And stay inside where it's safest, but of course it isn't." Owen said.

"Japanese networks are extremely safe. It's the earth that isn't, the sea that isn't, the sky filled with bombers that isn't. The trains filled with *gaijin* that isn't."

Owen studied her face looking for a tell-tale smile but she seemed fixated and looking through him toward some imagined spot beyond the scarred and punctured *shojii* of the smaller piano room. Owen remembered the entry garden had been freshly raked to mock zen serenity when he came in. "So it's *gaijin* that irritate you most, threaten you most. Mogens was the supreme *gaijin,* wasn't he? Is that why you engineered his delivery?"

"I engineered it? I hardly think so. Pastor Rielmann understood Japan needed something in return for preserving his sacred Kobe Union Church. Or if Japan didn't—we don't need anything from outsiders—then the Germans did."

"Ah, I see—the outsider—it was the German Ambassador who actually saved the church."

"He was a Christian. Of course he did, but he needed something, and he got it."

"It? Poor old Mogens." Owen said.

"Hardly poor. Not at all old. A very fit family man in his prime as you Americans like to say."

"Not at the end."

"Do we know the end?"

"Kawabata does," Owen said.

"Kawabata says he does, that's true enough, but Kawabata rearranges (your word) things, doesn't he? He's wonderful at playing the kindly old man, a little unsteady and unsure of mind, isn't he? As full of guile as the serpent in the garden, don't you think? Or is it you're not given to such thoughts, since you're guileless and pure yourself?" Mioko paused, smiling inanely. "Just how pure are you, apostle Mathias? Do you have impure thoughts? Do you imagine killing me for example?"

"You might long for it, but in fact I'm uninterested."

"But you are interested in that translator, aren't you? And she's interested in you, isn't she?"

"We're a match—indeed, an arrangement—made in heaven."

"I think not. Made somewhere else. Such matches never last, you know. Once the bodies have been examined, the end of that titillation means death. A little clean-up toweling and then everlasting night. Mixed marriages end up like used tissues, if they are lived out in Japan. Elsewhere they might work quite well, but not here."

"Is that why you spent time in California?"

"Of course it is. Once a Japanese woman gets out, she doesn't want to come back. Much less end up in a place like this." She took a swallow of the cooling tea and then pointed to the walls."No holes in the *shojii*. Are you familiar with that very Japanese saying? No holes in the shojii—meaning the children have gone, life is over. Life is over. All Mogens ever talked about was his children. Men, especially Danish men, like to think their eyes are looking back at them—they long for that, features they can claim as perfect versions of their own."

Owen thought — of course, it was Mogens' children that bothered her most. All that progeny, apparently a rebuke to her own lonely existence. Such fertility needed and merited punishment, was that it? On the cream colored ferries out of Kobe Mogens en famile could be seen waving toward the very diminished Danish crowd at the docks—four darlings in white and waving but in a controlled Japanese fashion, as if they had learned the stroke order for departure. In the thick sunlight clamping like a glass block the motionless Inland Sea.

"The children depart and every little project ends in ashes. Everything means death. I accept that," Mioko said in a kind of automaton delivery, each syllable evenly accented. "And so repentance is all that remains. Just like the tower at Siloam."

Owen listened and puffed out a slow breath. He remembered someone in graduate school pontificating on the necessity of belly breathing to avoid the emotions linked to error—fear, rage, love. Still the slow exhalation was not sufficient. "Repentance for what? Living? Getting through each day? Or taking deserved rest in the tower's shade. Or maybe selling out your closest, most intimate friend? Joyously....no! Angrily or maybe defiantly delivering him up to his most profound enemies so that decades ahead you can pretend not to understand when asked to recount the process you and Rielmann set in motion. Better yet, you can deny it all. Feign a charming innocence, as if the marauding *gaijin* and his Japanese harpy accomplice had come here to pester the elderly waif befuddled by any notion of guilt."

"We Japanese don't feel guilt—your experts say so, don't they? I surely do not."

"Yet, by your own words, you summoned me here."

Mioko let her hands play around the warm tea cup. After a pause long enough to make Owen anxious to fill in the silence, she said, "It's true I wanted somehow to share with you particularly what I knew of Mogens."

"An odd way to start sharing by denying everything."

"The denial was *tatemae*, we're just getting to the *honne*."

"Oh, don't toss that old saw on me. You should be ashamed to retreat behind that lame explanation. Don't the Japanese insist that at its basic level *tatemae* is *honne*? What is required in the formal situation, in the official and polite language, is in fact what is written on the Japanese heart? Denial was your real intention, even to yourself. Even now talking through your denial with this silly, ultimately harmless *gaijin* feeds your real intention. But I don't make you feel better, do I? I can't. I can barely get through the next day in this country. That I could deliver you to what passes so tortuously in this country as the 'legal system'—the 'judgment system' is really an absurd thought. And you know that all too well."

"Do you really imagine I ever cared for the 'Japanese system'? Look at me. Listen to me. We're both adrift on this silly Inland Sea. You imagine in your wondrous Western arrogance that I want absolution from you, Matthias, the replacement apostle. But it's the very opposite. You cannot actually accomplish what you imagine with your little translator—you cannot really make a union with a Japanese woman."

"What a fantasy life you have," Owen said, but that hardly slowed Mioko's explanation.

"You've felt our skin, so strangely smooth, so unbelievably inviting, especially on the inner thigh. You dream of a union transcending family and obligation, outside of everything—adrift in bliss. Mogens dreamed it with me constantly. He actually never tired of imagining how it could be, with one family in Denmark and our bliss here, as if I were a sheltered geisha he kept for visits from the country to the city." She paused, then said, "No. It was always, in his mind at least, far nobler than that, a new possibility—something individual, unique to us—"

"I have no such dreams and neither does Mariko," Owen said with a conviction that surprised him. "You're not happy unless you cheapen us. Maybe that's your real purpose in life to cheapen everything you touch, to soil it, to soak it in bile."

"So you live at some lower level of intensity. Good for you. But that does not make what Mogens dreamed of any less real."

"You don't expect me to believe that crap."

The door slid aside and Kawabata was standing in the doorway. "Crap. That is a very good English word, used, I know, often by Americans. Crap. Bird excrement, is it not? Waste. Often used in anger. I have brought cookies from Kiyomizudera." He put the long rectangular box gently on the low table. "But they're really nothing special."

"And probably stale," Mioko said.

"Stale? Not a familiar word to me. What is stale?"

"Your English is better than mine," Mioko went on. "Stop hiding behind language difficulties."

Kawabata smiled, and opened the box. He sampled a thin brittle cookie. "Perhaps stale, indeed," he said. He offered one to Owen who shook his head.

Kawabata put the cookie on the table and settled in cross legged before the low table. He seemed to draw sustenance out of the silence. Sunlight from the narrow windows lining the ceiling flashed across to the open doorway, and eventually Kawabata pointed to that illumination. "Late afternoons in Japan have a kindly light you don't get in Manchuria. Even Mogens remarked on that often." Kawabata looked first at Owen, then Mioko, as if to gauge whether mentioning Mogens' name would trigger something. "He was such a quiet thoughtful man. A very kind man. Even when he was shaking and sweating he seemed more worried about what I thought than his own condition. He didn't want me to suffer watching him, even if it was my duty."

"Your duty?" Owen said.

"What I was commanded to do. Not a pleasant job. So I tried to ease his pain, his vomiting. But when I helped him he only said, strangely: 'They flogged him.' I had to look up 'flogged'. Who was he referring to?"

"Our Lord," Mioko said.

"Ah," Kawabata said, "Jesus?"

"Surely," Owen said, "the Romans flogged him."

"And that made Mogens feel better, is that it?"

"Well, if you were vomiting and you imagined you could have been flogged, that might make you feel a little better—since you weren't flogged." Mioko said.

"And if you contrived to arrange it so someone else, rather than you, got flogged that might make you feel very good indeed." Owen said.

"Did he do that?" Kawabata asked.

"Never," Mioko said, "never. He was, as you said, a very gentle, kind man. He deceived no one but his own family."

Kawabata again smiled, poured himself some tea and glanced at Mioko as if to chide her about having to do so. "As he got sicker he talked more about Jesus."

"Christians do that," Owen said. "At least some Christians do."

"Perhaps not the Christians in this room," Mioko added.

"I am not a Christian," Kawabata said quietly.

"Therefore we expect no deception from you," Owen said.

"We expect none, but I know you are full of deception," Mioko added. "After all, we are Japanese and always saying one thing while doing another. It is our gift, isn't it?"

"Mogens said Jesus never deceived. He just was tortured and died, and rose from the dead. But no one rises from the dead," Kawabata said. "Wasn't that his deception?"

"Absolutely not," Owen said," others saw him after his death. I'm here to tell you that."

"Then you've seen him too?"

"Absolutely not. I'm here to testify that others saw him and recruited his followers to this present moment in this present room without seeing or hearing him," Owen said, again surprising himself.

"Mogens said as much, but I didn't believe him. He was sick and in terrible pain. When I tried to comfort him he said something rather odd, is that the word: odd? He looked at me with dim eyes and said, 'Not yet nails through my wrists.' What did he mean saying that?"

"Jesus died nailed to a cross," Owen said.

"Yes! Yes, I knew that but wasn't it through the hands? I've seen pictures and it's always through the hands," Kawabata continued.

"Mogens insisted it was through the wrists," Mioko said. "He was convinced of that and disputed that with Pastor Rielmann plenty of times, who said the placement of the nails was not significant."

"Not significant," Kawabata said slowly as if understanding the word syllabically. "Not significant—meaning I don't have to pay it much mind, is that it?"

"You should pay it attention," Owen chided. "Millions have."

"Yes, millions of wrist advocates versus millions of hand advocates—isn't that so, brother Matthias?" Mioko said impatiently. "And haven't hundreds of medical experts taken sides in this dispute. One side proving beyond all doubt that nails through the palms could not keep a body from falling off the cross. And another side volunteering, say in the Philippines, to be nailed through the palms and hoisted up to demonstrate you could suffocate eventually in that position without toppling down. And yet Rielmann's side arguing the controversy was not significant, was, in fact, unworthy of consideration. And all of us wondering why three people in one ten-mat room should be making such arguments two thousand years after the fact. Surely we have better things to do with our lives."

Kawabata moved out of his cross-legged position, briefly knelt conventionally, then slumped back on his calfs in the classic Japanese position. Watching him Owen was carried back to his Kendo lessons, when the exalted sensei lectured his minions kneeling before him in a long line. They listened without moving, save for the undetected criss-crossing of their big toes to keep circulation flowing in their feet. Was the old man assuming an acolyte learning pose? Perhaps Mioko's tone commanded such a posture from anyone caught listening to her? Owen heard the Kendo *sensei's* muted tone proclaiming *chotto matteh*! to stop his students from blessedly uncurling from their agonized kneeling. And then the *sensei* demanded that they slump back on their calfs for another ten minutes of arcane instruction in a Japanese dialect Owen could only occasionally penetrate. It was obvious Kawabata could kneel as long as required or desired. A benign, almost jolly presence flooded across his face, a sappy satiety Owen decided as if some uncomfortable internal organs had suddenly settled into place, yielding pleasure driving out pain.

After a while Kawabata said slowly, "This Jesus. Mogens kept saying his name."

"A name above all names," Mioko said.

"What does that mean, a name above all names?"

Owen said, "The most sacred, the most honored of all names. God's name."

"The name that cannot be named, cannot be said," added Mioko. "The name that is beyond names—the name that can only be gestured at, not spoken."

"Not spoken?"

"Of course not spoken," she answered.

"Like the Emperor?" Kawabata asked, smiling again beatifically.

"I suppose." she said.

"Not at all like the Emperor." Owen said.

"I'm glad to hear that," Kawabata said. "I'm not in favor of the Emperor. He sent me to Manchuria, to Harbin."

"Where there were no clouds," Owen said. "Why don't you tell us again what you did in Harbin. We've heard terrible things."

"Not from me," Kawabata said, shifting his legs, to a side sitting position.

"Mogens wrote me about terrible things," Mioko said. "But I'm not interested in them. I'm interested in what happened to Mogens. His fate. Can you tell us?"

Kawabata reached for a second cookie and seemed to savor it bite by bite. Finally he pointed to Owen. "He must have told you."

"No. He didn't tell me anything. I know only what Mogens wrote me, what you carried back from Harbin."

"All through the last illnesses he talked about Jesus. Sometimes when the sores were worst he seemed to be talking to me as if I were Jesus. He begged me to kill him. Pleaded with me to kill him. Once when Dr. Matsuo was with him he talked to him begging him to show me how to kill Mogens. But Dr. Matsuo insisted the research needed to be complete and thorough—that would be Mogens' gift to humanity. I didn't understand how, but Dr. Matsuo was very certain Mogens was enduring these illnesses for the betterment of all of us eventually. And Mogens kept saying a word I don't know."

"What word?" Mioko interrupted.

"Ex—something," Kawabata answered. "Maybe expiration—is that a word, expiration?"

Owen said, "Yes, it's a word. but probably not what he said."

"Then, what did he say?" Mioko said quickly.

'Maybe exasperation—with you Kawabata-sensei, since you seemed to be such an inept instrument of killing. Maybe he was exasperated with you."

"What is inept? He was always kind to me. Very kind. Very caring. None exasperation."

"I imagine so," Owen continued. "So it was another word, a better word. Did he ever claim to be Jesus?"

"No."

"Did he ever compare himself to Jesus, say he was doing something that Jesus would have approved of, that would have made Jesus happy or content?"

"No."

"Of course he wouldn't," Mioko said. "He was not an arrogant man."

"But a man anguished and in terrible pain. Fragile and probably broken. Feverish, retching, bleeding and festering. Pus pouring out of wounds all over his body. And Dr. Matsuo calmly telling him it wouldn't stop, but would continue and worsen so that the research would be complete. What memories he had were of children being dismembered or frozen or both and probably he confused them with his own children, the beloveds of his life. His purpose for living shredded while he watched. Wouldn't he want some explanation for his situation? Wouldn't anyone? And in such circumstances of course the word that would cover it all, cover his misery and Jesus's, the word that would surface like deliverance itself from the very slough of despond would be *expiation*—wouldn't it?"

"Expiration!" Kawabata shouted.

"No. *Expiation*."

"Yes, *Expiation!*" Mioko echoed.

"What is the difference?" Kawabata asked.

"Before you expire," Owen explained, "you need to *expiate*. *Expiation* means finding some justification for your suffering, some excuse that compensates and honors your misery, some purpose that extends beyond and through your pain and illness. *Expiation* answers the question who benefits by your anguish—who gets relief, who gets free because you experience endless torment and bondage."

"But who did get free?" Kawabata asked.

"Yes. Who did? "Mioko echoed staring at Owen.

Owen thought about listing Matsuo and Kawabata as beneficiaries but decided to let the question rest while the late afternoon sun weakened through the narrow wall-top windows. He imagined *expiation* lolled on the table top like a *maruta* awaiting evisceration. Doubtless Kawabata would interrogate its spelling and meaning; Mioko would wonder what possible positive could compensate for its atrocity, and Owen, hearing Archie's voice whispering to his belly, could only begin to laugh at the absurdity these two Japanese and one *gaijin* thrashing over a single English noun. What could the Japanese know of atonement? What could Owen understand about obligation?

And later Owen in turning over what happened did come to understand that it was Kawabata, as always, who rescued them from stasis and confusion—from the lock of culture fissure and absolute otherness. After a suitably satisfying interval of silence and emptying he began to recount his last terminal visit with Mogens.

With studied hesitancy he recounted how Dr. Matsuo instructed him in putting the syringe into the IV tube flowing into Mogens' wrist. Drawing back on the plunger to magnify the air bubble, and then the slow cascade forward so that the delivering devastation could stream down the line in a translucent bulge . And while he was rehearsing that in his mind and then undertaking the action, suddenly Mogens addressed him, calling him "Peter,"again and again, calling "Peter," and extending his wrist upward toward him, and saying: "Take me in from the Beautiful Gate, into the temple. I know you have nothing to give me but only this: in his name, Jesus Christ of Nazareth, rise up and walk."

Owen remembered that Mioko then remarkably completed the narration from Acts: "And he took him by the right hand and lifted him up and immediately his feet and ankle bones received strength. So he, leaping up stood and walked and entered the temple with them—walking and leaping and praising God."

"But he didn't walk at all," Kawabata had insisted.

"Of course he didn't" she had answered. "You don't walk, or leap, or praise God with a ruptured aorta."

And Kawabata had closed the discussion, typically, with questions, "Ruptured aorta, what is that? What is the meaning of those words?"

2

AT THE SEASON'S ENDING adult Sunday school class the P & G contingent doubled. Owen noted with some surprise that there were two blue serged suited fellows at the end of the gleaming oak table. And two flowery and fluffed out women like flanges at the corner edges. A solid phalanx of well tailored evangelical commitment to test his faith. Mid-table were Archie and Jenna, but as always Owen doubted they would rush to compensate for his incompetent leadership. Next to them were the Japanese women, joined this time by Mariko.

For the last two sessions the group had been going through Paul's letter to the Romans, buttressing the case for faith against works, a mild challenge to the self-sacrificing inclinations of the P & Gers. But this larger contingent presented a bigger, enticing target, and, moreover, Owen had mulled over, to a degree he himself found astonishing, Mogens final reference to Acts—a book Owen had often used to attack P & G's assumption that wealth accumulation made the world go round. Owen had assembled his justification for switching texts and was about to speak when he was pre-empted.

"Deb and I will be leaving Kobe in a month. Our tour is up, so I wanted to introduce our replacements, David and Mildred. They'll take over our Rokko homat, as well as our place here at the table."

"Welcome," Owen said and was pre-empted again.

"I've told them this is a challenging discussion group, sure to improve their faith commitment, even as it disturbs it some."

It seems, Owen thought, the sentence, the thought, had been rehearsed, considered and practiced before utterance, and that called for some rebuttal, but again he was pre-empted.

"I've told Dave to expect a new Christianity here in Japan, and an occasionally sour piety from long term *gaijin* dwelling in this country."

"Sour piety?" Archie suddenly said. "What does that mean? Jena and I have been here for twenty years. Does that make us suspect Christians?"

"Probably," the VP answered with cool obvious reserve and equanimity, "this is such a secular culture. Its pagan elements insinuate themselves everywhere."

Owen thought, he's operating from a script—perhaps a company orientation lecture?

"Jesus," Archie murmured, cocking his head.

"I mean no disrespect," the P & G said, "but I've noticed here, as in Bangkok and Jakarta, that sooner or later, if farang or *gaijin* linger too long they invariably 'go native.' They get infusions of Shinto or Buddhism or Samurai-whatever, and those ultimately make acceptance of the incarnation problematic."

"Problematic?" Jena said.

"Don't you remember, darling," Archie said, "the Disney people always referred to Tokyo as Sewer City. It's the same thing . . . . problematic. A simple, straightforward racism. God doesn't speak *kaigo*. It's inconceivable, nay . . . problematic, that his son should be Japanese, unless of course his father was. Was he?"

"Maybe David and Mildred could ask him." Jena said.

"What do you mean 'the Disney people?'" Deb spoke up from the flange position.

"Ah, you weren't here then. We were posted outside of Tokyo when the Disney corporation and the Oriental Land Company married to incarnate Tokyo Disneyland—the all-American town with a sheet metal roof over it, and 'cully-ricesoo' instead of buffalo wings. The Disney people insisted there'd be no alcohol in Tokyo Disneyland, but the Japanese said no one would come to a park unless they could drink there. 'It's not a park. It's Disneyland,' came the inevitable answer, from the Disney People. What was it darling that that wife of the Dancing Bears engineer said—'If the bears sing in Japanese, they're not the dancing bears.' Case settled. Sewer City dismissed. Get us out of here and soon."

"And the incarnation has something to do with the Dancing Bears?" The P & G said.

"Perceptible only if you're a 'a gone-native secular *gaijin*," Archie answered.

"So much for orderly exposition," the P & G answered.

After a full eight-count of silence, Owen said, "I think what is being asserted consists in the collision of two views of religion, isn't it, Jena? Disney versus Japan required a new amalgam somehow so that the two worlds reconcile in the creation of Tokyo Disneyland —a new world. The starting premises so divergent the amalgam can only be bogus, I suppose. Rag-tag, improvised, negotiated constantly, always misunderstood and somehow attractive enough to engage the very opposite entrepreneurs, who keep at the game giving, taking, yielding, dominating in their respective turns."

But to head off some saccharine consensus P & G asked, "How can there be expiation if there truly is no sense of sin?"

"After you've been here long enough—as long as we have you can't really imagine what it would be to be washed clean of any sense of sin," Jena said. "Yet, that's exactly the legacy of all Japanese. Freed of the notion of sin. Think about it. We stand in awe of it, struck dumb by it. Liberated. Freed, do you believe? Do you?"

"What on earth are you talking about?"

"The sinless need no savior. That's what I'm talking about. The Japanese know that in their stomach, before their mind settles on the issue. Savior is extraneous, marginal, rococo embellishment—good for music and maudlin mutterings, dark thoughts, *gaijin* despair but not much else." Jena said.

"Jesus is not much good for much else?"

"Certainly not for the role so called scripture assigned him. That's the role you fix on, since after all, he's absolutely terrifying as a moralist, or a financial advisor."

"Oh, well said, my pet," Archie said. "He's more apocalyptic than Mickey, can't we all agree? More loving than the Dancing Bears—even for Sewer City. And not really cut out for a *homat* on Rokko Island. He carries a sword swatting dismissal of wealth."

"You wish to chide us for where we live—a choice over which we have no control?"

"Of course we do," Archie said, "it's embarrassing wiggling in the eye of the needle."

"Scriptually it was a place, not a metaphor." P & G replied cooly again. "And you could get through it easily."

"All the way to a *homat* on Rokko Island," Archie said.

"Yes, if that was the Lord's plan."

"And was it the Lord's plan to snuff out Ananias and Saphira because they held back some of the loot from the sale of their *homat*?" Archie warmed to combat.

"What are you talking about?"

"Scripture. Nothing else. Scripture I suspect you haven't read or thought much about. Try Chapter Five of Acts." And suddenly Archie turned to Owen. "Have you thought about God's plan and Mogens' injection that finished off his glanders-soaked body?"

"And sinless Kawabata?" Owen asked.

"He did what social expectation demanded," Jena said. "Did it competently and efficiently and without a moral qualm, as any good Japanese would have. Only you have constructed his 'sin'—lovingly constructed it."

"And then, best of all, you've seized on your scripture to expiate your construction—invented an elaborate charade of the infinite father sending his infinite son to suffer human pain so that Kawabata might earn eternal blessing somehow. All of which the Japanese listening to that story are as dumb struck as the lovely P & G people listening to this conversation." Archie said. "Utterly struck dumb. So mystified as to throw up their immaculately washed hands and hurry off to save aborigines in the South Philippines. Or hustle back to their balconies on Rokko Island and sip madeira in the late afternoon and worry over the stewardship of their church's endowment."

"It's so unChristian to invade capital." Jena added.

The matter rested in the soft sunlight off the oak table top and finally Mariko said, "This seems like a family argument. I don't think we," she nodded toward Yasuko, "have much to offer the discussion."

"Except to offer prayers for the participants," Yasuko said smiling.

"And prayers for Mogens," Owen added.

"And who is Mogens?" Mildred asked

"Conceived by the Holy Spirit, born of a virgin, and butchered in Harbin, circa 1945," Archie said.

3

LORD, LEAD ME AWAY *from my sin, my incredible sloth and my steady denial. Free me from distraction to wander fully in mounting doubt amid ice pillars upholding cloudless sky and sun-shy emptiness. Lead me through sickness and shuddering fevers, through fields of nausea beyond brittle boys hacked from ice barrels, and softly undulant girls, belly-thighs of immersible swallowable sweetness. Lord, help me across inexplicable suffering and torture's drop-away murkiness. Lord, pump up and then detonate my confusion, so that its pellets shatter all windowpanes of hoped-for deliverance.*

Lord, let pain free me from spite and resentment; instead, let me cradle the soft heads of my children and dwell in the sweet clean smell of their freshness. Let me collect their sleeping smiles as arrangeable in my heart as flowers strewn across a tray, as overwhelming as cello notes in darkness. Lord lift me beyond the cracking ice and chill submergence of scoffing laughter at my chaffing and bursting heart. Lord, let me soldier toward the murderous bubble of your salvation.